Other Books by Karen McQuestion

i

KAREN MCQUESTION

From a Distant Star

THE EDGEWOOD SERIES
Edgewood (Book One)
Wanderlust (Book Two)
Absolution (Book Three)
Revelation (Book Four)

FOR CHILDREN

Celia and the Fairies
Secrets of the Magic Ring
Grimm House
Prince and Popper

FOR WRITERS

Write That Novel!

WRITING AS K. J. YOUNG

The Dark Hour

A Limited Run

Karen McQuestion

NIGHTSKY PRESS

Text copyright © 2022 by Karen McQuestion

ISBN: 978-1-7367888-6-8

*For my sister, Khris——reader,
podcast listener, and friend*

Felix Worthington Reportedly Buys
Montana Ranch for $19 Million

For the last six months, elusive billionaire Felix Worthington has been aggressively adding to his real estate portfolio, snatching up a Hawaiian estate, a condo building in San Diego, a penthouse apartment in Manhattan, and a mansion in Austin, Texas. Now recent reports speculate he's behind the purchase of an eight-thousand-acre property in Montana. Formerly used as a cattle ranch, the property has two houses, four outbuildings, miles of riding trails, abundant wildlife, access to the Stillwater River, and impressive views of the Beartooth Mountains. Although real estate agent Ann Marie Gruszkowski would not confirm Worthington as the buyer, eyewitnesses spotted him touring the property with his longtime trusted assistant, Milo Lappin, shortly before the deal closed.

Chapter One

Chicago

Meri walked into the convention hall, took off her sunglasses, and blinked at the great expanse of glass and light. Absolutely breathtaking. The interior of McCormick Place somehow managed to look both modern and classic. She imagined this was how large gathering places looked in heaven.

But were they having the event here? *Couldn't be.* There had to be some sort of mix-up. Perhaps the Uber driver had gotten things wrong. Maybe there was a smaller event hall in Chicago with a similar name.

She was about to open her purse to look at the email printout when she spotted an enormous banner proclaiming "A Little Slice of Haven—Haven Con" hanging off to one side, and below it, "One Day Only!—Saturday May 5, 2018." So she was in the right place after all. Below the words were photos of each of the cast members who'd agreed to come, including one of her. Good Lord, they'd used pictures from the TV show. She shook her head, thinking that the attendees were in for a shock when they saw how the four of them had aged. Twenty-five years could transform a person's appearance in a big way.

Meri herself now looked like the mother of the character she'd played. She'd always been thin, nearly wiry, and she still was, so that hadn't changed much. Her face was relatively free of wrinkles, but over the years her hair had gone from brown to white, and she'd embraced the change. These days, she kept it short and spiky. That alone made people who hadn't seen her in a while do a double take.

Before she'd had a chance to go to the information desk, Meri was approached by a brown-haired woman wearing a colorful belted tunic over narrow pants. "Meri? Meri Wetzel? You're early!" The woman pulled her into an awkward hug, greeting her as if they'd met before, but that was impossible, seeing as Meri would have remembered. After they pulled apart, the stranger held out the laminated ID tag that hung from her neck. "I'm Ruby Sapp. The fan club president?" Before Meri could respond, she kept going. "I expected you to come through the celebrity entrance."

Meri had seen the note about the celebrity entrance but hadn't thought she fell into that category. "Did I do something wrong?"

Ruby laughed. "Trust me, you can't do anything wrong, as far as I'm concerned. I still can't believe I get to meet all of you in person. I couldn't sleep at all. Wide awake the entire night! I was abuzz, simply abuzz. This is a dream come true for me. I am literally, like I mean literally, the show's biggest fan. Well, maybe except for my brother." She shook out her hands as if to cast off nervous energy. "Sorry to ramble, but I still can't believe this is happening. You're the first to arrive." Her eyes widened. "Imagine how I'll be when all of the Barlows are here. I'll probably pass out."

"Thanks so much for organizing this and inviting me," Meri said politely.

"Are you kidding me?" Ruby said, a grin spreading across her face. "The pleasure is all mine. And just between us"—she leaned in conspiratorially—"you're my favorite on the show. I mean, all of the Barlows are really great, but Marion is so kind and lovely to everyone, and from what I've heard, you're the same way."

"Thank you. I'm happy to be here." She was especially grateful for the $5,000 plus travel expenses. A huge windfall for a day's work rehashing an old acting gig, and she might even get to take in a bit of Chicago before she flew out tomorrow night. Maybe if she was lucky, someone would spring for an expensive dinner.

"Too bad one of your daughters couldn't make it," Ruby said with a sigh. "Ann is one of my favorites. I loved the episode at the school musical where the family first finds out she can really sing. Oh, my heart!" She clasped her fist to her chest. "I think I can relate to her because I'm a younger sister as well. So sad to hear she had a conflict and couldn't be here today. We offered to change it to a different date, but she never got back to us. That's a definite loss, and of course, everyone is going to miss dear Grandma. She's like the grandmother everyone wishes they had. I bet you loved working with her."

"She was a dear," Meri said, puzzled. It struck her as strange that anyone remembered the show, much less spoke about it with such warmth and enthusiasm. It had a short run and never did get much in the way of a following. A major corporation, Quellware, had bought the rights fifteen years after it ended, and that was the last she'd heard of it. There hadn't been any reruns. Jeff Greer, who'd played her husband on the show, had texted her about a year earlier to say the shows had been leaked online and there was a resurgence of interest, but she hadn't paid much attention. Hadn't even clicked on the YouTube link he'd sent. Jeff was always texting something or other, trying to lure her back in. Most of the time she only glanced at his texts and responded with an emoji. The thumbs-up, usually. Never the heart. Now she stared at Ruby's eager face and saw that Jeff had been right. "Have you seen *all* of the episodes?"

Ruby grinned. Was the woman always this peppy? "Every single one. So many times that I know all the dialogue by heart." She cocked her head to one side. "You know, if you weren't wearing glasses and your hair was brown and longer, you'd look exactly the same. I was secretly hoping all of you would come in costume, but I guess that's kind of unrealistic."

"We didn't get to keep the wardrobe." Not that Meri would have wanted it, even if it had been offered. The 1940s clothing had been a pain. So many buttons! The woman in charge of wardrobe had delighted in finding vintage dresses for her and the girls. When Meri had suggested the addition of zippers, saying they did have zippers in that era, she'd been shot down. There wasn't the budget or time for alterations. In their roster of shows, *A Little Slice of Haven* was not a huge priority for the network. Getting picked up for a second season had been a miracle. They hadn't been about to spend a penny more than was necessary.

"Too bad." Ruby tilted her head to one side. "You know, I just thought of something. Your name is Meri, and you played Marion. Wow, those names are close. Did they do that on purpose?"

"Just a coincidence." Meri smiled politely. "Do you have any idea how many people will be attending today?"

"We sold out in the first twenty-four hours," Ruby said proudly. "Eleven thousand tickets. Unfortunately, the Arie Crown Theater booked for the discussion panel only holds four thousand people." With a shake of her head, she added, "Going to be a lot of disappointed people in the Haven fandom today. Those folks who didn't get tickets for the panel discussion will just have to get in line for the photo meet and greet."

The Haven fandom. Thousands of people who wanted to see and hear them talk about a TV show from more than two decades ago? Meri felt like she'd been dropped into an alternate reality. Her acting career had stalled after the show ended. She hadn't been offered anything significant in film or TV. After they'd been canceled, she did snag some guest spots, and when those opportunities had dwindled, her agent had been able to book some commercials and voice-over work. After her agent retired and her manager lost interest, she had been left without representation.

More recently, she'd turned her walk-in closet into a makeshift recording studio and started narrating audio-books from home. It wasn't glamorous, but it put her acting talent to use and paid the bills. Living in Southern California wasn't cheap, and for more than twenty years she'd been a single mother, without the benefit of child support. Every penny came from her, and every month it was a struggle to pay her bills. Sometimes it seemed like it would never end. "That's quite a turnout," she finally said. "Hard to believe there are so many people interested."

"Believe me, for every person who shows up there are thousands who wish they could be here. *A Little Slice of Haven* is *a thing*. It started with the shows being leaked online last year, one dropping every week, and the excitement just built from there. I got hooked early on, and I could tell by the comments I wasn't the only one getting into it. You could see the enthusiasm climbing. And you wouldn't believe the discussion forum!" She took a breath and kept going. "People have joined from all over the world. Everyone has an opinion too. When viewers started creating their own merch, I knew it was time for Haven Con." Ruby pointed to the sign. "I organized nearly all of this myself. Booked the space. Got the vendors lined up, arranged the ticket sales, ordered the banners—and invited all of you, of course."

"Do you know who leaked the episodes?" Meri asked, her eyes on the banner. Appearing on *A Little Slice of Haven* hadn't been a happy time in her life. She'd put all of it behind her, and now all she cared about were the royalties she wasn't getting. If people were watching it, she should be paid. Besides appearing at Haven Con, she hadn't made a dime off the show since it last aired.

"They obviously don't want anyone to know," Ruby said with a shake of her head. "The person posts as 'Haven

Maniac.'" She leaned in with eyebrows raised. "It's all very secretive."

"I wish I knew who it was." Meri wondered if it was worth hiring an attorney, then discarded the thought. Let Jeff or one of the others pursue it if they wanted to. She didn't have the energy or the money to see it through.

Ruby looped her hand through Meri's elbow like they were old friends. "Shall we go back to the celebrity entrance and greet the others? I'm sure you're just as eager to see them as I am."

"Certainly." It had always struck Meri as odd how viewers assumed they knew actors based on the characters they played, when nothing could be farther from the truth. Oh well. Time to put her acting skills in gear in time to show the Haven fandom a happy reunion.

Construction Begins on Felix Worthington's Montana Property

A structure resembling a warehouse is currently being built on the Montana ranch purchased by billionaire Felix Worthington four months ago. Three stories high and measuring more than a mile in each direction, the massive building has windows running the length of the top floor. Construction permits give no specifics as to the intended use of the building, and workers on site won't divulge any details. Neighbors who were contacted said they did not object to the project. One resident, Pat Werths, divulged that she was told the building was temporary and would be dismantled and removed by the end of the year.

Chapter Two

Jeff wasn't surprised that Meri was already there when he arrived. In the two years they'd worked together, she was always on time and always knew her lines (and most everyone else's too). She ate healthy food, took vitamins and other supplements, and exercised regularly. Her go-to workouts were rock climbing and hiking. The cast had once been invited to an industry event at an executive's house that featured a vertical rock-climbing wall. It was so difficult that most of the younger partygoers gave up in short order, but not Meri. Even wearing palazzo pants and sandals, she was able to scramble all the way up. The entire party had gathered to watch, applauding when she reached the top and rang the bell.

Maybe it was her mind-body fitness that allowed her to keep calm under pressure. She always knew the right thing to do and say in any situation. He hadn't realized it at the time, but Meri had been his guiding light, both personally and on the set. No wonder he felt like such a mess in her presence. No one could compare favorably. She was perfection. Twenty-five years later, sporting spiky white hair and round tortoiseshell glasses, she even managed to make getting older look sexy.

Meri gave him a small smile when he walked in the door, but he was waylaid by the fan club president before they could speak. The woman squealed and said, "Gerald Barlow, is that you?" She held her hand over her eyes as if shielding them from the sun.

"If it isn't, we're both in trouble," he said, which sounded like something his character would say.

She grinned and held out her hand. "Ruby Sapp, your biggest fan and the organizer of this event. I'm thrilled you could make it." Her voice trilled with excitement.

He shook her hand and gave her arm an affectionate squeeze. "I'm excited to be here." Jeff had been glad to leave LA to come to Haven Con. Returning with the money earned from this event would literally be a lifesaver. Like an idiot, he'd acquired gambling debts playing poker three weeks earlier and now owed $12,000. When he couldn't pay on the spot, he'd promised he'd settle up next time and went home thinking it was over. He found out too late that these guys took it seriously. A week later, they sent some thug to corner him in a grocery store parking lot, of all places. The dude came out of nowhere and slammed him against the driver's-side door with one meaty hand. He said the next time they sent him out he'd beat Jeff to a pulp. "My boss isn't big on second chances," the hulk had said.

So the offer to appear at Haven Con had come at just the right time. Hopefully, today's money would buy him more time. Jeff grinned to show his appreciation and made small talk with Ruby, and then Dominick and Amanda arrived and he was left behind as Ruby went to greet them. Jeff took this as an opportunity and sidled up to Meri. "Good to have the whole crew back together again, don't you think?"

"Should be fun," she said distractedly. Her eyes were aimed on the kids—or at least they'd been kids when they'd worked together, but now they had to be on the other side of forty. Jeff had kept track of them after the show but hadn't been in touch. Dominick was now a DJ on a Los Angeles radio show, one of those outrageous morning shows, which was a good fit. The guy had been born with brass balls and never ran out of things to say. A real motormouth. He'd aged well, with his head of thick curly hair only starting to go gray. As if Dominick knew it was his best feature, he often rested his hand on the top of his head or raked his fingers through it when making a point. If it wasn't his actual hair, it was a damn good wig, but Jeff suspected it was Dominick's own. Lucky guys tended to stay lucky. Dominick would probably drink and smoke for the next fifty years and die peacefully in his own bed.

Amanda had improved with age, morphing from a lovely teenager to a self-assured, beautiful woman. He knew from googling that she was working as on-air talent for a local news program at a station in Sacramento. He'd even watched a few clips online, noticing the confident way she bantered with the other anchors. Good for her. She'd managed to stay in front of the cameras without having to deal with all the crap that came with acting in Hollywood.

The show's youngest daughter, played by Lauren Saunders, was the only one who'd dropped out of sight, but that was no surprise. Even during the show she'd seemed distant and miserable—the victim of a pushy aunt.

Jeff hadn't anticipated the warm rush of feelings he'd have upon seeing all of them together. For a time, they'd been a family, albeit a dysfunctional one. During the filming of the show, he'd spent more time with these people than his own wife at the time. And the younger actors could be stand-ins for the kids he'd wanted but never could have.

After the fan club president finished exclaiming over all of them, the four cast members hugged it out, exchanging greetings in the way of old friends. Dominick poked Jeff's belly. "Getting fat, old man!"

Jeff responded, "Watch yourself, son. I can still take you down any day of the week." They each raised their fists in a mock fight.

"Boys!" Meri said, playing the mother role. "Be nice."

Ruby clasped her hands together. "I feel like crying. I'm so privileged to be witnessing the family getting back together again." She wiped her eyes with her fingertips and watched them interacting. When the small talk died down, she said, "Why don't I give you a tour of the hall and talk you through what will be happening today?" Without waiting for a response, she led the way, gesturing for them to follow.

They wandered through the convention hall, where booths had been set up and vendors were in the process of organizing their inventory. As they walked, Jeff tried to take Meri's hand, but she frowned and shook him off. He tried not to take it personally. Her attention was on the merchandise: T-shirts, miniature cars like the ones on the show, dollhouses exactly like the Barlow homestead, postcards, magnets, bumper stickers, bookmarks, clothing in the style of the show. They went down aisle after aisle, and there seemed to be no end to all things Barlow family.

"Good grief," Meri said under her breath. "It's like a cult. How did this happen?"

"I told you it was a big deal now," Jeff said. He'd texted her countless times in the last year and had even sent her links to articles and to the discussion group, but the speed with which she'd responded—always a thumbs-up—made him suspect she hadn't even bothered to read his words. Now he was certain of it.

One vendor, a silver-haired woman in her sixties, caught sight of the group and stopped stocking her shelves. Her face broke into a wide grin. "I can't believe it. Marion and Gerald Barlow! And the kids—Dorothy and Tom, all grown up!" She put her hand to her heart. "If only Ann and Grandma and Bud were here, my life would be complete." She asked for a photo, and the next thing Jeff knew, all of them were crowded behind her while Ruby took the picture.

Other vendors caught wind of it, and suddenly a crowd of thirty-some people gathered around them, all wanting pictures and asking questions about the show. After about fifteen minutes, Ruby called out, "Five more minutes, and that's it." Her voice had gone from adoring fan to drill sergeant. "We don't want to wear out the Barlows before the day's even begun!" She herded them away from their admirers, holding out a raised hand to stop those who wanted more.

A young woman with a braid over one shoulder called out, "I love you, Dominick Ingrelli! I named my dog Tom Barlow after you."

Dominick smirked. "That must be quite a dog."

As they left the convention hall, Meri said, "It's like we're the Beatles." Her voice was filled with wonder.

"The Beatles? How old are you?" Dominick muttered with an impish grin.

Meri gave him a light punch in the arm. "Okay, Beyoncé then. Or Taylor Swift or whoever else is such a big deal that they get mobbed when out in public." She grinned. "You knew what I meant."

Overhearing, Ruby said, "To the fans, you're bigger than any of them. The fandom for *A Little Slice of Haven* is a force." A slow smile stretched across her face. "You'll see."

Chapter Three

Dominick snuck out the back of the auditorium and through an exterior door marked "Do Not Open Door, Alarm Will Sound." Earlier, during the tour of the convention hall, he'd pushed it open on a whim and discovered that the sign was a lie. There was no alarm. Now, needing to have a smoke break and wanting to avoid the fans, this seemed like a good option.

Once outside, he propped the door open with a brick presumably left on the pavement for just such a purpose. Dominick fished a cigarette out of his pack, put it between his lips, and leaned over to touch the flame from his lighter to the tip, watching it glow as he inhaled. The official story was that he'd quit smoking, but the truth of it was that he had one or two a day. One of these days he'd swear off them completely, but for now, they were his reward for things well done and his consolation prize when things went the other way.

Leaning back, one foot flamingoed against the brick wall, he marveled at everything that had happened today. He was used to attention. On his radio show, *The No Bull Show with Dominick Ingrelli*, it was his job to get attention. The difference today was that he was getting an actual outpouring of love. He enjoyed the love but wished it wasn't for something he'd done as a kid, a role he wasn't particularly proud of.

Weird.

He'd always thought of his two years on the show as one of the low periods in his life. He'd taken the job because it was a foot in the door, but a feel-good family drama didn't fit his bad-boy perception of himself. The show was lame. The show's creator had based the town and interior shots on the movie *It's a Wonderful Life*, but there was nothing wonderful about it. One critic called it "a treacly melodrama" and criticized the acting as ham-fisted. And that had been one of the better reviews. Back then, the show had been a flop. So odd that it was finding a following so many years later.

Dominick wasn't the only one who'd thought working on the show was a slog.

On the set, tensions had been high. Jeff Greer, who'd played his father, had a tendency to be depressed or drunk, or both. Jeff wasn't shy about talking about his real aspirations. He wanted to do edgy parts, roles that had a lot of meat to them. Playing the patriarch in a family-friendly TV drama was beneath him. Luckily, they also had Meri Wetzel in the role of his mother. She was a natural-born diplomat, good at smoothing things over when there were conflicts on the set. If anyone ever nominated her for sainthood, Dominick would give her his vote. Usually, Meri could coax Jeff through a scene, but as the show went on, he just got worse. His issues were so prevalent that no one seemed to notice that the rest of them were miserable as well.

What Dominick most remembered from the day-to-day business of the show was fooling around with Amanda. She'd been cast as his younger sister, but they were actually the same age. Sparks had flown between them from the first meeting, and he'd spent most of his time on set trying to figure out how to get her all to himself. During the interminable waiting that happened on set, they'd sneak off together, but they never managed to get much beyond some groping, French kissing, and dry humping. The costumes had too many buttons, and Amanda was always worried about her hair. Once they'd been in a closet behind some wardrobe racks, so close to having sex, nearly there, when they'd been interrupted by Lauren, the girl who'd played his other sister. Thinking about that incident vividly brought back the sexual frustration of the moment.

Stupid Lauren, always wanting to pal around with them. Why a fourteen-year-old would think two eighteen-year-olds would want to be friends was beyond him. To make it worse, Lauren had thought it was funny to call him Dom-Tom. Stupid kid didn't even know what she was saying. And wouldn't you know it? The moniker stuck. By the time the show was canceled, no one in the cast or crew called him Dominick anymore. He might as well have had Dom-Tom tattooed on his forehead.

The fourth kid in his fictitious family had left the show midway through the first season due to an injury. What was that kid's name? Dominick scrunched his forehead in thought. The character's name was Bud Barlow, but that was the best he could come up with. He could picture him, anyway. Little Bud Barlow, all of seven or so. Stick thin with a perpetual look of confusion. Not an actor, that was for sure. After the kid left the show, they carried on as if he'd never even been there in the first place.

There was a grandma too, but she spent most of her screen time in a rocking chair, dispensing pithy wisdom or petting the dog, Beau, a beautiful golden retriever. Dominick only talked to Grandma in character as Tom. They never exchanged a word beyond the scripted dialogue. The actor's name had been Catherine Sedgwick, and she was ancient even back in 1994. She had to be long dead at this point, which meant she was missing the best part of the whole thing—this strange religious fervor over the revival of the show twenty-five years later.

He'd read the posts in the discussion forum and knew the fans were rabid, but he still wasn't prepared for this day. During the Q and A after the panel discussion, one teenage girl's voice had quivered and she'd looked as if she might faint. It was clear that all of those in the audience had watched the TV show multiple times. They knew the dialogue by heart, and their questions concerned trivial things, like the grandfather clock in the front hall and the locket Gerald gave Marion for their anniversary.

Of the four of them, Amanda was the smoothest. So many years in front of the camera at her news job had given her a practiced ease. She charmed the crowd. When a guy about their age asked her to marry him, she said, "I'm sorry, but you know my heart belongs to George Bonner." Dominick had all but forgotten the storyline about Dorothy Barlow's unrequited crush on the neighbor, George, but Amanda had come prepared, launching into a speech right from the show. A speech that clearly resonated with the women in the audience. The men seemed to appreciate her too. It didn't hurt that Amanda, who'd been pretty as an eighteen-year-old, was now drop-dead gorgeous. Dorothy Barlow had grown up to be sophisticated and sexy. And the crowd loved her.

But even though Amanda had memorized some lines ahead of time, Dominick was no slouch. He got in a few good ones of his own. What he lacked in prepared dialogue he made up for in anecdotes, telling the crowd about the time one of the old cars failed to start and how they did the scene anyway. "Three of the crew members pushed it from behind, and the cameraman kept them out of the shot." He mentioned how he got physically sick during the Thanksgiving dinner scene because there were so many takes that he'd overeaten mashed potatoes and gravy. "Mashed potatoes used to be one of my favorites, but after that I couldn't eat them for a long time." That line got a big laugh. He'd neglected to explain that Jeff was the reason for all the takes. He'd shown up unprepared and sloppy drunk again.

Dominick could give Jeff credit now, though. Today his gray eyes were clear and bright, his attitude upbeat. Clearly, he was glad to be here. He wore a crisp white shirt, pressed pants, and shiny dress shoes, like an old guy going on a date for the first time in years. He'd heard Jeff had gone through rehab about ten years ago, and from the looks of him, it had stuck. Good for him. Meri also looked great for a woman her age. She had a sexy librarian vibe, but she also appeared almost shell-shocked. "My daughter told me she'd been watching the show online, but I didn't know it was such a big deal," she'd said. Meri was in a state of disbelief at all the audience members who knew specifics about the show, details that the four of them had largely forgotten.

The Q and A could have gone on and on, but luckily Ruby cut it off after they'd been on stage for an hour and a half. "Always leave them wanting more," she'd said backstage. "Let 'em sign up for the meet and greet if they need more Barlow time."

Dominick took one last drag from his cigarette. During the previous years, he'd had three kids from two different baby mamas. The relationships hadn't lasted, but the kids weren't going away, and the child support payments were killer. The first woman had been reasonable, kept her job and didn't push for any more than she was due. Those two kids were into the double digits age-wise, so the end was in sight. The second one, Jaime Carter, the mother of his three-year-old son, Nick, hadn't worked since the day she gave birth. She'd had a thriving acting career, guest roles for the most part, and gave it all up to sit on her butt at home. They'd had screaming matches over this, with Jaime claiming he'd promised to marry her and Dominick telling her to get a job. She was sucking him dry, and he still had fifteen years to go until the kid reached adulthood.

And to make it worse, rumors around the radio station indicated his contract wasn't going to be renewed at the end of the year. He had a clue this was coming, of course. His role as a shock jock was antiquated. As one of his friends had said recently, "No one is shocked anymore." His numbers had been declining for a while now, so hearing he was being phased out didn't come as a surprise, but he was still unprepared. It would be different if he had some money set aside, but managing his finances had never been his forte. He liked to live large, so this job and the money that accompanied it would help keep him afloat while he came up with a plan.

He dropped the cigarette to the ground and snuffed it out with a twist of his shoe, then got out his phone to see how much time he had before the meet and greet. As he looked at the screen, he heard the ping of his notifications telling him he'd gotten an email and a new text. As it turned out, both messages were identical:

Hey, Dominick! Milo Lappin here, contacting you on behalf of Felix Worthington. He has a business proposition—ten days of your time in exchange for $2 million. Interested? Get back to me and we'll schedule a meeting.

Curious, he called the number.

Chapter Four

Meri, Jeff, and Amanda sat around the table in the conference room reserved for the cast members, drinking coffee and talking. Ruby had plunked them there earlier, then left in a tizzy, saying she would come and get them when it was time for the meet and greet. It wasn't a bad place to pass the time. The room had typical commercial carpeting, making it quiet. The chairs had padded seats and wheeled casters. A beverage cart held a coffee urn along with pastries and cut fruit.

And of course, this gave them time to get caught up on what had happened in their lives after the show. Meri felt an odd sense of déjà vu listening to Jeff ask Amanda questions about her dating life. She'd forgotten that he was such a skilled conversationalist. He really paid attention, which was saying a lot, and he gave the impression he cared as well. He'd always had a good rapport with the kids on the set. At least when he wasn't wasted.

"I go on plenty of dates, but I'm too busy for a relationship," Amanda explained. "My hours are crazy. Early mornings. Split shifts. Being called in at the last minute when there's some kind of big news event. I don't know how I'd even work a boyfriend around that schedule." She tucked a strand of hair behind her ears.

"You should figure out a way," Jeff said. "Or else you'll wind up being like me—old and alone. The years go by in the blink of an eye. It's lonely, right, Meri?" He reached over and gave her arm a squeeze.

Meri set down her mug, startled. "I'm not lonely."

"I don't mean all the time, but evenings are tough, don't you think? And holidays?"

"Not for me. I have a daughter, and we're very close."

"Well, sure." He tented his fingers together. "But she's an adult and doesn't live with you, right? So you're essentially alone. Or is there something I don't know?"

She stiffened. "Since you haven't spent any time with me since 1994, I would guess there's a lot you don't know."

There was a long awkward pause, which was only broken when Amanda said, "I hate it when Mom and Dad fight," which made them laugh.

"We're not fighting, honey. Sometimes grown-ups just disagree." Jeff broke into a grin, and Meri saw it, then, a glimpse of his old self, his rugged good looks and youthful impishness peeking through his older exterior. People were almost always the same underneath; it was just the outer shell that withered and aged.

Dominick came through the door, back from his bathroom break, smelling of cigarette smoke and holding his phone aloft. "I just got the craziest text. It was from Felix Worthington's assistant offering me two million dollars."

"I got that one too," Amanda said, stifling a yawn. "A few minutes ago."

"Just like this?" He showed her the screen.

"Exactly the same." She waved a dismissive hand.

Dominick nodded. "Jeff, you and Meri should have gotten a text as well."

Each of them pulled out their phones to take a look. Jeff said, "Well, what do you know?" He held up his phone. "Felix Worthington is offering me two million dollars."

"The same for me." Meri stared at the screen. She rarely got texts, not even of the spam variety. The only one who ever texted her was her daughter, Hailey. Weird that whoever this was had the phone numbers for all four of them.

Amanda said, "Just delete it. Trust me, it's nothing. Spam."

"That's what I thought too, at first, but then I called the number." Dominick paused for dramatic effect, a triumphant look on his face.

Meri was the first to break the silence. "And?"

"It's legit. I FaceTimed with both Felix Worthington and his assistant, Milo. It was definitely them. Turns out that Felix is a huge fan of the show, and he wants to meet all of us to talk about this opportunity. He wouldn't say much about what's involved, but it's a ten-day commitment, and when it's over each of us will get two million dollars."

Jeff leaned back in his chair. "Son, I hate to break it to you, but this sounds really sketchy. I've lived a long time, and no one just gives you two million dollars."

Dominick shrugged. "I think it's for real. Felix really loves the show. Said he discovered it online recently and has binge-watched it over and over again. He wants to fly us out so he can pitch his proposal in person. He'll take care of all the travel arrangements, and we can stay with him. I say we do it. It's one weekend. What do we have to lose?"

If Dominick had one outstanding personality trait, it was his know-it-all confidence, accompanied by a charming smirk. Still, he wasn't wrong.

"If he's paying for it, we could at least go and hear him out," Meri said. It had been a long time since she'd done anything outside of her usual routine. At the very least it would make a good story for the next time she had dinner with friends. Felix Worthington, the mysterious billionaire. Little was known about him. She'd heard he was a teetotaler who refused to serve liquor at his companies' events, despite owning one of the largest distilleries in the country. He was rarely seen in public and almost never gave interviews. Meeting him in person would really be something.

Amanda crossed her arms. "If I'm taking time off from work, I need to know more before I'll commit to doing it."

Dominick pulled out a chair and took a seat. "He wants us to come out to his ranch in Montana, says we'll love it. Stunning views, complete privacy. We can use the pool, go horseback riding, hiking, whatever we want. His gourmet chef will prepare our meals. He only needs us for one night, but we can stay longer if we want. Even if we don't want to take him up on his proposal, it'll be like a free vacation. He's open to any days that work for all five of us."

Jeff raised his eyebrows. "All five of us?"

"Five?" Meri repeated, looking around the table.

"That's the one sticking point." Dominick sighed. "It's all five of us or not at all."

"And the fifth one would be?" Amanda tapped her fingers on the table.

"Lauren, of course. He wants the whole Barlow family there, including Lauren."

Meri shook her head. "Lauren's never going to go for it. I tried keeping in touch, but she wasn't receptive at all. She even sent back my Christmas cards with a note asking me not to contact her anymore." That had stung. Meri knew that Lauren had been miserable working on the show and had tried to give her some extra attention and help, but was blocked by Lauren's aunt, who had also served as her manager and guardian on set. The woman was a nightmare, browbeating the poor child when she forgot her lines, as if that would magically make her a better actor. At fourteen, Lauren had been so tiny that playing a twelve-year-old wasn't much of a stretch. She was a little fair-haired pixie, blonde with blue eyes, and when she smiled, really smiled, Meri thought she was prettier than Amanda. But Lauren rarely smiled, and Amanda, who was all attitude, was a showstopper. Poor Lauren. During the second season, the writers had relegated Lauren's character to a supporting role. It was an act of mercy, but her aunt hadn't seen it that way.

Meri repeated, "She's not going to go for it."

"Leave it to me," Dominick said. "I can talk her into it."

Chapter Five

Montana

Milo and Felix had FaceTimed with Dominick using the oversize computer monitor that covered one wall in Felix's office. The size of the screen made his face look monstrously large, but also highlighted the emotion as it played across his face. Dominick's eagerness was unmistakable. During the conversation, Felix had let Milo take the lead, only chiming in when clarification was necessary. Milo sat closer to the screen, while Felix stayed in the background behind his mammoth desk, a replica of the Resolute desk in the Oval Office.

Milo was a large, beefy guy with broad shoulders, a sharp contrast to Felix's pencil-thin physique and unassuming ways. With Milo doing most of the talking, someone would have thought he was the boss and Felix his trusty assistant. Felix had his reasons for letting Milo handle the call. Milo knew it wasn't from a lack of self-confidence—quite the opposite. Felix believed in a low-key presence. When people underestimated him, it gave him the upper hand.

Working for Felix had surpassed all of Milo's expectations. He was paid well and loved the travel. The work was interesting, since no two days were alike.

In talking to Dominick, Milo had been vague about what the ten-day commitment would entail, but he'd spoken enthusiastically about Felix's love of the show and the weekend meeting at the ranch. To drive the point home, he mentioned the $2 million more than once. Dominick was practically salivating by the time the call ended.

After they hung up, Felix turned to his assistant and said, "That went well."

"He was impressed that you are a fan of the show." Milo smiled. "I would guess that most of the fans are women."

"That sounds a little sexist, Milo. I would guess that most of the fans are people who yearn for a simpler, gentler time," Felix said. "They see the family they'd love to have. The town of Haven is idyllic. Who wouldn't want to live in a place where everyone is a friend and looks out for you?"

"Not me," Milo said glumly. "The fewer people involved in my life the better. Sometimes I even find group chats overwhelming." After a long pause, he said, "Well, one down, four to go. What are the chances you'll get all five to agree to participate?"

"I'd put our chances at one hundred percent." Felix tapped the eraser end of a pencil on his desk. "Without a doubt."

"You really think so?"

"I know so," Felix said confidently. "Soon enough they'll be back in Haven playing the roles they were meant to play."

"Because of the money?" Milo himself looked unsure.

"That," Felix said, "and because the story needs a conclusion."

Chapter Six

Kansas City, Kansas

Dominick had never been here before and was certain that, after this one visit, he'd never come back. If it weren't for the $2 million being dangled in front of him, nothing could have lured him away from the coast and into the nondescript, suburban middle of the country. He drove from the airport in a rented black Toyota Camry and headed straight to Lauren's house. No need for a hotel room. This was a day trip, completely spur-of-the-moment, driven by the prospect of a financial windfall.

The money had become all the more attractive when he'd realized there was a possibility he wouldn't have to share any of it. Neither of the mothers of his children would know about it, so they'd go along with the existing child support agreements based on his salary. Of the two, Jaime would certainly take him back to court for a higher amount if she knew. But there was no reason for her to find out, not if he could be discreet about it.

Now all he had to do was get Lauren to agree to go to the weekend meeting with Felix Worthington. The other three were already on board. All of them had doubts about his trip to Kansas. "I just don't think you'll be able to talk Lauren into it, not even for the money," Meri had said with a shake of her head. "She's married now and has kids. She's moved on." He saw her point, but what Meri didn't know was that Dominick was highly motivated. Lauren had to agree, that's all there was to it. He was going to make it happen.

Now he drove through the suburban outback, letting the GPS lead the way. The car wended its way past houses that all looked the same to him. Generic two-story houses with attached two-car garages and small front porches. As far as he could tell, there was no specific style, or at least no notable architectural characteristics. Lined up, they appeared generic, each one looking like a builder's special from twenty years before. The basketball hoops in the driveways and the glimpses of playground equipment and trampolines in the backyards told him all he needed to know about the neighborhood residents. This was where nonachievers went to live their lives. They worked at boring jobs, got married, had two kids, and lived out the rest of their days coming home after work to mow the lawn and take the children to soccer practice. He shuddered at the thought. Yes, he had kids, but when he spent time with them—which, granted, was infrequently—they had fun. Dominick took them to theme parks and sporting events. When they were in his company, they took part in experiences that enriched their lives. He made sure their time together was always positive. No forcing kids to do homework or chores on his watch. He wasn't that kind of dad and never would be.

Lauren's house was the last one on a dead-end street. Dominick pulled into the driveway and gave the property an assessing glance. A lawn you could golf on, bordered by perfectly manicured landscape beds. Yep, Lauren had embraced the life of the middle class. Probably saving up for retirement, setting aside part of every paycheck and dreaming of the day she and her husband could finally enjoy themselves. If they lived that long.

Two million dollars could go a long way toward saving a person from that kind of drudgery.

Dominick shut the car door behind him and strode up the walkway, a look of practiced good cheer on his face. It was Saturday; hopefully Lauren and her family would be home. He was most interested in meeting her husband and seeing his face when he heard about the amount of money his wife could make for two weeks' work. The husband's influence could make all the difference.

Ringing the doorbell, he heard the scuffle of activity from inside before the door opened and he came face-to-face with a girl who looked to be about eight. Blonde hair, blue eyes, wearing blue jeans and a T-shirt with a panda on it. A Lauren clone. An older girl, who was clearly her sister and a teenage version of their mother, came up behind her, saying, "Charlotte, you're not supposed to open the door unless you know who it is."

Charlotte, not taking her eyes off Dominick, pointed. "I know who it is. It's Dom-Tom from the show."

Dom-Tom. Hearing that nickname from a Lauren looka-like made his stomach clench. Politely he asked, "Is your mother home?"

Before they could answer, he heard Lauren's voice calling out, "Girls, who is it?" Then there she was, Lauren, but twenty-five years older. Her shoulder-length blonde hair had darkened somewhat, making her look less washed out, and her blue eyes were more striking than he remembered. She'd gained a bit of weight too, which actually improved her appearance. As a kid she'd always looked waiflike. Underfed. Since then, she'd been transformed into a completely different person.

Spotting him through the gap in the open door, her expression hardened. "What do you want?"

Dominick turned on the charm. "Is that any way to greet an old friend?"

She frowned, then turned to her daughters. "Charlotte, please get your sandals on. Emily, would you mind grabbing my purse and car keys off the counter? We're running late." She turned back to Dominick. "Sorry, can't talk. You caught us at a bad time. Take care now." And then she closed the door in his face.

WTF? He'd flown in all the way from the coast and she actually *closed the door in his face?* Dominick pressed the doorbell repeatedly, listening as it chimed inside the house. He got some degree of satisfaction in knowing that she wasn't going anywhere until she gave him a chance to make his pitch. His car was parked right in the center of the driveway. She'd have to drive over the lawn to get around it. He kept ringing the doorbell, until finally she yanked open the door and said, "Are you kidding me? Just go away, Dominick. Whatever you want, I'm not interested."

He held up a hand. "Just hear me out. I came to confirm that you're on board with the Felix Worthington offer. It's a really great opportunity, don't you think?"

"I don't have time for your nonsense. All I know is that we're late getting to the humane society, so you need to move your car."

Now he could identify the expression on her face. Absolute disgust. Still, he kept trying. "Just give me two minutes. That's all I need."

"If you don't move your car, I'm calling the police." This time, the door slammed shut.

He didn't remember Lauren having such a forceful personality. On set, he'd once made her cry when he'd called her a pest. "Go away," he'd said after she followed him and Amanda one too many times. "No one wants to hang out with you. You're just a pest." He still recalled the way her face had crumpled and the convulsive sobbing that came afterward. Her eyes had been so red and puffy that they'd had to put off taping a scene in which she'd played a key role. She hadn't even outed him as the cause of her crying, that's how docile she'd been at the time. Hard to reconcile that memory with the woman in front of him. Clearly, she'd changed.

Dominick dutifully returned to the car and backed down the driveway. He parked on the street a few houses down and waited until he saw Lauren drive past in a tan minivan. The older daughter, Emily, sat in the passenger seat next to her mother. Presumably the younger one, Charlotte, was in back, although it was hard to see through the tinted windows. He pulled away from the curb to follow the minivan, then called Meri, putting her on speaker phone.

"She wouldn't even talk to me," he said after she answered. "Shut the door in my face."

Meri sighed. "I'm sorry, Dominick. I know you must be disappointed."

Disappointed? She didn't know the half of it. Lauren was standing between him and his future. "I'm not giving up yet. I'm going to try her one more time."

"Good luck," Meri said, sounding doubtful. "Let me know how it goes."

"Will do." He slowed as he approached an intersection with a red light. There was only one car between Lauren's vehicle and his own. If he lost sight of her, he could always look up the address for the local humane society, but he preferred to tag along behind her. The light changed and he zipped ahead, following when she made a right turn onto the interstate. He stayed a few car lengths behind until they reached an exit that led to a country road, then reduced his speed, allowing her to get farther ahead so as not to look too obvious. When they reached their destination and he finally turned into the humane society lot, she and her daughters were already getting out of their vehicle.

Dominick parked and then approached her, calling out, "Hey, Lauren, do you have a minute?"

She held out her arm and stepped in front of her daughters as if he was a threat, which was ridiculous. "Emily and Charlotte, go inside," she said firmly. "I'll be right there."

"Mom," Emily said, "I'll stay with you." Her eyes darted from Dominick to her mother, a look of concern on her face.

"No." Lauren's tone was decisive. "Go with your sister. I've got this covered."

As the girls reluctantly walked toward the building, Dominick called out, "Nice meeting you, Emily and Charlotte."

"You aren't allowed to talk to my daughters," Lauren said, her arms crossed.

"I'm sorry. I won't talk to them again, but I find it interesting you named them Charlotte and Emily," he said, trying to find common ground. "Old-fashioned names like in the show. So you must have some good memories of that time?"

"My daughters were named after Emily and Charlotte Brontë, two of my favorite authors. Not that you'd know anything about reading books."

"You're probably right." He spoke agreeably, hoping it would bring her temper down a notch.

"I can't believe you followed us. Do you have any idea how creepy that is?" Her voice got louder with every word. "I don't see you for years, and then you freakin' show up at my house without any notice and stalk me and my kids?"

"I didn't mean to stalk you. They seem like nice girls, by the way. Beautiful, like their mom." He gave her his warmest smile, the one that endeared him to everyone, despite his shock-jock bluster. "What are you doing here? Adopting a puppy?"

"We volunteer twice a month, not that it's any of your business."

Sensing she was softening, he went right for the meat of the matter. "I came all the way out here because I want to make sure you know about the two-million-dollar offer Felix Worthington is making to all of us in the cast. Each of us will get two million dollars, Lauren! For a ten-day job. Easy money. Imagine how life-changing that would be for you and your family." She didn't say anything, so he continued. "You could pay off the mortgage, go to Disney World, pay college tuition for the girls."

"I got the text and the email, Dominick. I've been informed."

"So you know. I know it sounds unbelievable, but I can tell you that I've spoken to Felix and his assistant, and this is a legitimate offer." Out of the corner of his eye, he saw a police car turn into the lot. Lauren stepped away from her van and waved it over. His mouth dropped open. "You called the cops on me?" His incredulity had more to do with being outmaneuvered than anything else. He wouldn't have thought Lauren had it in her.

"Nothing personal," she said. "I'd do it for anyone who follows me and my daughters after I've warned them to leave me alone. I don't know how it is where you live, but stalking is a crime in Kansas."

Getting out of the car, the officer called out, "Are you Lauren?" He was a beefy man in his thirties, in full uniform.

"I am," she said, walking toward him. "And this is the man who followed me after I told him I wasn't interested in talking to him."

As the policeman got closer to Dominick, his expression changed and he broke into a big grin. "Wait a minute! Aren't you Tom Barlow from *A Little Slice of Haven*?"

"That would be me," Dominick said, giving him his signature smile. "Are you a fan of the show?"

39

"I've seen it for sure, but it's my wife who's your biggest fan. Oh, she's going to die when I tell her. She's seen every episode a million times." He shook his head in disbelief and then did a double take looking at Lauren. "Good grief, you played Ann Barlow on the show, right? This is incredible!"

She let out a frustrated sigh. "Yes, we were both on the show. But he's harassing me now, and I'd like him to leave me alone."

"I get it—a little sibling fight." The cop smirked and elbowed Dominick. "You need to respect her space, man."

"I just wanted to tell her about an opportunity related to the show. I'm only here for the day. I flew in from LA this morning and went straight to her house without calling, which wasn't the right way to do it. I get that now. It's totally on me. I guess I was just so enthused about seeing her again and the possibility of doing another project with the whole cast that I wasn't thinking clearly. Honestly, I didn't think she'd be so alarmed when I turned up at her door." He turned to Lauren. "I apologize for upsetting you. I just wanted to let you know about the offer in case you weren't aware."

Lauren spoke directly to the officer. "Are you going to arrest him or give him a ticket or what?"

He pointed a friendly finger in her direction. "You live here? In Kansas City?"

"Yes," she said, a look of resignation crossing her face. "I haven't been in show business since I was a kid. I'm married and teach third grade now."

"Really? I had no idea you lived in the community!" The officer turned to Dominick. "I tell you what, if you take a selfie with me and promise to go straight to the airport, I think I can let this go." He turned to Lauren. "What do you think? We'll give him a pass if he agrees to leave and not come back? It will save all of us a lot of time."

Lauren nodded. "As long as he goes."

The cop waved Lauren over to join them in the selfie. After the photo was snapped, Dominick went to pull Lauren in for a hug. Surprisingly, she allowed it. He whispered into her ear, "Please promise you'll think about the Worthington deal. It affects more than just you."

She responded, "All of you can go straight to hell." She turned away from him and walked toward the building, not looking back.

So that was it, then. Inwardly, Dominick felt a wave of relief mixed with disappointment. Lauren was never going to come around, but at least he could get the hell out of Kansas without getting into trouble with the law.

By the time Dominick had gone through security and found a seat in the terminal, the photo of the cop posing with a sullen-looking Lauren on one side and a smiling Dominick on the other had already been posted by the officer's wife on the *A Little Slice of Haven* discussion forum. She'd written: "Guess who had an impromptu reunion in the parking lot of our local animal shelter? That's right, it's Ann and Tom! My husband is a police officer and got to meet both of them!"

Several commenters proclaimed how lucky her husband was to meet them, and from there the discussion led to speculation on the reason for the reunion. One person wrote, "Wouldn't it be great if they're meeting because there's a movie in the works?" That comment led to hundreds more, all of them eager to see the Barlows back together again.

Lauren Saunders was a fool, Dominick decided. The public had a short attention span. Who knew how long the fandom would feel this strongly about the show? The offer from Felix Worthington was a once-in-a-lifetime opportunity for all of them to become rich. He sighed.

Stupid Lauren. It was one thing for her to turn it down, but didn't she realize she was screwing it up for all of them? *Selfish bitch.*

Chapter Seven

Los Angeles

When Jeff got the phone call from Dominick informing him that Lauren had unequivocally said no, his stomach dropped. He'd had realistic expectations and knew it was a long shot, but apparently on some level he'd hoped that she might agree to join them. "Maybe if I talk to her?" Jeff said.

"Her last words to me were, and I quote, 'All of you can go straight to hell.'"

"Probably not, then." It was clear Lauren held grudges.

Dominick excused himself from the call to give the news to Meri and Amanda and ended with: "I'll text Milo Lappin too and let him know." And that was it. After the call ended, Jeff wandered into the kitchen and found himself opening the empty cabinet where he used to keep the bourbon. He hadn't had a drink in more than ten years, but it was times like this that the dragon reared its ugly head, the urge coming on so strong that he knew he was one step away from being out of control. Jeff could almost feel the taste of the liquor on his tongue and the comforting warmth as it slid down his throat and entered his bloodstream. Oh, he wanted it. Bad.

The problem was that no matter how much he drank it was never enough. He'd be craving the next swallow before the first was even down his gullet. One sip began an endless cycle of craving that only ended up causing him pain and misery. Drinking hadn't served him well, but it sure would take the edge off now. Thank God he didn't keep it in the house anymore.

The day after Haven Con, he'd handed over the $5,000 payment to his gambling creditors, with the promise of paying off the balance by the end of next month. Reluctantly, they'd gone along with the arrangement. The problem was that he had no idea where he could get that kind of money on short notice except from his brother.

And wouldn't Scott love that? Jeff had been the shining star in their younger days, but he'd managed to royally screw things up. Meanwhile, Scott had stayed in their hometown on the outskirts of Albuquerque working in the local hardware store. Over the years, he'd quietly progressed from stock boy to assistant manager to manager, finally buying the business when the owner wanted out. Now Scott was sitting pretty. Writing a check for $7,000 would be easy for him, but it came at a price for Jeff. He'd have to repay Scott, of course, and he'd never hear the end of it, not even after the debt was settled. Scott would gloat until his dying days.

Getting beaten to death might be preferable.

If only Lauren had agreed to the Worthington deal. Jeff wondered if it would have gone differently if someone else had contacted her. Dominick and Lauren had never really connected.

It was a shame, but not all family members got along.

Jeff settled in front of the TV and flipped channels, looking for a distraction, but nothing grabbed him. Sometimes he wondered if he'd developed attention deficit disorder over the years. It took so much to hold his attention lately. He set the remote down at the same time his phone buzzed, letting him know he had a text.

It was from Milo Lappin:
Looks like we have a quorum! All five of you have agreed to meet at Felix's Montana ranch to discuss the opportunity at hand. I'll be in touch soon to set up travel arrangements.

Seconds after that, Jeff got a flurry of other messages on their group text.

Dominick:
What the hell? How did this happen?

Amanda:
Jeff or Meri, did you call Lauren?

Meri:
Wasn't me.

Jeff:
Me either. Maybe she changed her mind after you left, Dominick?

Dominick:

Not likely. I'm calling Milo to find out what happened. Sit tight.

Jeff went into the kitchen, set the phone on the counter, then rummaged around in the fridge. Finally, settling on a can of Coke, he popped the top and took a swig before going into the living room to take a seat. Within a few minutes, Dominick was back with an answer.

Dominick:
Turns out Felix Worthington reached out to Lauren himself and got her to agree.

Interesting. Jeff sat back and read the thread as the others went back and forth, wondering what Felix Worthington could have said to change Lauren's mind. Amanda thought it was all about the money, while Dominick floated a different theory.

Dominick:
Her daughter called me Dom-Tom. If her kids know the show, maybe she's doing it for them?

Amanda:
I don't get what you're saying.

Dominick:
Like she wants to impress them? She teaches elementary school now. It's not like she's got much going on.

46

Meri:
Possible.

Amanda:
I still think it's the $. She didn't realize the offer was legit until Worthington called.

Meri:
So what do you think the project is?

Dominick:
A reunion movie. Gotta be.

Meri:
A movie in only ten days?

Amanda:
Hard to do in that timeframe. Plus, we're all so much older.

Dominick:
Doesn't matter. They do it all the time. Worthington's going to call it ANOTHER SLICE OF HAVEN!!

True to form, Dominick kept riffing, coming up with more titles and story premises until Amanda, most likely wanting to make it end, conceded he was probably right in that there was a reunion movie in the works. Jeff had forgotten how exhausting Dominick could be. Amanda excused herself, saying she had to answer a call, and Dominick bowed out too, saying he had somewhere else to be, leaving just Jeff and Meri to talk on the thread.

Meri:
You've been quiet. Everything okay?

Jeff:
Never better.

And he meant it too. The forthcoming money couldn't have come at a better time. An added bonus? Seeing the whole gang together in Montana. Thank God for Felix Worthington and the Barlow reunion. It was the lifeline he needed.

Meri:
Good. See you in Montana!

Jeff typed: **Can't wait. Good night, sweetheart.** He stared at it for a second, then deleted the word *sweetheart* and replaced it with her name. There would be plenty of time in Montana for him to make amends and try to resurrect the old feelings between them.

Chapter Eight

Montana

At the airport, Amanda was glad to see the driver ready and waiting at the designated pickup area. Easy to spot in his chauffeur's uniform and crisp cap, he held up a sign with her name in bold black letters: **Amanda Waddell.**

"You're right on time," she said.

He nodded. "Of course, miss. We don't want our guests to wait." His name tag said Oswald, and he had a pleasant persona. Trim build, clean-shaven, a smile on his face. Deferential, but not overly so. Just the way she liked supporting staff.

"Are the others coming soon?" she asked.

"Everyone else arrived earlier. They're all waiting for you at Mr. Worthington's place."

Since Amanda only had a carry-on, there was no need to make a stop in the baggage claim area, so the driver escorted her to the exterior doors and asked her to wait while he went to get the car. She was looking down at her phone, wondering why no one would answer her on the group text chain, when he returned to escort her to the vehicle parked at the curb. "Right this way, miss," he said, holding the car door as she slid into place.

"Is this a Rolls-Royce?" she asked as they drove away from the airport.

"Yes, miss, a Rolls-Royce Phantom."

Amanda nodded in approval, then cast her attention back to the screen. Colleagues had accused her of being obsessed with her iPhone (Sheri Powers, the meteorologist at the station, had said Amanda loved her phone like most people love their babies), but that wasn't entirely true. It was just so damn convenient to have on hand. It was her link to the world, her way of staying in touch with family and friends. An avenue for keeping track of details for work. An easy mode for shopping and playing word games. She wasn't addicted, though. There'd never been a time she hadn't muted it at a restaurant, and right before she went on the air, she always tucked it into her handbag and stowed it in her locker.

When the car slowed to a stop, she looked up in time to see the driver roll down his window and punch a code into the security box. Ahead of them, rustic gates swung open, allowing them entry. "We're here?" she asked, amazed. Clearly, she'd lost track of time.

"We're here," he said. "Welcome to the Worthington ranch."

The dirt-packed driveway went on for another quarter mile, passing through a grove of trees, and then, coming out the other side, she could see that, almost magically, they'd arrived. Amanda got out and shielded her eyes, taking in the bright blue of the sky and the backdrop of majestic mountains. Off in the distance to her right were more trees and behind them a massive squared-off building. Ahead of her was the house, mansion-sized, but ranch-style in design, with a fieldstone exterior on the first floor and rough timber siding for the two floors above. The columns holding up the massive front porch overhang were rustic logs as well. Not Amanda's preferred style, but still impressive.

"Follow me, please," Oswald said, leading the way into the house. They went through the tall entryway, notable for an enormous antler chandelier in the center of the tray ceiling, and continued on until they approached a large room, where she saw the rest of the cast sitting around a U-shaped sectional sofa, along with a man she didn't recognize.

All eyes were on her as she entered, and Jeff called out, "Amanda!" as if they hadn't seen each other in decades. He leaped up off the sofa and gave her a hug in greeting. Normally Amanda wasn't much of a hugger, but Jeff always had been, so she went along with it. He said, "So good to see you."

"Thank you. I'm thrilled to be here." She peered around Jeff's shoulder. "Good to see all of you."

Oswald said, "I'd be happy to take your bag up to your room, miss." Amanda stepped back from Jeff's embrace and handed over her bag.

The strange man on the sofa said, "Miss Waddell will be in the Stillwater Suite." Oswald nodded. After he left the room, the man stood and introduced himself. "I'm Milo Lappin, Mr. Worthington's assistant. Come and take a seat."

Sitting down next to Jeff, Amanda noticed that all of them were clustered to one side except for Lauren, who sat apart from the others. "Hello, everyone," Amanda said in greeting, making a point to look at each face, ending with the only person she hadn't seen at the convention. "Hey, Lauren, it's been a long time." When they'd worked together, the age gap between them had felt like more than four years. Lauren, who'd been small and fragile in appearance, had made Amanda feel as if she were the adult and Lauren the child. She wasn't prepared for this new version of Lauren, all grown up, casually dressed, poised and present.

Lauren wasn't relaxing into the sofa like the others. Instead, she sat on the edge of her seat, back straight, feet together. She didn't respond, just nodded in acknowledgment. *So that's how it's going to be.*

Milo stood to face them, then rubbed his hands together. "With everyone in attendance, we can now get started."

Dominick held up a finger. "When is Mr. Worthington arriving?"

"Mr. Worthington was unexpectedly called away on business, so unfortunately you won't be seeing him today," Milo said smoothly. "But he's entrusted me to walk you through his proposal, so no worries there."

"But we're going to meet with him eventually?" Trust Dominick to ask what everyone else was wondering.

Milo's smile was wide. "I can't speak to that, but I can fill you in on an exciting opportunity that will leave each of you two million dollars richer."

Dominick frowned and turned to Meri. "I don't know about you, but I was looking forward to meeting Felix Worthington."

"Oh, for crying out loud!" Lauren's voice rang out, filling the room. "Could you let the man finish talking?" They all turned to her, shocked at the outburst. She rested her hands on her knees and met their gazes. "What?" she said. "All of us dropped everything and flew out here. I can't be the only one who's curious what this is about."

Meri addressed Milo. "Please go on. We'll be quiet." She gave Dominick a maternal look of warning.

Unfazed by the interruption, Milo proceeded. "The ten-day project will take place here on this property. All of you have to agree to it, and all of you have to see it through. You'll be here for the entire time and won't have any contact with the outside world. If anyone drops out midway through, there will be no payment for any of you."

"That hardly seems fair," Dominick muttered under his breath.

"So what exactly is the project?" Meri asked, peering up at him through her round glasses.

Milo nodded. "I think it would be easier to have a visual while I explain it." He extended his hand, waiting for the group to follow him out of the room. "I want to show you something, and I predict you're going to be absolutely amazed."

Chapter Nine

He hadn't oversold it, not in the least. All five of them were amazed.

After Milo's proclamation, he'd led them outside, where they found the driver waiting in a minivan similar to the one Lauren drove on a daily basis. Getting into the van, Dominick had joked, "I think this is the part where some hoodlums come and put cloth bags over our heads."

On the ride to the far side of the property, all of them were quiet with anticipation. When they got closer to a warehouse-sized building and realized the size of it, there were a few murmurs of awe. Milo opened the door to the vast building, led them inside along a short hallway to some interior double doors, then ushered them through.

"Welcome to Haven," Milo said, with a broad sweep of his arm. "Welcome home."

They were back in Haven. More precisely, they stood on the corner of Bailey Street and Sycamore Drive. In front of them was Doc Tarter's home, the very house they'd visited when little Bud Barlow, the long-absent fourth child, had gotten a fishhook caught in his hand. A row of houses fronted by a sidewalk continued down the tree-lined street. Birds could be heard chirping off in the distance. Overhead there was a lovely blue sky dotted with puffy white clouds. It was summertime, based on the abundance of flowers in every yard. More flowers than Lauren had remembered on the set, each planting bed popping with color and meticulously arranged. The trees, too, were perfect, their limbs reaching up to the sky.

Inexplicably, a slight breeze gusted, making the leaves tremble. Lauren knew they were inside a building, but everything about it felt as if they were outdoors. She'd been transported to small-town America in the 1940s. More specifically, they'd somehow landed in Haven as it would have been if it were real. She suspected that if they kept walking straight, they'd arrive at the Barlows' house.

Unbelievable.

Each of them had a different reaction at seeing Haven re-created before them. Meri blinked once, then twice, as if she couldn't quite fathom this television world come to life. Dominick said, "Holy crap!" Jeff grinned, while Amanda looked at the buildings within a building and back at the door they'd just walked through as if they'd somehow gone through a portal.

Lauren, who'd gotten most of the details from Felix Worthington ahead of time, still had a question. "How did you do this?"

Milo gave her an appreciative look. "It was no small thing, believe me. Mr. Worthington had a team who worked for the past year to ensure it was as accurate as possible. We were able to purchase some of the sets from the actual show, which we used to get an idea of the floorplan of your house.

We bought props from the show as well, but most of it has been re-created." He pointed down the street. "This version of Haven extends a mile and a half in length and width."

Jeff whistled. "I guess if you have enough money, you can do anything."

"Would you like a tour?" Milo asked and then flushed red. "Wait! I guess you don't need a tour. You've lived here."

"The sets were on soundstages. They weren't actually arranged like a town," Lauren explained.

He nodded. "Of course. I knew that."

"I want to see all of it," Amanda proclaimed, and then they were off as a group, walking down the middle of the road. The houses were picture-perfect, with wide porches and mullioned windows. Milo pointed out a side street that led to the downtown area. "When we're up and running, you'll be able to go to the pharmacy and visit the soda fountain, get yourself an ice-cream soda. It's right next to the Keenalynn Bakery, just like in the show. And of course, Aden's Garage is there for all your mechanical fixes, just in case your car breaks down. Everything will be completely operational."

"So what's this all for?" Amanda asked. "For filming a movie?"

Milo said, "No. Guess again."

"You said when it's up and running people can visit the soda fountain. Is this a theme park for the fans?" Meri asked, speaking for the first time since they'd arrived.

"No." Milo shook his head emphatically. "This is most definitely not a theme park, and it's not for the fans. It's for all of you."

"I don't understand," Meri said. "How is it for us?"

Before Milo could answer, Dominick asked, "I'm guessing we're supposed to stay here for ten days?"

"Very good, Dominick!" Milo grinned. "The answer is yes. You'll spend ten days here, living the life of the Barlows."

"We'd just live here?" Jeff said to Milo. "Why? What would be the point?"

"I'd love to tell you right now," he said, "but Felix really wanted you to get a feel for what he's done here first. He made me promise I wouldn't tell you until we get to your house. Once we're there, I'll lay it all out and answer any questions you might have."

They spotted the house from the end of the block, and without saying a word, all of them quickened their pace until they'd arrived at 442 Bailey Street, home of the Barlow family. There it was, two stories of nostalgia fronted by a long porch and set off by a white picket fence. Most shocking of all, Grandma sat in the rocking chair on the front porch, gently rocking, her hand resting on the head of her loyal dog, Beau. If seeing the town had amazed them, spotting Catherine Sedgwick waiting for them shocked them to the core.

"What the hell?" Dominick said quietly. "I thought she was dead."

Milo laughed, a short, barky sound. "Come and see." He opened the gate and, despite his large size, bounded like a child up the walkway to the porch. "She's an animatronic representation of the character, and so is the dog."

"Now that's creepy," Amanda said.

"Holy crap," Dominick added. "And she just rocks like that continuously?"

"The rocking is intermittent," Milo said. "Grandma also talks, and sometimes she pats the dog. On occasion her eyes close and she dozes off. Just a little light snoring. Periodically you'll hear her dispensing advice or giving consoling words in the actual voice of the actress. The dog is also equipped for sound, sometimes barking or whining."

They gathered on the porch and inspected both. Catherine's double had been outfitted in a housedress, a loose-fitting floral print with two large pockets on the front. Identical to her costumes on the show. Lauren remembered Catherine protesting, wanting something less shapeless and more flattering, but wardrobe had held firm, saying the garments they'd chosen were accurate for grandmothers at the time.

"Did you get permission from Catherine Sedgwick's estate to do this?" Meri asked. "I don't think Catherine would like this." Her eyes had a worried look to them. Lauren understood her concern. Catherine, despite her sweet grandmother persona on the show, had been a hard-edged woman who didn't tolerate much. Known for talking back to the director, she'd often made disparaging comments to the children if they messed up their lines. There was no way she'd go for having a robot version of herself dressed as Grandma Barlow rocking into eternity. Lauren wouldn't be surprised if this animatronic version blew a fuse and burned the whole house down in retaliation.

"No need to worry about the legalities," Milo said. "Mr. Worthington has made sure to get the necessary permissions." He opened the screen door. "Time to go inside and see the rest of the house."

Lauren wasn't prepared for the surge of emotion that came over her as she walked into the house. The two years working on the show had been dreadful for her, had crushed her soul, in fact. She'd never wanted to be an actor, ever. It had been Aunt Jackie's dream, and initially Lauren had gone along with it.

After her parents died in a car accident, Aunt Jackie had taken her in and forced her into acting classes. She'd done a commercial for Barbie's Dreamhouse, which admittedly had been fun, so she'd agreed to do more. Somehow her audition for the show had gotten her the part. From there it only got worse. Despite what most people thought, acting wasn't a glamorous job. The lights were bright and hot, and she had a crippling fear of not knowing her lines.

Later, as an adult, she liked to point out to friends that it was the only profession she knew of that actually allowed child labor. They nodded as if they understood, but really, you had to be there.

She understood early on that this wasn't for her. When she'd learned that she'd gotten the part, a sick sense of dread came over her and she'd run to the bathroom and vomited. Her aunt wrote it off as excitement. Anytime Lauren expressed her concerns about acting, Aunt Jackie had told her she was being selfish. "Do you know how many girls would die to get this role?" So she did it, but her lack of passion showed. When the show was canceled it was a relief, and she'd refused to go to any more auditions. And after that, her aunt had shipped her off to Kansas to live with her grandparents. Washed her hands of her ungrateful niece.

Standing in a house that looked so much like the set, but had none of the negative emotions attached, was strangely cathartic. Jeff, Meri, Dominick, and Amanda were just people she'd once worked with. Lauren was an adult now, and none of them had power over her anymore. Being here broke the spell.

They all separated and explored the house. The parlor had the same configuration of identical-looking furniture. No television set because this was the 1940s, but there was a wood-clad radio the size of a dorm refrigerator and an upright piano, sheet music spread out on the ledge above the keys. The sofa had a large crocheted doily across the back, as did the wing chair. In the kitchen, Meri called out, "My apron is hanging right where it always was!"

Lauren did a slow lap around the lower level, peeking into Grandma's bedroom in the back of the house. She heard Dominick and Amanda exclaim over knickknacks that were exact replicas of those on the show. "Holy crap!" Dominick said. "Remember the episode when I broke that vase and glued it together so Dad wouldn't find out?" He held up the vase, complete with cracks that had been glued. "How in the hell did you guys do this?" This question was addressed to Milo.

A slow grin spread across Milo's face. "Mr. Worthington insisted on complete accuracy."

Lauren slid her hand along the banister and slowly walked up the steps to the second floor. On set, the stairs had led nowhere. The top landing had extended another ten feet on either side, ending at a wall. When the kids were sent up to their rooms, they'd climbed the stairs and waited out of sight until the scene finished. So many times, Dominick had tickled her, making her laugh and getting her into trouble with both the director and her aunt. The stairs in this house, unlike on the set, presumably led to actual bedrooms.

She went from room to room, taking it all in. The parents' room was identical to what she remembered, right down to the chenille coverlet and the dresser topped with a framed black-and-white wedding photo. She stared at the photo, mentally comparing Jeff and Meri to their fictitious counterparts, Gerald and Marion. Both Jeff and Meri had aged well enough since the show. Jeff's face was a bit craggy, and he carried more weight, most of it in his gut. By Hollywood standards he'd let himself go, but he'd blend right in with his age group in Kansas. Meri, on the other hand, was stunning. If anything, she looked better than ever. She made being sixty-something with white hair and dark-rimmed glasses look like the epitome of cool. *Good for her.*

In Tom's room, sports pennants and ribbons hung on one wall. Lauren went over to the nightstand and opened the top drawer, then smiled when she saw the Bible sitting inside right where it had always been. Tom Barlow had so many spiritual dilemmas that episodes often ended with him cracking open the good book, looking for answers. She doubted that Dominick ever read the Bible, then or later. If Tom Barlow had an evil twin, it would have been Dominick Ingrelli.

Lauren continued on to the girls' room. In the show, Dorothy and Ann had shared a room. Two twin beds separated by a lamp-topped nightstand. She stood between them for a moment, taking in the patchwork quilts covering the beds. On the show, they'd been sewn with loving care by Grandma Barlow. Lauren ran a hand over the quilt on what had been her bed. It looked the same, but the feel was not quite right. Her brow furrowed as she tried to work out the difference. The fabric had a smoother feel. More synthetic, less cotton, maybe? She shrugged. Close enough.

Going to the window, she smiled upon seeing the tree just outside the glass. It was fake, of course, but the re-created version was spot-on. The tree was part of one of Lauren's few fond Haven memories. One of the storylines had involved having Dorothy climb the tree for the purposes of looking through George Bonner's bedroom window. Amanda, who had an intense fear of heights, had refused to be hoisted that high, even with the security of a harness. After a lot of brainstorming, the director came up with a solution. Lauren, wearing a dark wig, was filmed from the back, supplemented by close-ups of Amanda's face surrounded by tree limbs. That day, the director had given her a high five and said, "Way to go, Lauren!" For once he'd actually called her by her name, instead of referring to her as Ann. She'd saved the day and felt like a hero. Of course, that was before the tragic accident. After that, the tree took on a more menacing association.

The last bedroom belonged to Bud Barlow, the younger brother who'd only been on the show for six episodes. He'd actually been her favorite in the cast. A sweet child. The two of them were the only ones who had to attend school on set, and she'd also helped him with his lines. He had a quick mind and a phenomenal memory, but difficulty reading. If she read his lines aloud, he had no trouble memorizing and delivering them, but left on his own, he struggled. And he was left on his own a lot. His mother, who was pregnant at the time, and Lauren's aunt had spent more time socializing with each other than overseeing their young charges. Lauren realized years later that her fictitious little brother must have had dyslexia. Poor kid.

She wasn't sure if Bud had ever been shown in his bedroom on the show. It didn't look familiar, anyway. This version had a teddy bear on the bed and a baseball bat leaning against the wall in one corner. Framed prints showed original illustrations from the Wizard of Oz book series. That's right, she remembered now—Bud Barlow had loved those books. She pulled open the drawers of his bureau to find shirts and sweaters neatly folded inside. She pulled out a sweater and held it up for inspection. Just the right size for a seven-year-old boy. Milo hadn't been kidding about complete accuracy.

Lauren heard Dominick and Amanda coming down the hall, laughing and exclaiming over the contents of the rooms. She sighed. It hadn't taken long for the two of them to reconnect. Refolding the sweater, she returned it to the drawer.

"What's this room for?" Amanda asked from the doorway, sounding puzzled.

"It's Bud's room," Lauren said. She'd thought it was obvious, but maybe not. She sat on the edge of the bed.

"Bud?" Amanda repeated the name like someone who was learning a foreign language.

Lauren clarified. "Bud Barlow."

"Squiggles," Dominick answered, using the nickname he'd given the kid. "Remember him? Overly sensitive, big eyes, trouble hitting his mark?"

"Oh yeah. I forgot about him." Amanda tucked a strand of hair behind her ear. "I wonder why they bothered to give him a bedroom? He wasn't on the show for very long at all."

Not saying a word, Lauren got up. Skirting around them, she headed to the stairs.

"What's her problem?" she heard Dominick ask.

"Who knows?" Amanda answered.

In no time at all they'd reverted back to their teenage selves. Part of Lauren wanted to respond, "I can hear you," the way her own daughters would have, but she was the bigger person now.

Besides, karma would eventually even things out. She was sure of that.

Chapter Ten

Once they'd finished exploring, the group gathered in the parlor so Milo could spell out the terms of the proposal. He stood in the entrance of the room, in full view of everyone. Jeff, Meri, and Amanda took their places on the couch, while Dominick plunked himself down in the wing chair, one leg slung over the arm. Lauren claimed the piano bench, dragging it a little closer to the others, but not quite joining them. Jeff stood up to offer his spot on the couch to Lauren, but she just shook her head.

There was something about Lauren that Jeff couldn't quite figure out. She'd come to Montana, which meant she was open to whatever this was, but she hadn't embraced being in the company of the rest of the cast. No friendly greetings or casual conversation. He knew she had bad associations from the show, but that had been so long ago. Besides, there'd been some good times on set too, something she seemed to have forgotten. Jeff sighed. Time had softened his view of the show, but apparently Lauren didn't see it the same way. People seemed to selectively filter their memories to fit their own purposes.

Milo clasped his hands together. "Now that you've all seen the miracle we've created, it's time to answer all of your questions. As I stated before, the project you've been invited to attend will happen here, in Haven. You'll live in this house and live the lives of the Barlows, not breaking character the entire time." He paused, beaming, and glanced around the room to take in their reactions.

Dominick raised his hand. "Why?"

Milo's eyes narrowed in confusion. "What do you mean?"

"What is the purpose?" Dominick asked, emphasizing each word. "Is Felix Worthington going to be living next door, waiting to hang out with us, or what?"

Milo laughed. "No, nothing like that. Felix is looking forward to watching your creative take on this very different acting experience, but he won't actually be here. The whole town is outfitted with cameras, so he can watch off-site."

Amanda whispered, "Creepy." The word came out in a loud hiss. If she was trying to keep quiet, it wasn't working. Everyone in the room heard it.

"I realized as I said it that it came off the wrong way," Milo said, a smile in his voice, "but if you give it some thought, it's not that different from the cameras that taped the show. You did it before as paid actors—this is very much the same."

"Where are these cameras going to be?" Dominick asked.

"Everywhere except the bathrooms." Milo pointed up at the light fixture in the middle of the ceiling. "Every room, every building, and every street in Haven is already equipped with cleverly hidden cameras. You should assume they'll be recording everything you say and do. Think of it as reality TV or a social experiment. This is unprecedented. You'll be part of something that's never been done before."

They were all quiet, thinking. Now that they knew they were being recorded, the cast appeared to be weighing every word and facial expression. Amanda sighed, and Lauren shifted on the piano bench. Through the screen door, the creak of Grandma's rocking chair broke through the silence.

Finally, Jeff spoke up. "So, we'll have ten days' worth of pages to learn ahead of time?" This could be a deal breaker. He hadn't memorized dialogue in years and wondered if he still had the mental capacity to commit so much to memory. Even during his best acting days there were times he'd flubbed his lines, and his brain certainly hadn't gotten any sharper with age.

Milo shook his head. "That's the best part! You won't have to learn any lines. Every morning, a letter for each of you will be waiting on the entryway table just inside the front door. You'll only be allowed to open your specific envelope, the one with your name on it, and you can't show it to anyone else. The letter will have vague instructions, a sort of outline for the day. You'll follow the directions, improvising as you go. All in character, of course. It might say something like 'the Barlow kids plan a surprise party for their mother's birthday,' and Tom's might say his role in this is to bake the cake. That's just something I made up," he added hurriedly. "You won't actually see that particular scenario, but it gives you an idea of the kind of thing you might encounter. And just to be clear, we'll provide the clothing, food, toiletries, and anything else you might need. You can't bring anything with you, including cell phones. We're keeping it accurate to the 1940s."

"So all of this is just so a billionaire can watch a reenactment of his favorite show?" Amanda asked. "I mean, if so, that's okay by me. I can be Dorothy Barlow for ten days for that kind of money, but I'm having trouble understanding what his motivation is."

"It's simple, really. His motivation is linked to his passion for the show. He's just doing what most of your fans would be doing if they had the money. They'd all love to see you together again. To catch up with the Barlows and see what they're up to now."

Amanda didn't look convinced. "Who's going to be watching us besides Felix Worthington? Is this going to be broadcast?"

"I promise you it will not be broadcast. We do have a tech crew who will be monitoring the cameras and recording it as it happens, and I might be watching on occasion, but other than that, no one will see it. This is a private event."

"Completely private?" Meri asked. "Or is it going to be aired at some point?"

"Private for now," Milo said. "When the ten days are up, Mr. Worthington will assess if there's enough good footage to create a movie or a limited series. Either way it will be a limited run, and if that's the case, all of you will be able to see the end result ahead of time for your approval. And if he decides to move forward with this, it will be a separate deal. You'll be able to negotiate your terms at that point."

"Terms? Like more money?" Dominick asked.

Milo nodded. "Correct. It could potentially be a lot more money, and all five of you have to agree to it, or it won't happen."

Lauren stood up. "I have a question. If the show was set in the 1940s and twenty-five years have passed since then, does that mean that this so-called experiment takes place in the 1960s?"

Good question. Jeff nodded while wondering about the ramifications of moving the timeline forward. Would the Barlows now be attending civil rights demonstrations, flashing peace signs, and wearing tie-dyed T-shirts?

Milo said, "Time has stood still for the Barlows. You'll be playing your roles as if Ann and Dorothy and Tom are still teenagers living with their loving parents and grandmother." Seeing their dubious expressions, he smiled and added, "I know you're all that much older, but just go with it! Believe me, it'll work out great."

Lauren sat back down, and Meri raised her hand and asked, "Besides acting out scenes, what else will we be required to do? Will I have to cook meals? Do housework?"

"Absolutely not," Milo answered. "Fully cooked meals will magically be delivered to your home when you're away from the house. All you'll have to do is reheat them. As for the housework, you'll only be required to do it if it's part of that day's scenario. It's unlikely to be more than a few minutes' worth."

Meri had more questions. "Will we have to do anything illegal or immoral? Will there be nudity or violence in the storylines?"

"No. Absolutely not. This project is aligned with the core values of the show. Gerald and Marion will share a bed the way it was done in the show, but just for the sake of sleeping."

Jeff asked, "Will there be other actors, or is this just us?" He thought of all the others who'd worked on the show, some on a regular basis.

"Excellent question!" Milo said enthusiastically. "Haven will be populated, just like in the show. We were able to hire some of the same actors who worked with you back in the day. Others will be lookalikes, and still others will be brand new, chosen to fill out necessary roles. We have a fabulous collection of talent, and I think you'll be very pleased."

"Is everything here real, or are some of the buildings false fronts?" Jeff asked.

Milo gave a shake of his head. "Every building here is fully realized, with furniture, plumbing, and electricity. The local stores will be stocked with food and other items. You'll have money to make purchases. Everything will be provided."

"Am I right in assuming we'll be wearing costumes for the entire ten days?" Amanda asked, not sounding thrilled. "Those dresses with the stockings and the uncomfortable shoes?"

"We'll see what we can do about the shoes," Milo said with a sweep of his hand. "Obviously, we were able to pull this together, so comfortable footwear should be doable."

Jeff tried to size up the others, knowing they were processing what they'd been told. He was prepared to sign on the dotted line and knew that Dominick felt the same way, but the rest of them? It could go either way. He thought Amanda was on board, but Meri still looked doubtful, and

Lauren's face was completely impassive. She'd make an excellent poker player, Jeff thought.

"One more thing!" Milo said, giving his ear a scratch. "I almost forgot to talk about hairstyles. We'd like to create the look you had on the show, whether that requires haircuts, coloring, extensions, whatever. It will be done here ahead of time at no cost to you."

Meri groaned. She'd mentioned at Haven Con how liberating it was to finally have short hair. Not only was it less time consuming, but it just felt right. She'd said, "I look in the mirror and it finally looks like me." Jeff had no idea what she'd meant, but he hoped that some hair dye and extensions weren't the only things standing between him and $2 million. He gave her a nudge. "It's just for ten days. It'll be fun." Her lips twitched into a small smile, but she didn't look as if she was fully on board.

"Any more questions?" Milo asked, and then it seemed that everyone had something they wanted to know. The younger generation was stuck on not having a cell phone, even for emergencies. Each of the three had their reasons. Lauren mentioned being away from her kids for ten days; Amanda brought up her dad, who had health issues; and Dominick said he worried about not being able to get in touch if there was an unexpected problem at work. Apparently, there was the potential of a radio show emergency requiring intervention on his part. It didn't surprise Jeff that Dominick thought he was just that important.

"It's part of the process," Milo said, explaining. "You'll go into a changing room and leave all your modern-day things in a locker. When you come out, you'll be dressed as the characters, and our transport van will deliver you to Haven. Once you step through the door, it all begins, and you'll be fully immersed in your identities as the Barlows for the entire time. Not having anything from your actual life will help you make a full transition into the role. Cell phones are just a distraction. Believe me, you're better off without them."

"But what if my dad has a heart attack?" Amanda asked. "Or there's a death in the family?"

Milo smoothed things over. "Of course, if we hear from your family and there's a compelling need to get in touch, we'll respect that. But really what are the chances? It's only ten days." He grinned. "People always talk about taking a vacation from the internet. Some people pay big money to go to spas or retreats that don't have Wi-Fi connectivity. You'll be doing just that and getting two million dollars in the process!"

It was hard to argue with that kind of logic. Jeff, who had a history of high cholesterol, had a different concern. "What if someone is injured on the set or has a medical emergency?"

Milo was ready with an answer for this one too, telling them that Mr. Worthington had already considered this and would have a doctor embedded in the cast. "He's a young guy who'll be working with old Doc Tarter. Dr. Reed. If there's any kind of medical concern, he's available. And if he decides it's an emergency, he'll make arrangements for an ambulance. At that point, you'll leave this building and go to the closest hospital."

Jeff nodded. "Fair enough."

When they were out of questions, Milo said, "So what do you think? Are you ready to sign the paperwork and lock this deal in?" He held out his arms, as if wanting to sweep all five of them into an embrace. "I know what my decision would be."

Before anyone else could speak, Lauren stood up and loudly said, "I'm in."

Jeff raised his hand. "I'm in as well."

A slow grin stretched across Dominick's face. "I want to read the agreement, but if the paperwork checks out, I'll do it." He turned to Amanda. "What do you say?"

"Why not?" She gave him a smile. "I've been in a rut lately. Might as well make it four."

Jeff turned to Meri. "What do you think? We've done this before, and now we can do it again. I'll be Gerald and you'll be Marion." He rested a hand on her arm. "Should we do it for old time's sake?"

Chapter Eleven

Meri felt the weight of five sets of eyes boring into her. She knew that they wanted her to agree to what she was starting to think of as the Worthington Proposal. The Crazy, Too-Good-to-Be-True Worthington Proposal. The other four had clearly been lured in by the promise of $2 million, as almost anyone would be. Anyone but Meri. She thought she'd put *A Little Slice of Haven* and Jeff Greer behind her years ago, and now both had come back to haunt her. It was bad enough that Jeff had cozied up to her on the couch. As he'd moved closer, she'd wedged her purse between them. Not much of a barrier, but at least he wasn't touching her. What would it be like sleeping in the same bed for nine nights? Even conversing with him now was strained and difficult. Could she keep it up for more than a day?

"It does sound intriguing," she said, breaking the silence. "But I can't help wondering what the catch is."

"There's no catch," Milo said. "It's a straightforward offer. Just exactly what I told you."

"But you said we only get the two million dollars if all five of us stick it out for the whole time. Did I understand you correctly?"

"That's true, but it's more of a requirement than a catch. Without the full cast, it won't be a success. The fans love all of you."

"I don't want to ruin it for everyone else, but the truth is, I'm not sure I want to do this." She saw their disappointed faces and felt the ebullient mood in the room leak out, like air leaving a balloon. "I'd like to make a phone call, if you don't mind."

Milo's face darkened. "What I told you is confidential. Mr. Worthington doesn't want this divulged until he's ready. He specifically does not want this leaked to the media."

"But we can tell our families, right?" Amanda asked. "They're going to want to know where we're going and why we can't be reached. I have to tell my parents. They'll worry."

"Of course, you can tell your immediate family as long as they know to keep it under wraps until the project is over with."

"I'm going to call my daughter. Believe me, she can be trusted to keep a secret." Meri rose to her feet and looped the purse strap over her shoulder. "I need some privacy, so I'll be outside." Milo stepped back, letting her pass. She pushed her way through the screen door to the porch, where the sight of Grandma, still rocking, gave her such a jolt that she almost screamed. An animatronic Catherine Sedgwick. It was bad enough when the woman was alive. Creating a facsimile of her was an abomination. What kind of mind even came up with this kind of thing? Too bizarre.

She left the porch and went down the walkway, passing through the gate. Pausing on the sidewalk, she got out her phone and took a picture of the outside of the house, a close-up of the Grandma figure, and a few more aimed down the street, so several of the neighborhood houses were included in the shot. Hailey had to see this. Her daughter had watched all the episodes recently and had heard her mother's stories of all the behind-the-scenes drama, so she had a special interest.

Meri kept walking, stopping when she got to Gloria Youngbauer's house. Gloria had been her best friend in the neighborhood on the show. She remembered when little Bud Barlow had run away from home, he'd ended up hiding out at Gloria's house. Now she saw that the exterior looked exactly as she remembered it, the porch swing hanging to the left of the door. It was, she decided, the perfect place to sit during her phone call. Getting settled on the swing, she texted the photos to Hailey, then gave her a few minutes to look them over before hitting the button to start the call.

"Hey, Mom!"

"Hailey." She exhaled in relief. "I'm so glad you answered."

"Of course. I've been dying to hear!" Her daughter had such an exuberant personality that Meri often envisioned her words punctuated with exclamation marks and bracketed by smiling emojis. "What's the deal with the pictures of the set?"

"That's the interesting thing. They aren't from the show." Meri went on to explain the whole thing, ending with Milo's caution about confidentiality.

"You've got to be kidding," Hailey said. "How many people did it take to build Haven inside a warehouse? And the staging and casting all the other townspeople? And he thinks he can keep this a secret? A ton of people must know about it already. There's no way this isn't getting out."

"I hear you, but it hasn't so far." Meri leaned forward, making the porch swing sway. "So if you would keep it to yourself for now . . ."

"I won't say a word," she promised. "So you're going to do it?"

"Maybe? I don't know," Meri said. "Maybe not. I'm so conflicted. On the one hand, two million dollars could buy an incredible retirement." Down the street she heard the church bells chime. "And I could pay off your student loans. We could take some trips. Honestly, I'll never get this kind of opportunity again."

"Yeah, but . . ." There was a grin in her daughter's voice.

Meri smiled. "*Yeah, but* is right," she said. "It will resurrect all kinds of emotional garbage that I don't think I'm ready to deal with. Or even want to deal with. I mean, it's Jeff." At one point in her life she'd vowed never to see him again. How could she share a bed with the man? She shuddered at the thought.

"But if you're staying in character couldn't you just think of it as you being Marion and him being Gerald?"

"So you think I should do this?"

"Only if you want to," Hailey said. "I'd love to have my student loans paid off, but not if it forces you to do something traumatic. A smart woman once told me, *Life's too short to get mired in the muck.* Don't worry about me. I'll be fine either way."

A burst of laughter escaped Meri's lips. "I'm not so sure about *smart*, but I stand by what I said. Life is too short."

She ran a hand over the top of her head, loving the familiar soft brush of hair against her palm. "I'd have to go ten days without working out. You know how crazy I get if I can't challenge myself physically." She'd been rock climbing and hiking for years. It was part of who she was. "Marion isn't much for exercising."

"I know you'll miss it."

"My muscles will be pudding by the end of the ten days."

Hailey said, "You'll have noodle arms."

Despite herself, Meri chuckled. "The thing that bothers me most is the isolation. Not having access to a phone is pretty drastic. I can't imagine not being able to call you for ten days. I mean, people who do reality shows can still call home, right?"

"Right." Hailey exhaled. "Well, not on all of them."

"If it weren't for the phone issue, I'd be more inclined to do it." In the background, Meri heard the ding of the microwave. Hailey could never just talk; she always had something else going on. The consummate multitasker.

Amid the sound of the microwave door opening, Hailey said, "And there's really no reason to cut you off from using your phone. I mean, you called me just now. So clearly the signal in Montana is strong enough. Sounds like Felix Worthington is a control freak."

"Most billionaires are."

They talked for a few more minutes, with Meri anguishing over her decision and going over the pros and cons.

"Seriously, Mom, whatever you decide is fine with me."

When they finished the conversation, Meri told Hailey that she loved her and would call her when she returned home. Then she powered down the phone, got up from the porch swing, and went back to the sidewalk.

On a whim, she continued down the block, walking away from the Barlow house. Dandelions grew through the cracks in the pavement, something she hadn't noticed originally. The attention to detail was astounding. Felix Worthington had to really love the show to create the whole town with such precision. Looking at each house and the cars parked in some of the driveways, Meri got a sense of having traveled back in time. Without the bright lights and the push of getting everything filmed on a tight schedule, she could almost understand what the fans must feel when they watched the show. Haven was peaceful, sweet. Populated with quirky, loving folks. She could see the appeal.

Milo had said there were cameras everywhere, so she assumed that everything she'd said and done since entering Haven, including her conversation with Hailey, was being observed. Amanda was right. It was creepy, but not as creepy as if they hadn't known. She turned around and headed back, strolling leisurely. She was in no hurry. Let them wait.

Meri thought she'd reached a decision, but now that it was time to give her final answer, she vacillated. Two million dollars was a lot of money. And it was only for ten days work. She didn't have an agent or a manager anymore, so she wouldn't have anyone else taking a percentage off the top. It would all be hers. For her and her daughter, the money would be a boon now and a nest egg for the future. But she did have some objections that couldn't easily be discounted.

As she approached the front gate in front of the Barlow house, Hailey's question played in her head. *But if you're staying in character, couldn't you just think of it as you being Marion and him being Gerald?"* That was an approach that might work, or at the very least help her get through the days. But then there was the matter of her hair. She wasn't looking forward to getting her obnoxious long hair back. Still, it would be temporary. Lastly, she wasn't thrilled with the idea of being cut off from the outside world. That was a big roadblock. Her fingers curled around the phone still in her hand. The idea of handing it over and going without it for the duration was terrifying.

But maybe there was a way around it.

Coming up the path and onto the porch, Meri went right to the animatronic Catherine Sedgwick. The figure was still rocking back and forth, her loyal dog at her side. It would be impressive if it weren't so lifelike and eerie. "Oh, Grandma," she said in a loud whisper and leaned over to embrace her. Inwardly, Meri cringed. It was galling to have to hug Catherine. Even touching the fake version was like touching a corpse. She wouldn't have done it unless it was absolutely necessary. "I wish you could be here in person," she said, slipping her phone into the pocket on the front of the fake Catherine's housedress. Then, mustering all her acting ability, she added, with a tear in her eye, "We had so many good times together. You are missed." She straightened up, wiping her eyes with the tips of her fingers. After giving Catherine a fond once-over and a pat on the arm, she opened the screen door and went inside.

Her entry back into the acting world had officially begun. Time for her close-up.

Chapter Twelve

Two days before the experiment was to begin, Felix and Milo set out to perform a final inspection. As they walked the streets of Haven side by side, Milo kept his gaze locked on his tablet, verbally checking things off a list. "The crew double-checked all the electrical and plumbing, and everything is in working order," he told Felix. "The same is true for the phones. Each phone has a phone directory next to it with the pertinent numbers."

"Only local calls within Haven can be made, right?" Felix asked.

"Yes."

"What about the weather?"

Eyes still on the screen, Milo answered. "It's been programmed to fluctuate somewhat but will be temperate enough that the actors will be comfortable indoors or out. We have precipitation set for the day you requested."

Felix nodded. "Very good." Milo had noticed a change in his boss in the previous few days. Normally driven and focused, he seemed less keyed up and more relaxed. The attitude of a man about to see the culmination of a long-held dream. Felix turned right on Lara Avenue and stepped over the curb and onto the sidewalk.

Milo followed him, still talking. "All the pantries and refrigerators are stocked. The stores are full of merchandise. All of the ladies' purses have the necessary items, including money. The men's wallets are full of cash as well, and the bank is set up for withdrawals and deposits. Although I doubt we'll see anyone making a deposit." From a nearby tree, he heard the chirping of a bird, one of the many who'd been brought in to provide authenticity.

Felix linked his hands behind his back like a college professor deep in thought. "You've done an excellent job of coordinating all of this." He paused, and although the sun wasn't on the brightest setting, he shielded his eyes with the flat of his hand and gave the neighborhood a long look. "It's just the way I imagined it. Thank you."

"My pleasure, sir." They turned onto Bailey Street. "All of the homes have extra blankets in their dressers in case the actors get chilled at night. The mail carrier has done a few trial runs, both in delivering and in picking up mail from the collection mailboxes. The supporting actors have been briefed."

"I watched the orientation. I was glad it was emphasized that they can't leave for the duration and that they have to stay in character, no matter what," Felix said. "I noticed that the supporting actors seem glad to be taking part in this."

Milo thought that *glad* was an understatement. The actors who were returning from the show were overjoyed, and the supplemental actors couldn't believe they were getting such a well-paying gig doing something so fun and unconventional. The excitement in the room had been palpable. "Very much so. This is a unique acting experience and a great opportunity. And of course, they're all hoping it ends up becoming a movie or a series. I'm sure they're dreaming of this making it big on some streaming service and giving their careers a boost."

"Hmm."

Milo took a deep breath and then read off the remaining details. "The radios have been programmed and are synchronized. We were able to find original recordings for some shows, others were re-created. We included commercials." His voice took on an apologetic tone. "We tried to come as close as possible."

"I have no doubt of that."

They walked the rest of the block in silence. When they got to the Barlow house, Felix opened the gate and headed up the walkway, with Milo right behind him. The animatronic Grandma, Felix's pride and joy, patted the head of the dog as she gently rocked back and forth. Felix sat down on the top step, his back to her. "So it sounds like we're good to go, then."

"Yes, sir. Everything is in place. Tomorrow the supporting cast will arrive, and the Barlows will come the next day." He sat down next to Felix. For a few minutes, they were quiet. Milo, aware of the gentle breeze, took in the view. Every house had a neatly tended yard, complete with flower beds and large leafy trees. Personal touches abounded. One house had a bike lying in the yard, as if a kid had come home and thrown it down before heading in for dinner; another residence had a hose attached to a spigot on the side of the house, the length of it leading to a flower bed, as if someone had just watered the marigolds. American flags dotted the neighborhood, both on flag poles and mounted on porch columns. Tomorrow a newsboy would ride his bike down this street, tossing newspapers onto each of the porches. Housewives would come out the front doors to shake out their mops and greet neighbors. The uniformed mail carrier would be traversing this very sidewalk, a cap shielding his head from the sun, a bag filled with letters and catalogs slung over one shoulder.

"It's all very idyllic, isn't it?" Milo said, taking a deep breath. "So peaceful and perfect. Who wouldn't want to live here?"

Chapter Thirteen

Amanda sat on the bench in the changing room and finished lacing her shoes, then stood up to assess her appearance in the three-way mirror. "Not too bad," she said aloud, even though no one else could hear her. Just by putting on Dorothy Barlow's clothes she'd been transported back to an earlier time. At forty-three, her teenage years were far behind her, but this costume definitely made her appear more youthful, girlish even. The stylist had added curled hair extensions that would be easy to pin up to create a 1940s look. Between the hair and the dress, she'd been transformed. If she squinted, the laugh lines around her eyes visually melted away, making her look, she thought, exactly as she had on the show.

She stared at her image and grinned. Maybe someone should bring back 1940s style trends, the laced shoes with the clunky heels and the belted dresses that fit snugly against the waist. The shoes were more comfortable than she remembered, and the dress more flattering. She turned from side to side, looking at herself from all angles, and gave an approving nod. This was going to be fun as well as profitable.

It had only been a week since they'd all met at the ranch and gotten the lowdown on the requirements of the proposed deal. When Meri had left to call her daughter, there was something about her determined look that made Amanda certain she was going to ruin the whole thing for all of them. But something must have changed in the fifteen minutes she was gone, because when she returned, Amanda spotted her through the window hugging and talking to the animatronic Grandma, a serene expression on her face. The exchange was touching, especially given Catherine's prickly personality, but then again, this was Meri, who never had a bad word to say about anyone. When Meri had come into the room to announce that yes, she'd do it, Jeff had jumped up and given her a hug. "That's my girl," he'd said, then turned to shake Dominick's hand and give Amanda a high five. From the other side of the room, Lauren was strangely silent, but that was par for the course.

Lauren, Lauren, Lauren. Some people just couldn't let go of the past.

Seven days. They'd each had seven days to get ready to put their lives on hold. Milo had given them a contract, a map of Haven, and a listing of the rules, which they'd all read immediately, even though they were allowed to take the paperwork home with them. The documents seemed straightforward.

The contract essentially said they needed to abide by the rules, that they acknowledged they knew they were being filmed and recorded at all times (with the exception of the bathrooms), that all five of them were required to stay on site for ten days (from Sunday afternoon, May 20, until

Tuesday evening, May 29), that they would not be required to do anything illegal or immoral, and that at the end of that time, they'd be paid $2 million, which would be wired into their bank accounts immediately. The only provision was a statement saying that if any one of the five had to leave due to illness or injury, an exception would be made, and the others could carry on without them.

At the top of the page of rules, there was a reminder that all the rules applied to all five of them at all times and that breaking them could result in the contract being voided. Amanda knew what that meant. No money for those who'd violated the agreement. She'd committed the list to memory, so fearful was she of violating said rules. Mentally, she played them back:

1. Each cast member had to stay in character for the duration.

2. No details of the project could be divulged to the public until after the ten days were completed.

3. All personal effects and clothing must be relinquished prior to the beginning of the project and would not be allowed in Haven.

4. Any questions or concerns during their stay in Haven could be sent to the management in the form of a written letter, which could be dropped into the mailbox on the corner of Darcy Street and Crossen Lane. Responses would be delivered by mail as soon as possible.

5. At the end of the ten days, the group would be shown footage of possible violations to the rules and told if their actions or words disqualified them from getting the payout. Felix Worthington would have the final say in this matter.

6. Each member would receive a one-page directive, a general outline of their activity for each day, which they were required to follow as closely as possible. They would be assisted by other residents of Haven, who would provide prompts to guide them.

For the last one, Milo had said, "It'll be like doing improv. You're gonna love it!" Amanda, who was used to occasionally ad-libbing as an anchor at the TV station, wasn't one bit worried. She was born to talk and loved impromptu banter. She had a feeling Lauren might not fare as well.

Milo had told them to feel free to show the contract to their agents, managers, or attorneys, although he didn't think it was necessary. "There's no fancy legalese," he'd said. "Just straight talk." Amanda hadn't bothered having anyone else vet it. She was committed regardless. In fact, it was as good as done. She was so certain that when her boss balked at giving her the time off on such short notice, she'd tendered her resignation. *Screw them.* She didn't need their approval. Soon enough, she'd be a millionaire.

As she viewed herself in the mirror, she wondered if the actor who'd played George Bonner would be participating. What was his name? She looked up at the ceiling, as if the answer would be printed above her head. She was fairly certain his first name was Neal, but she couldn't come up with a last name. At one point she remembered having looked him up on IMDB, but that was a dead end, since he didn't have any other acting credits after *A Little Slice of Haven*. Not that it mattered. If anything, a change of career made him even more attractive. Yes, she'd be happy to see Neal again. Of course, she wouldn't be calling him by that name, in any event. They'd be interacting as George and Dorothy in the greatest bit of role-playing ever.

On the show, Dorothy's love had gone unrequited. In a bit of life mirroring art, Amanda's teenage crush on the actor had gone unnoticed as well, even after she'd pretended to be interested in Dominick to make him jealous. In the years since then, she'd matured into the kind of woman who eschewed game playing in favor of a direct approach when it came to men. If Neal proved to be single, straight, and just as attractive as his younger self, she planned to invite him out after all this nonsense was over with. They'd start with one drink, and after another, and a few more, who knew what might happen? She smiled, thinking of all the possibilities. She'd spent so many years pouring everything into her career that she'd neglected to become a fully realized person, but that was going to change. Once the ten days were over, she'd have more time and money than ever before. Her personal life was going to take center stage.

When Milo had delivered them to a large building on the far side of the ranch property, Meri hadn't been surprised to see that the changing area was actually five rooms, each door sporting a large gold star and the name of a cast member. Felix Worthington apparently thought of everything.

By that point, they'd all had their hair done by a stylist, with Meri having the most drastic change. When the chair had been spun around and the young guy, Trent, handed her a hand mirror to see the back, she'd barely recognized herself. Her hair, now long and chestnut brown, had been arranged in a sort of pompadour on the top, the ends curled under and just brushing her shoulders. The result had flipped a visual switch, changing her from Meri to Marion. This new version of herself looked uncannily like her daughter, Hailey, something she found shocking. She'd always thought Hailey had her own look, resembling neither parent, but now she saw what everyone else had been saying since her daughter was a toddler. Except for Hailey's gray eyes, which were clearly from the paternal side of her DNA, she was the spitting image of her mother.

After Meri got dressed and tucked her personal belongings in the locker Milo assured them was secure, she looped Marion's handbag over her arm, then stood motionless in front of the mirror. Staring at her reflection was a way to delay her entrance into Haven. She'd already made the commitment, signed the papers, and told the others she was doing this. It was, sad to say, too late to back out.

Her stomach churned with anxiety. Ten days. She took a deep breath and declared to herself she'd get through this. One minute at a time, one hour at a time, one day at a time.

Maybe it would work out like summer camp when she was a kid. She'd been incredibly homesick and out of place at first, but by the third day it had gotten easier, and by the time it wrapped up she'd grown to love it. It was doubtful this experience would prove to be the same, but a person could hope.

In the changing room next door, Jeff felt anticipation and excitement building from the soles of his feet to the top of his head. He looked through the wallet he'd been issued, complete with a driver's license, photos of Marion and the kids, and a wad of cash. Old currency that looked new. He tucked the wallet into his back pocket, then whistled as he slipped the cuff links into his dress shirt and kept on whistling even as he adjusted his tie tack. When he put on his suit coat, he finally fell silent, taking in his reflection. "Why, Gerald Barlow, you're looking better than ever," he said with a devilish smile.

He'd gained weight since his days on the show, but whoever managed wardrobe had compensated well for his extra girth, giving him a slimming silhouette. Along with his new neatly parted hairstyle, and some magic done by the stylist to cover the gray and fill the thinning across the top, he now looked years younger. He planned to use this time in Haven to play his part as if life depended upon it, because he had two things at stake: reviving a dead career and winning back Meri Wetzel.

Meri was the most important of the two. Over the years, he'd often thought of her as the one who got away. At the start, they'd just clicked, and to this day her laugh was his favorite sound in the world. He'd been married during their brief affair, something that had tormented Meri more than him. His wife had eventually divorced him. Not for his infidelity, curiously enough, but for his drinking, and who could blame her? He wasn't an angry drunk, just a sad-sack, depressed, worthless piece of crap. He couldn't stand himself, so he didn't blame anyone else for feeling the same way.

But Jeff had changed in the years that followed. He'd done a lot of work on himself over the last decade and had become a better man. He and Meri had ended things on terrible terms—they'd had a big blowout fight where he'd called her a liar and she'd wound up throwing a shoe at him. The shoe had left a mark on his forehead that proved to be a challenge for the makeup artist. Before that he couldn't have imagined Meri becoming angry, but clearly she had the capability for it when provoked, just like everyone else. Luckily, this had been close to the end of the second season, so they didn't have to work together for too long after that. Seeing the wounded look in her eyes killed him, but he was too far into the bottle to make amends. Most days he could barely keep it together. Looking back, he knew he didn't deserve a second chance, but he still hoped she'd give him one.

Today he looked like the banker he was going to play. A respectable family man. He slipped on Gerald Barlow's wedding ring. One last detail to make the image complete.

Originally, Lauren had had no intention of taking part in this Haven reunion. She'd left the series behind her and was glad of it. Getting married, she'd taken her husband's last name, Pisanelli, happy to cast off her identity as Lauren Saunders. In her mind, the name was associated with her childhood acting career.

When she heard from Milo Lappin, she'd found his offer amusing. She showed the text to her husband, Aaron, and they both laughed before she deleted it. There wasn't enough money in the world to make her work with those four people again. She was now Mrs. Pisanelli, wife, mother, and teacher of third graders. She loved her life in Kansas.

She'd never sought out the limelight in the first place.

On the set, she and Sean, the actor who'd played Bud Barlow, were the only kid actors, which meant they had to balance their schoolwork with learning lines and sitting for hair and makeup, and the tedium of filming scenes, sometimes over and over again if Jeff was having a bad day. And if Jeff was having a bad day, they all had a bad day. The director never bothered to learn their names, calling her Ann and yelling "Bud!" when he wanted Sean. How rude was that? After Sean was written out of the series, she was the only minor left of the regular cast. Funny that the new fans of the show had the impression they were all one big happy family. That notion was so far from the truth it was laughable.

Working on the show was a job. A job like any other miserable job. Meri got along with everyone, but even with her Lauren could tell it was still just an acting gig. That's

93

what the viewers failed to realize. The relationships they saw were creations. The actors were no more likely to be friends than the employees in any given office or store. Throw together a bunch of different personalities and it was like magnets—some would stick while others repelled. There wasn't much sticking on *A Little Slice of Haven.*

After Dominick had come to see her and she'd called the cops on him, she thought the subject was closed, but later that day, while she was unpacking groceries, her daughter Charlotte answered Lauren's phone. When Charlotte held out the phone, she said, "It's Felix Worthington, Mom."

This was unexpected. How could it be that mysterious billionaire Felix Worthington was calling *her* cell phone? Worthington sightings were rare. He never spoke to the press, and he rarely appeared in public. But here he was calling her, a schoolteacher in Kansas. She could hardly refuse to talk to him. If nothing else, it would be interesting to hear what he had to say. She set down a bag of apples and took the phone out of her daughter's hand. "Hello," she answered, leaning her elbows on the counter. "This is Lauren."

The phone call turned out to be a complete surprise. Talking to Felix Worthington was as comfortable as speaking to an old friend. She listened as he explained how important it was for him to get the cast together again in Haven. And when he reiterated that the pay would be $2 million, he added that if she agreed to his proposal, she'd get the money even if one or more of the others dropped out early. "Just don't tell the others," he said. "And if you don't want to be featured prominently, we can make sure you're more of a background character. I'm willing to do whatever it takes to get you on board." By the time they'd ended the conversation, she'd done a complete turnaround. She was in.

Now she stood in front of a three-way mirror, wearing a chocolate-colored dress with white piping, her hair curled and pulled away from her face in a style her daughters called "half up, half down." On the show, she'd had braids. Luckily, they'd agreed to let that one go.

Lauren's character, Ann, was the plain daughter in the family, while Amanda's Dorothy wore floral prints, her dresses more apt to have ruffles or fancy collars. Lauren was happy to let Amanda be the center of attention. Lauren's focus had always been on her students, her family, and her church. It was enough. She loved her life so much that even though she'd only been away from Kansas for a day, she missed her home life already. She consoled herself, thinking Aaron and the girls would survive without her, and maybe even appreciate her more upon her return. The next ten days would put old hurts to rest and then she could close this chapter of her life forever.

Chapter Fourteen

Dominick had actually groaned after receiving his haircut. He'd known his curly hair wasn't quite as thick on the crown of his head but hadn't realized he actually had a quarter-sized bald spot. Having his hair cut Tom-style brought it to light. The stylist had offered to provide a weave, but he'd waved away the suggestion. The spot wasn't that obvious, and he didn't want to have to deal with something new on top of sliding back into Tom Barlow's character.

Dominick hoped that Milo hadn't been lying when he'd claimed the changing rooms would be camera free. No way could he go ten days without nicotine, so he'd smuggled it in. He was clever about it, hiding nicotine patches on the inside of his thigh, sealed beneath a large Band-Aid, the kind with a four-sided adhesive seal.

He justified breaking the rule by equating it to essentials like food, water, and air. If Worthington wanted a good performance out of him, he had to stay level.

Dominick put on a shirt and deftly buttoned it, then pulled on the high-waisted trousers, tucking in the shirt and adding the belt. Socks and shoes completed his attire. Frowning, he took in the sight. The clothes were similar to what he'd worn on the show, but on a grown man they looked ridiculous. He turned sideways and looked over his shoulder into the mirror, but the new angle didn't improve things.

"Damn." He shook his head and tried to look on the bright side. At least he didn't have to wear a suit and tie like Jeff. That would bite. Besides, it was only for ten days, and when all was said and done, he'd be $2 million richer and able to wear whatever he wanted for the rest of his life.

After getting dressed, he strapped on a wristwatch, an accessory that came with the clothing. It looked both vintage and new, and he found he liked the way it looked on his wrist. When this was over, he'd have to ask if he could keep it.

Outside the changing room, he stood next to Milo and watched as the others appeared, one by one, each of them made over to resemble their character. Jeff, as Gerald Barlow, looked every inch a 1940s small-town banker in his wide-lapelled suit, pressed shirt, and tie.

Meri had changed the most, but surprisingly, her darker hair made her look almost dowdy. Younger, yes, but also very nondescript. Lauren, in her brown dress, was forgettable, while Amanda was now smoking hot. The dress hugged her curves like her own clothing never had. She knew it too. When she caught him looking, she struck a pose, setting one hand on her hip and giving her hair a flip before asking, "So what do you think?"

"Sexy!" He whistled. "All the boys in Haven are going to be chasing after you."

Jeff frowned. "Don't forget that you're supposed to be brother and sister. We have to stay in character."

No kidding. Dominick sighed. "I'm aware, Jeff." The man was taking his father role a little too seriously. They all knew what was at stake. Dominick wasn't about to jeopardize the payout of a lifetime for a piece of tail, even one as top-notch as Amanda's. Maybe afterward, if anything. Besides, they weren't in Haven yet, so the rules didn't apply.

Milo, tablet in hand, said, "Remember, no cell phones allowed in Haven. Has everyone left their clothing and personal items in the lockers?"

He was greeted by nods and a chorus of yeses. "Mr. Worthington is giving you some time to ease into the experiment. That's why we're launching late afternoon. You can settle into the house, get your instructions, and go from there. Okay?"

When they all confirmed that they understood, he asked, "Any questions before we head out? Last chance."

Meri raised a timid hand. "I was wondering what we do about the Grandma figure. Are we supposed to bring her in at night and lay her on the bed?"

Dominick gave her credit for thinking ahead. He hadn't even considered moving the old bag. If one of them had to do it, he'd nominate Jeff.

Milo smiled. "Good question! The answer is no; she can be left right where she is. In fact, moving her would cause problems with the functioning of the unit. And since Grandma Barlow was often seen rocking on the porch late into the night, the assumption will be that she stayed up late or got up early. Interacting with her is optional, unless she speaks or asks a question in your presence. In that case, you should definitely respond." He paused to look at each of them in turn. "Does everyone understand?"

They nodded, and Jeff pointed to his forehead and said, "I've filed it all away up here," which made them laugh. The line was a favorite of Gerald Barlow's.

"Anything else?" Milo waited, and when no one broke the silence, he said, "Very good. Let's begin."

They followed him out of the building and into a waiting van. Once seated, Amanda chattered away to Milo, telling him she'd watched the shows again online to refresh her memory. "I was surprised at how charming the storylines were! I can see why the fans are so enthused."

In the back, Jeff and Meri spoke in low voices. To Dominick they sounded friendly but guarded. A conversation between two people just getting acquainted. Or reacquainted, in this case. Dominick wound up sitting next to Lauren, who was silent as usual.

He gave her a nudge. "I know you're nervous, but you really shouldn't be. Remember, we're all in this together."

She turned to meet his eyes. "Why would I be nervous?"

Her response caught him off guard. He smiled and said, "It's just that you've been out of the acting game for a long time now. I just thought—"

"You think you know everything, don't you?" She folded her arms. "You pulled into my driveway and saw my girls and now you think you've got my number, but actually you know nothing about me or my life."

"I know a little bit," he said defensively. "You have great kids, and you seem very happy. Which, hey, good for you!"

"That's all surface," she said. "Did you know that since the show ended I earned my degree, got married, took care of my elderly grandparents, and then after they died, I settled their estate and arranged for their funerals? I've been happily married for the last fifteen years, gave birth to two babies without anesthesia, and am raising my daughters to be good citizens. At work, I deal with twenty-six third graders every school day. I think it's a safe bet you wouldn't last an hour in the classroom."

"Maybe not," he said, trying to lighten the mood. "Even as a student an hour was a long time for me."

Lauren kept going as if he hadn't spoken. "And what is it you've done with *your* life, exactly? Become some big shot on a radio show and fathered children you don't live with?" Her blue eyes stared intensely.

"Ouch," he said. "That was harsh."

"Maybe a little bit." Her tone was regretful. "I'm sorry."

"I'm trying to extend an olive branch here. We're going to be working together for the next ten days, doing something neither of us has ever done before. I wanted you to know I'm here for you."

She gave him a long look, as if debating whether to answer, and finally said, "Thanks, but I won't be needing your help. Trust me, I can pretend to be Ann Barlow." She turned away and rested her palm against the glass. "Just worry about yourself."

"Can I ask you a question?" He spoke to the back of her blonde head.

"Sure." The answer sounded begrudging.

"What do you have against me?"

"Are you serious?" She turned to stare at him. "You're really asking me that?"

"Yes, I'm really asking you that. I know I kidded around a lot on the show, but I didn't do anything that drastic. We were kids, and it was a long time ago. I'm trying to be nice here, and all I get is attitude from you."

"Attitude?" Her voice had such an edge that everyone else stopped talking to listen. "Are you kidding me? You're actually saying that to me with the way you are?"

"And what way am I, exactly?" Trying to make a joke, he said, "And please don't soft-pedal it. Give it to me straight."

"Here's what I have against you." Her eyes flashed with anger. "You're cruel and don't think of anyone but yourself."

Dominick had asked for the truth but wasn't expecting this outpouring of hatred. "I know I'm not perfect, but I don't think I'm that bad. Tell me one time I was cruel." If he knew what she was referring to, he could at least defend himself.

"Not only are you cruel, you apparently have a very convenient memory," she said. "If you don't know what I'm referring to, there's no reason to continue talking." With that, she shifted away from him in the seat and returned her gaze to the window.

Chapter Fifteen

Climbing out of the van, they found themselves at a different entrance than the one they'd used previously. Milo opened the door by pressing the combination on a keypad. Inside, they encountered an airport body scanner and two young men dressed in khaki pants and polo shirts. With their un-lined faces and baseball caps, they looked like high school students to Jeff, but then again, he'd noticed that people were starting to look younger all the time. "Please line up, and wait your turn to enter the scanner," one of the men said, directing them. His colleague stood to one side, his eyes on a monitor.

Without discussing it, they automatically lined up in order of age. After Jeff had successfully made it through, he stood off to the side, watching nervously. He wasn't worried about Meri or Lauren, but he wouldn't have put it past Amanda or Dominick to try to sneak in a phone. When all of them were finished, he took a deep breath of relief.

Milo beckoned for them to follow him to an interior door, where he solemnly punched some numbers into a touchpad. When the green light above the door went on, he turned to them with a smile and said, "Go straight for three blocks and then turn left on Bailey Street to get to the house. If anyone asks, the five of you are going on a family walk. Your directions for this evening will be on the table near the front door. Don't forget to have fun!"

With a flourish, he opened the door and directed them through it. Once they were all inside Haven, when the door clicked shut behind them, Jeff saw a look of panic come over Meri's face, and he knew she felt trapped. The door had no handle on their side, and the outline of the opening was concealed in a mural of the farm fields outside of town. As they walked forward, a row of shrubbery rose up out of the floor behind them, obscuring the entrance even further. He leaned over and whispered in her ear, "It's going to be fine." She allowed him to take her hand, and he led the way, with Dominick, Amanda, and Lauren trailing behind them on the sidewalk.

As amazed as they'd been before, now that Haven was populated, they were awestruck. Cars drove down the street, and kids rode bikes or tossed balls in the yards. The sound of someone playing a piano wafted out of a living room window. In the back of one of the houses, Jeff spotted a woman hanging laundry on a clothesline.

A grade-school boy ran across the street with a fistful of flowers in his hand, taking them to an old woman sweeping her porch. On the sidewalk across the street, two little girls, about eight years old and dressed in 1940s dresses, each jumped rope side by side, chanting, "Ice-cream soda, lemonade punch, tell me the name of my honey bunch . . ." Jeff wondered what the girls had been told in order to stay true to the era. How many times had they practiced jumping to that particular rhyme? He imagined a 1940s class where kids were schooled in playing jacks, marbles, and kick the can.

As they approached a man washing his car in his driveway, Jeff called out, "Good afternoon!"

The man hailed them, holding up a drippy sponge. "Good afternoon, Gerald. Marion." He nodded his head toward them. "Look at this weather." He glanced up at the sky. "A perfect day for outdoor chores," he said, then turned back to scrub the whitewall tires.

Jeff broke into a grin. By God, Worthington had pulled it off. Haven had jumped off the screen and come to life. The entire place gave off an otherworldly feeling, ripe with possibility. Could this be sustained for ten days? They were about to find out. Personally, he already felt like Gerald Barlow, a small-town businessman taking a pleasant Sunday stroll with his lovely wife and three children. The life he could have had, under different circumstances. This place was incredible. He couldn't believe he was getting paid to do this. Given the choice, he might live here forever.

By the time they reached the house, they'd already exchanged greetings with three other people, including one man who told Gerald he'd see him tomorrow morning at the bank. A coworker or customer? Hard to say. Jeff grinned and played along. "See you tomorrow," he said, waving the hand that wasn't holding Meri's. He was happily surprised she hadn't let go by now.

As he was striding up the walkway to the house, the Grandma figure on the porch scared all of them by calling out, "You're back, finally! Thought you musta got lost." All of them stopped in their tracks. Her head and lips moved as she spoke, the raspy voice sounding so much like Catherine Sedgwick it was shocking. Afraid that one of the kids might comment on the creepiness factor, he went right into character. "Sorry if we worried you, Mother. Did you need something while we were gone?"

She didn't respond right away, and he wondered if maybe he wasn't supposed to ask her questions. Was she capable of listening and responding? Milo hadn't covered that part. Just when he was going to walk past her into the house, she said, "I was fine, but Beau's water dish needs to be filled." The dog figure whined in agreement.

"I'll take care of it, Grandma," Dominick said, sliding right back into being Tom. He picked up the empty dish at her feet. "Be back in a jiff."

As they walked into the house, Grandma said, "Thank you, Tom."

Inside on the table, underneath an oval mirror, a letter labeled "To all the Barlows" sat waiting for them. After Tom returned from setting the water dish on the porch, Meri opened it, and they all gathered around to read. It said:

Greetings! Welcome back to Haven, the place where it all happened. This evening's assignment: Gerald and Marion will take the children out for a chicken dinner at Charlie's Family Restaurant. The Buick's in the garage waiting for you!

Chapter Sixteen

As they headed out, Jeff invited Grandma to come out with them. "We're going to Charlie's for a chicken dinner. Would you like to come along?"

Robot Grandma shook her head. "I'm not feeling up to it, son. My arthritis has been troubling me something fierce lately. But you go ahead and enjoy."

"We'll bring something back for you," Lauren said, in a nice bit of improvising.

"Thank you, Ann." Grandma nodded. "You're so thoughtful."

Opening the double doors to the garage, they found the old Buick Eight waiting, polished to a high sheen, chrome gleaming the way it had when it came off the assembly line. Getting behind the wheel, Jeff didn't say a word, but Meri could tell he was relieved that the car had been converted to an automatic transmission. The kids slid into the back, with Lauren graciously sitting in the middle, the spot no one wanted. Meri couldn't remember if they'd ever filmed a car scene when the fourth child, Bud, had been around. Probably not, because it would have been logistically difficult to fit all four in the back.

Jeff gave her a smile right before he started up the engine, and after he'd finished backing out of the garage, Dominick grudgingly got out to close the garage doors. So far everyone was playing their parts to perfection. Mentally, Meri started to think of them as their characters. Gerald, Tom, Dorothy, Ann. She wasn't sure if using the wrong name would be a deal breaker, making them all ineligible for payment, but she wasn't going to risk it.

As they drove down the street, the dialogue began. In the back seat, Dorothy chattered away, saying she hoped some of the kids from her high school would be at the restaurant. Tom gave her arm a light punch and said, "You aren't fooling anyone. George Bonner's the only one you care about. You're sweet on him."

Marion looked back to see Dorothy smile. "If anything, George is the one who has a crush on me. I've caught him looking. He's obviously waiting to make his move."

"You wish." This from Ann, who spoke quietly.

"I don't need to wish," Dorothy said. "I'm not a child like you."

"Kids, be nice," Gerald warned, his eyes still on the road.

Watching the three adults function as teenagers struck Marion as both ludicrous and endearing. They'd slipped into their old roles with such ease that she felt a mother's pride at seeing them all pull together for the sake of the collective.

Marion marveled at the storefronts as they passed. The window display in front of Bonner's Sewing Store was particularly bright and cheerful, with two mannequins wearing housedresses covered by aprons, quilts stacked to one side.

The Buick drove smoothly and slowly down the streets of Haven, and like a tourist Marion took in the people sitting on their porches and children playing outside. One lone girl in pigtails played hopscotch on the sidewalk, while a man—her father, presumably—pushed a lawn mower nearby, a lit cigarette between his lips. When they turned the corner and the church came into view, Marion noticed a prominent sign near the street that said the building was closed for repairs. Scaffolding surrounded the steeple and the walkway leading up to the front doors was roped off. She said, "Looks like the church is under construction." Then realizing this was something she should have known, Marion added, "I would have thought it would be done by now."

"It takes time," Gerald said, cruising slowly past. "But once the steeple is fixed and the inside is done, it'll be perfect. Good as new."

Down the street, they went by a two-story brick building. If not for the sign that said, "Haven Memorial Hospital," she would have thought it was an elementary school. A white automobile shaped like the *Ghostbusters* vehicle was parked in front and identified by a red cross and the words "Haven Memorial Hospital Ambulance" on its side door. Marion didn't remember there being a hospital in the show. Worthington's people were thorough, she'd give them that much.

"Oh look, the hospital!" Dorothy exclaimed.

They had to come up with better dialogue, she thought. So far, none of this was going to get them on prime time. "I don't know about the rest of you," Marion said brightly, "but I'm starving."

"Me too," Tom said. "I'm so hungry I could eat a horse."

Marion reflected on the fact that people actually used to talk like this. Simpler times. Jeff pulled into the parking lot of the restaurant and found an available space close to the front door. The words "Charlie's Family Restaurant" were stenciled on the brick side of the building below a spotlight that looked like it may have contained a camera. They got out of the car and walked silently to the door. This, she knew, was the true test. Interacting with the other actors would either throw them off course or help them rise to the challenge.

Gerald held the door open for the family. Inside they were greeted by a woman who knew them, even if they didn't know her. "The Barlows!" she exclaimed. "And right on time." She picked up a stack of menus and said, "We reserved your usual table. Right this way."

Marion was overwhelmed by all the customers eating, drinking, and talking as if they lived in the 1940s in Haven and had just opted to go out to eat that Sunday evening. They were led to a round table in the back corner, where they quickly seated themselves. The hostess handed each of them a menu, and when she was done, her hand rested on Gerald's shoulder as she said, "Your waitress will be right with you."

When the waitress arrived, she said, "Hello, everyone. So good to see you again. Did you want to start out with some drinks?" Marion blinked and managed to stifle the exclamation of surprise that rose upon realizing that their server was Ruby, the fan club president. There was no mistaking her identity, even in her waitress uniform with the frilly apron, a matching cap pinned to her hair, a notepad in one hand,

and a pencil behind one ear. Her name tag even said *Ruby*, and she was every bit as cheerful as when they'd previously met.

Gerald didn't miss a beat. "Hello, Ruby. Can you tell us about the blue plate special?"

"That would be an excellent choice. Tonight we have the roast chicken, with mashed potatoes, gravy, and green beans. I highly recommend it." She took the pencil out from behind her ear and held it above the notepad.

"Sounds delicious," Gerald said. "We'll have five specials and five Coca-Colas."

"Very good." Ruby gathered up the menus. "I'll put your order in right away."

Marion waited for one of the children to object to the choice of food and drink, but all of them were on their best behavior. Under other circumstances, she would have wanted to choose for herself too. Did Gerald always make the decisions on the show? Upon reflection, she thought that maybe he had. It seemed that Marion did a lot of agreeing with and supporting of the children and Gerald in their respective endeavors. Perfect Marion.

"Look," Tom said, nudging Dorothy. "George Bonner is over there with his mother."

Marion glanced over to see the actual actor who'd played George on the show, now older, but still trim with dark hair. He sat at a table across from a woman who looked only vaguely like his mother. A replacement. The Bonner storyline came back to her now. George was the man of the family since his dad had died. He helped his mother run a shop in town that sold fabric and sewing machines. "How

110

nice," Marion said. "He's always been such a thoughtful young man."

As she glanced around the restaurant, she recognized old Doc Tarter with a younger man who had to be the real doctor, Dr. Reed, and several other people who had a familiar look, probably lookalikes brought in to fill the roles of minor characters. Ruby brought out a tray with sodas, each glass accompanied by a striped straw. She set down the drinks, and Marion noticed the beverage had been poured over crushed ice. After the waitress walked away, they each picked up their drinks to take a sip.

"So sweet," Dorothy said, her mouth puckering in disapproval. Marion was willing to bet she never drank anything but diet soda in her real life.

Tom and Gerald made an attempt at fake conversation, going on about the local baseball team and how the weather had been so perfect lately. Listening to them, Marion died a little inside. Would they be able to keep this up for ten days? She knew this foray into the restaurant was just an entry-level assignment, but she found it straining, and anyone viewing the footage would see how awkward all of them were. She imagined Felix Worthington watching them in some booth somewhere, remarking on how they'd squandered his money with their lame attempts at re-creating the show he adored. She smiled wider to make up for her own shortcomings. An attempt to show how happy she was to be here.

It was a relief when Ruby approached the table, holding a tray of food over one shoulder. She set it down on a nearby tray stand and delivered a plate to each of them. When finished, she asked, "Can I get you anything else?"

Again, Gerald answered for all of them. "I think this will do. Thank you, Ruby."

"Enjoy!" She sounded so pleased to deliver food to the Barlows that Marion could only imagine how happy she'd been when Felix Worthington's team had contacted her and offered her the role. From fan club president to resident of Haven—an impressive leap.

The food was delicious. The smell had made Marion's mouth water, and with every bite she realized that she'd been overly hungry, having not eaten much in the previous few days. The conversation at the table switched to talking about the creaminess of the potatoes and how perfectly cooked the chicken was, the meat moist and skin crisp. If Haven's food was consistently this good, she was sure to gain weight.

Ruby checked on them after the first few bites. "Is everyone enjoying their dinner?" One by one, they assured her everything was perfect, and she smiled in approval before walking away. Marion noticed that Ruby waited on other tables as well, which sucked if you really thought about it. Well, hopefully it would only be when the Barlows were there, which would be infrequent.

Dorothy said, "Have you noticed that George has been staring at our table?" She smiled demurely.

While everyone turned to look, Ruby returned and rested her hand on Marion's arm. "Can I take your plate?"

"Yes, I'm quite finished, thank you."

As Ruby leaned closer to pick up the dish, she whispered into Marion's ear, "Be prepared to expect the unexpected. Things are not what they seem." It happened quickly, first the words of warning, then the lifting of the plate. Ruby was gone before Marion could respond or even register what she might have meant. She glanced around the table to see if anyone else had overheard, but they were still so focused on George Bonner that no one else had witnessed the exchange.

Marion couldn't even imagine what Ruby meant. As the waitress at the local restaurant, Ruby was just a bit player, not privy to any of the workings behind this project. Maybe she just wanted to stir things up, add some intrigue to the storyline. But why? There was no plausible reason.

By the time Gerald had paid the bill and they'd driven home, Ruby's words had receded in importance. As they walked up the path to the front door, Tom whispered, "We forgot to bring food back for Grandma." Luckily, Grandma's eyes were closed and she was snoring quietly. There would be no need to tell her they'd come back empty-handed. It wasn't like she could eat it anyway.

Chapter Seventeen

Crawling into bed that night, Meri had a mini panic attack and thought about calling the whole thing off. She imagined bolting out from under the covers and taking to the streets in her bare feet, finding her way back to the edge of town and pounding on the door until someone let her out. This was an unprecedented experience. Although she and Jeff had been in bed together as their characters and had had sex during their own short-lived affair, they'd never slept together. The idea of actual sleeping, the closing of eyes and drifting off, accompanied by the inevitable snoring and shifting around in the night next to someone else, especially Jeff, made her feel vulnerable. She was used to having the whole bed to herself and secretly feared she'd throw her arm over him in her sleep, thinking he was one of her extra pillows.

It didn't help to know they were on camera as well.

After the kids had changed and gone off to their respective rooms, she'd decided it was time for her own nighttime routine. She'd washed up, brushed her teeth, and changed into a granny nightgown in the bathroom. The floor-length nightgown, which came up to her neck and covered her arms to her wrists, provided the right amount of coverage, but she still felt exposed. When she left the bathroom and came out into the hallway, Jeff went in to take his turn, carrying the men's pajamas he'd found in the dresser. He smiled as they passed each other, and in her mind the expression was a leer. If he thought this was the beginning of something, he had another think coming.

When he joined her in bed, she had the covers up to her chin and was staring at the ceiling in the dark. She felt his weight jostle the mattress. He whispered, "What a day, huh?"

"Quite a day." She would have loved to discuss the experience with him so far, but as Meri and Jeff, not as Marion and Gerald. That wasn't an option. She wasn't sure if whispers could be picked up by the audio equipment, but it was best to assume they could. She spoke in code instead. "Gerald?"

"Yes, sweetheart?"

"Do you have any regrets?"

"About what?"

"About our commitment and our family." She hoped he could read between the lines.

"Marion, I cherish every minute spent with you and the kids. As far as regrets, I would only change one thing. If I could, I'd go back in time and treat you better when we were first together. I was young and immature back then. I said and did things I've regretted every day of my life since." He reached out under the covers and brushed his fingertips against the palm of her hand. "I know I've let you down, but knowing you has changed me for the better, and because of you I strive to be a better man."

She cleared her throat, not quite knowing what to say. He'd given her a Gerald speech, when she'd hoped to reach Jeff. "I'm not sure what you mean. You've never let me down."

"Oh, but I have." He moved his hand back to his side of the bed. "I promise to make it up to you."

"Don't worry about it," she said. "I'm not sure I even know what you're talking about. Every woman I know envies me for being married to you. Gloria once told me she'd trade Clarence for you anytime."

He laughed, a real laugh, and the sound of it warmed her heart. "Please don't trade me."

"I promise I won't."

"Good night, sweetheart."

"Good night, Gerald. Sweet dreams." She turned over on her side, facing away from him. For the longest time she stayed awake to listen. Only when she heard his breathing change did she allow herself to sink into sleep.

Chapter Eighteen

At home, Amanda had a self-imposed bedtime regimen that consisted of yoga, facial exercises, washing up with a special oil, and applying expensive cream around her eyes. She always finished up with three different procedures for oral health: using a Waterpik, flossing, and brushing with an electric toothbrush. She loved how clean her mouth felt when she was done.

In Haven, her nighttime routine was reduced to washing up with bar soap, brushing her teeth the old-fashioned way, putting on a nightgown, and going to bed. So freakin' weird. It was like revisiting her childhood. No wonder women used to age so rapidly. Soap! Everyone knew that was the worst thing you could use to clean your face. She felt her pores rebelling already. Thank God Felix Worthington had made this project financially worth her while.

Back in the room, she claimed the bed Dorothy had used in the show. Not that she had any choice. Lauren was already in Ann's bed, staring up at the ceiling, her fingers interlaced over her stomach.

She turned off the bedside lamp, and as Dorothy, she said, "Such a great day. First a family walk and then going out for dinner." She climbed under the covers.

"It was nice for Mother not to have to cook a big meal," Ann answered. "And Ruby gave us excellent service."

Typical. Ann always had been a Goody Two-shoes. Thinking of others was her most defining personality trait. "So you didn't enjoy it?" Dorothy asked.

"Of course I did. Dinner was delicious. And it was fun to see people I knew at the restaurant. Jimmy Curtiss from church was there with his folks, and I saw Doc Tarter there with the new doctor."

"And George and his mother."

"Yes. Them too." Ann yawned.

"Good night, Ann."

"Dorothy?" Her voice floated over in the dark.

"Yes?"

"Do you remember when Bud was climbing the tree and he fell?"

Amanda sucked in her breath. Why was she bringing this up? The accident she was talking about hadn't happened on the show—it had occurred on the set to the actor who'd played Bud. The stupid kid had fallen out of the tree, the same tree represented by the one outside their window right now. How could she get the actor and his role mixed up? Less than twenty-four hours into this project and she was already breaking character. "I think you must have dreamed that, Ann. It never happened."

"I'm pretty sure it wasn't a dream. I remember it happening." Her voice was matter-of-fact, almost as if she was doing this on purpose, to jeopardize all of them. But why?

"That never happened to Bud. You're thinking of someone else," Dorothy said firmly. "Go to sleep. Tomorrow will come soon enough."

"I must have gotten confused. Good night, Dorothy."

"Good night, Ann. Sweet dreams. See you in the morning."

Emotionally it had been a big day, making her exhausted. Even knowing there was a camera taping nearby, it was easy to close her eyes and sink into the pillow. Dorothy was almost asleep when the sound of a sudden tap sent a jolt up her spine. *What the hell?* Her heart skipped two beats and then sped up while her mind scrambled to find the source of the noise.

It happened again, but this time the bounce of a projectile against the glass was more pronounced. Ann sat up and said, "It's coming from the window."

"A bird?"

"I don't think so." Ann quickly rose from the bed and slid open the drapes. Dorothy got up and stood behind her, getting a view of George Bonner, sitting on the limb of the tree a few feet away from the window.

"Took ya long enough," he said with a grin. The streetlight provided enough dappled illumination that Dorothy could see the glint of his eyes and the neat part in his hair. He held out his fist and opened it, releasing a handful of pebbles. The very tree she'd been terrified to climb on the show apparently wasn't a deterrent for her love interest.

119

Dorothy hissed, "Are you crazy? What if my parents wake up?" Secretly, she was proud of coming up with this bit of dialogue, considering she'd been half-asleep two minutes ago.

"I wouldn't worry about it too much." George scooted forward on the branch. "If they're anything like my ma, they're sound asleep by now."

"What do you want?" Ann asked.

He spoke quietly but with enthusiasm. "I want to know if you'd accompany me to the Haven fair later in the week. There's gonna be rides, dancing, cotton candy. I might even win you a stuffed animal playing darts. I've been practicing."

Dorothy folded her arms. "I'm not sure I want to go to the fair with you, George. I'll have to think about it."

"Not *you*." His eyebrows knit together as he frowned. "I'm asking Ann."

"Ann?" she said, her eyes widening in disbelief.

"Me?" Ann took a step back. "I'm sure my father wouldn't allow that."

"Could you ask him?" George gave her the puppy-dog eyes. "I'll be a complete gentleman, promise."

"Ann's too young to go on a date." Dorothy wasn't entirely sure how old Ann's character was supposed to be, but she'd started the show as a twelve-year-old. Even allowing for the two-year run, she'd currently be no more than fourteen. Regardless, George was supposed to be part of *her* storyline. Felix Worthington had messed up big-time.

"Just ask," George said, ignoring Dorothy. "We can go as friends if you want. I just think it would be fun to spend time with you."

Ann waved for him to get back from the window. "Go home, George Bonner. We're supposed to be sleeping."

"Promise you'll ask, and then I'll go."

Ann sighed. "I'll ask, but he's going to say no."

"I think he'll say yes," George replied, his voice cocky. He turned around on the branch and climbed nimbly down the trunk of the tree. His last words drifted up from down below. "Talk to ya tomorrow."

Shutting the window and yanking the drapes shut, Ann said, "What a pest."

A few minutes later, when they were both back in their own beds, Dorothy whispered into the night, "Ann, are you still awake?"

"Yes."

"Did you know George was going to ask you to the fair?"

"No idea. If it makes you feel any better, I have no interest in George Bonner. You're welcome to him."

A crack between the drapes let in a thin sliver of moonlight, making shadows on the ceiling. "I don't care about George," Dorothy said. "I just wondered."

"Well, you don't have to wonder anymore." Ann turned over on her side, facing the wall.

"Ann?"

"What?"

"Are you mad at me?"

Ann's sigh cut through the darkness. "I'm not mad at you, Dorothy."

"Are you sure? I mean, we used to be more like friends than sisters, but lately it seems like things have changed."

"I think things changed when I realized that we're not very much alike. Don't worry about it." Her voice had softened with the beginnings of sleep. "Good night, Dorothy."

Dorothy remembered so many instances in the past when she'd given Ann the brush-off, preferring to hang out with Tom or others. Most of the time she hadn't given it much thought at all, but in retrospect, she had to admit she'd been unkind. If she wanted her time in Haven to go smoothly, she should probably make amends. She whispered, "I feel terrible that I haven't always been nice to you. I promise to do better. Can we start over?" She ran a finger over the bedspread. "Ann?"

From the other side of the room, there was only the sound of rhythmic breathing indicating Ann was asleep. Maybe tomorrow she'd try again.

Chapter Nineteen

The main house on the Montana property had a twenty-five-seat home theater with a full-size commercial screen. A remote control had the capability to open the heavy drapes across the screen, turn the overhead lights off and on, and show that day's footage, backward and forward. Milo found the room impressive, but his boss found it merely adequate for their purposes. The front row, which was set up with reclining loungers with built-in cup holders, was where they watched the events of that day in Haven. Despite the fact that Felix had viewed most of it in real time, he wanted another opportunity to study a few select scenes. "I don't want to view small talk or footage of the cast walking or driving. Life is too short for minutiae. What I'm really interested in is anything surprising or tension-building."

Milo took charge of the remote, while Felix sat back, sipping a green smoothie. They'd glossed over the dinner scene at the restaurant and fast-forwarded to where Dorothy and Ann conversed in their bedroom after turning in for the night. The light was dim, but luckily both women slept on their backs, making their faces somewhat visible. In the midst of their conversation, something Ann said was notable. "Do you remember when Bud was climbing the tree and he fell and broke his leg?"

"This part here," Felix said. "Turn it up."

"Will do."

They watched in silence as Dorothy, seeming to realize Ann was referring to something not on the show, made a quick and creative attempt to cover for her. When they wrapped up the conversation and said good night, Felix said, "Let's see that again."

They went over it three times in all, stop-start, stop-start, and when they were finished Milo said, "Are you thinking Ann broke character and is no longer eligible for payment?"

"Not necessarily," Felix said. "I just found it of interest."

"But it wasn't on the show, right? Was she referring to something that happened on the set?"

"Did you come across anything like that in your research?"

"No," Milo admitted. "Just a small article saying the boy left the show due to family issues." Not much more was known about the actor, Sean Knight. He didn't have any acting credits prior to his stint on the show or afterward. Just dropped out of sight. Maybe he couldn't cut it. Not unusual for a child actor, and that particular boy hadn't been a stand-out as far as acting went anyway. The name was common enough that Google brought up tons of results. "The article quoted Jeff Greer as saying Sean would be missed but that the Barlow family would carry on. Do you want me to do some more investigating?"

"No. It's not our concern right now."

Milo nodded. "You're right. Bud was only on for part of the first season, so I guess we should focus on the cast that's here."

Felix took a sip of his smoothie, which Milo knew would serve as his dinner this evening. His boss was so health minded that he never drank alcohol, and only consumed food and drink with the objective of providing fuel for his body. He didn't even partake of anything with caffeine, and that included chocolate. Milo admired him, but he set the bar far too high to emulate. Felix set his drink in the cup holder. "Next let's go to the part where there's the tapping on the window."

"That might be a fun scene for a reunion movie," Milo said, fast-forwarding. The look on Dorothy's face when she realized George was asking her sister for a date was priceless. Ann, too, had played it just right, not being the least bit interested. They watched for a few minutes, and then Milo rewound the segment and played it again. This was, he thought, a bit of plotting genius on the part of Felix Worthington.

No one else was privy to the actors' written prompts. Felix had insisted on writing all of them himself. He then sealed each letter in the appropriate envelope and had embedded members of his team deliver them. He'd said, "I want the results to be as much a surprise to the team as it is to the cast." Initially, Milo had felt funny about being in the dark. He'd been so involved in every detail of building Haven, from casting the supporting actors to working with engineers to make it all possible, that being kept out at the last moment was a letdown, but Milo found what his boss had done so far fascinating and couldn't wait to see more.

When they were done, the screen went blank, and Milo turned on the overhead lights, then asked, "Just between us, is Ann's father going to give permission for her to go to the fair with George?"

Felix slowly shook his head. "You'll just have to wait and see." He sucked down the last of his smoothie and handed the empty cup to Milo. "I'll see you tomorrow. It's time for me to head to bed. Morning starts early in Haven."

Chapter Twenty

Meri was surprised at how quickly she'd managed to become Marion. She answered to the name and had no trouble staying in character. Each of the five knew to look for their letter sitting on the top of the entryway table and read it discreetly before starting their day. When Gerald left for work in the morning, Marion gave him a peck on the cheek and sent him off with a wave from the porch. "Have a good day!" Grandma Barlow called out and added, "Don't take any wooden nickels," then laughed at her own joke.

"You're silly," Marion told the animatronic figure. While Beau barked in agreement, Marion reached down and discreetly patted the front pocket of Grandma's dress to confirm that the cell phone was still right where she'd left it.

On Monday, Marion and Ann went to the grocery store in the morning, and later they did some minor household chores that took them outside, where they were greeted by the neighbors. It was all very pleasant, if a little bit boring. Gerald was proving to be a bit of a problem, hugging her tightly and whispering words of love in her ear when no one was around. Even when the others were in the room, he'd take every opportunity to touch her, trailing a hand across her back or squeezing her hand when sitting next to her at the table.

That evening the family listened to the radio, and when the intro music to one of the shows came on, he insisted on twirling her around in the living room. She agreed to this improvised dance number because she wasn't sure if it was part of the script or just his own idea, but it was awkward. When the song ended, she suggested a stroll through the neighborhood, which suited him just fine as he could hold her hand and claim her as his own. As they ventured down the block, he proclaimed, "I'm the luckiest man in the world." His voice was a little too loud, in her opinion. "A beautiful wife and family. What more could I want?"

Good grief.

She knew where he was going with this. Behind Gerald's mask, it was really Jeff hoping he'd charm her into falling in love with him again. Did he think she could just forget what had happened between them? In her greatest time of need he'd called her a liar and discarded her, all the while insinuating that she'd set out to threaten his marriage, as if she'd been the instigator when he'd actually been the one to pursue her. If he'd even apologized somewhere along the line, she might have been able to forgive him, but that had never happened. Time passed, but his treatment of her had left a deep mark.

Prior to that, she'd given people the benefit of the doubt. Being called a liar by someone she'd loved had changed her outlook completely. By the time Hailey was born, she'd sworn off men entirely, and if it weren't for this Worthington project, she would have stuck to it.

Now that he found himself alone and heading toward old age, suddenly a life with her was looking pretty good. Well, she had news for him. Life with her would have been pretty good, but it wasn't something she was going to share with him at this point.

On Monday, the first full day of the project, Tom and Dorothy had gone off to visit with friends, the way teenagers presumably did during summer vacation, but on Tuesday they found out they each had a job, Dorothy manning the counter at the soda fountain and Tom working to set up the fairgrounds for the coming event at the end of the week. So off they went, adults faking being teenagers working at summer jobs.

Marion's chore for Tuesday was to help Gloria, her friend and neighbor, who was recovering from foot surgery. Before she left, Marion put her daughter Ann in charge of Grandma and the household, then went next door, where she and Gloria traded stories about their fictitious families and nibbled on baked goods that had been dropped off by fake well-meaning relatives. When Marion couldn't stand it anymore, she suggested a walk around the neighborhood and helped Gloria into the wooden wheelchair parked in the corner of the parlor.

Once they were outdoors, Gloria took a deep breath. Holding out her arms as if to encompass the day, she said, "It feels wonderful to be out in the fresh air, Marion. I can't thank you enough. You're the best friend I ever had."

Gloria did appear grateful, Marion thought as she propelled her down the block—and no wonder, given her cumbersome plaster cast. The warmth that spread through Marion's heart was so genuine that she had to remind herself that none of this was real, even if it felt completely authentic.

If she were being honest, Marion thought later that day, she would admit that she envied all the other cast members. Their storylines were so much more interesting. Gerald always seemed to have some anecdote to relate about the people who came to do business at the bank. That evening at dinner, he told the story of how a local mechanic had been paid with a counterfeit bill. "Completely bogus!" he announced. "I knew the minute I saw it. The police arrived, and there was quite the hoopla. The feds are sure to be investigating."

Tom arrived home from the fairgrounds sweaty and fatigued and late for dinner. He'd obviously put in a good day's work, but if he resented it, it didn't show. She'd been so bored at home that she yearned to hear all about what had happened at the fairground, but when she asked, he begged off, saying he was too tired to talk.

Dorothy, too, seemed to enjoy working at the soda fountain. Marion had no idea what Ann did all day long while left at home with a mechanical senior citizen, but her guess was reading movie magazines and taking a nap. Although, to be fair, when she came home from Gloria's, Ann had dinner in the oven, so that was something.

Two days down, eight to go. She steeled herself for the days ahead, then reminded herself that in the scheme of things, this wasn't too bad. For her daughter's sake, she could do it.

Chapter Twenty-One

Tom had opened his letter on Tuesday to see: *Report to the fairgrounds to start your new job!* Below the words was a small map with a line from his house to the destination, marked with a star that ended at Haven's one and only park. Walking distance, but of course everything in Haven was within walking distance. The brevity of the message surprised him. Somehow he'd thought they'd get detailed instructions on how to go about their days. The lack of directions made things easier, but it was also a bit unnerving, leaving him with the concern he might accidentally mess up.

He shouldn't have been worried. When he arrived at the job site, he was greeted by half a dozen men who addressed him by name:

"Tom's here!"

"Hey, Tom!"

"Howdy, stranger! It's good to see ya."

"Tom Barlow? Whaddya know! Looks like they'll let anyone work here!"

Even though he had no idea who these men were, the camaraderie put him at ease. He hadn't felt that kind of instant acceptance since his school days. An older man wearing work pants, a short-sleeved shirt, and suspenders walked up to him and shook his hand. "Happy you're here, Tom. We need all the help we can get." He let go of his hand and gestured for him to follow him. "My name's Herman McAvoy. If you do everything I tell you to, we'll get along fine. Have you ever done this kind of work?"

Tom thought, trying to remember if he'd ever had a job on the show, but he couldn't recall one. "No, sir, Mr. McAvoy, but I've been to the fair many times."

Herman hooted and leaned over to slap his thigh. "That's a good one, son." He straightened up, his six-foot frame still shaking with mirth. "You'll find that doing the setup and working at the fair is completely different than walking around eating cotton candy."

Tom grinned. The old guy really had a knack for playing his character. "I'm a hard worker, sir. Just tell me what to do."

"You can drop the *sir*. Just call me Herman."

"Okay, Herman."

"Right this way." And from there Tom was introduced to the crew, so many names he couldn't possibly remember them all, but he got the sense it didn't matter. This whole set piece revolved around Tom Barlow. It was more important that they remember who he was than the other way around.

A surprising thing happened halfway through the day, though—somehow the physicality of the work made him forget this was just a re-creation. In unloading trucks and setting up booths, tents, and rides, he became part of a group, working together to get things done. He couldn't remember the last time he'd done physical labor, much less worked with a team. There was something about it that felt just right, all of them coordinating their efforts, muscles straining. Unlike his radio job, he could step back and actually see what he'd accomplished: a tent raised, a dance floor built, booths ready to be manned.

By the end of his shift, his muscles ached and his shirt, wet with sweat, clung to his back, but instead of feeling worn out, he had a sense of euphoria. He'd been part of something bigger than himself. Lauren's words played back in his head: *And what is it you've done with your life, exactly? Become some big shot on a radio show and fathered children you don't live with?* Harsh, but she wasn't wrong. Once his contract expired, he should explore some different career options, maybe spend more time with the kids. Less talking and more doing.

Maybe then Jaime would get off his back. Besides nagging him about money, she constantly complained about his lack of involvement in their son's life. As if a man had to be there every minute to make a difference. Jaime was relentless, never letting up. What she didn't know was that her constant criticism made him feel less like helping her out.

When Herman declared they were done for the day, all the men gathered, sitting on wooden pallets, wiping their faces with their shirts or handkerchiefs. One of them brought out a metal cooler and handed out bottles of Blatz beer. They each took a turn with the bottle opener, passing it around from hand to hand, and then all of them took a handful of ice to rub their faces and necks.

133

Herman said, "Just don't tell your old man we let you have beer, Tom." The men laughed and ribbed him about drinking.

But then Tom saw one of the men light up a cigarette, and he felt the craving come over him. He rubbed the sleeve that covered his nicotine patch, but the smell was too strong. He wanted the real thing. What would his character do? Tom Barlow was a good son, but he also had a reputation for getting in trouble from time to time, necessitating a good talking-to from his father. He'd gotten into a fight at school and once snuck out of the house at night. Smoking a cigarette, he decided, wouldn't be outside the realm of possibility for Tom. He'd never considered himself to be nicotine dependent, but even with the patches he'd been edgy since landing in Haven, and a cigarette would satisfy his craving. With that in mind, he bummed a smoke from the guy with the pack of Marlboros.

"Smoking and drinking?" One of the other men raised an eyebrow.

Another guy chimed in, "Now you know you're a man, son."

Herman said, "Better take it easy there, slugger."

"Don't get drunk and be gettin' us in trouble!" This from a guy named Tex.

Tom played along. "I've always wanted to try smoking. And I've had beer before." He grinned and took a swig.

A gangly dark-haired man with a scar across his left cheek said, "Sipping from your dad's beer when he ain't lookin' don't count!" All of them laughed uproariously, as if this was hilarious.

"Got me good with that one," Tom said.

After that, all of them went on about the fair, mentioning the rides they'd be erecting the next day and the jobs they'd have once the fair began. From what Tom could tell, the jobs were assigned by the boss man, Mr. Dineen. "He likes to mix it up, so you never know what you're gonna get," Tex explained to Tom. From the way they were talking, Tom would be working at the fair as well.

The man with the scar was adamant that he wasn't going to work the dart-throwing booth. "You can't get me to do it, not for love or money."

"But that's an easy one!" another said with surprise.

"You think so? Then you try blowing up the damn balloons."

The first one nodded. "I see what you mean."

When the beer was gone, the men set down their empty bottles and drifted away, one by one.

"See you tomorrow," Herman called out as they left.

Tom got up to leave too, but no one was heading his way, so he walked home alone. Halfway there, a car pulled up alongside him and a lady's head popped out the window. "Tom, do you want a ride?" It was Ruby, the fan club president and waitress from the restaurant.

He hesitated. Was this something he was supposed to do? "It's so kind of you, but I'm very sweaty from working all day. I don't want to smell up your automobile, so I'm going to say thank you, but no."

Ruby hopped out of the car and opened the back door, gesturing to the interior like featuring prizes on a game show. "Good clean sweat doesn't bother us. Hop on in!"

135

Tom slid into the back seat. "Thanks." The driver was a man who looked familiar, but he couldn't place him. From the restaurant, maybe?

After Ruby got back in and the car moved forward, she said, "My husband and I were just coming back from the hardware store, and I said, 'I think that's Tom Barlow,' and sure enough it was you."

"Yes, ma'am," Tom said. "Just walking back from work."

The driver, her supposed husband, said, "Your father told me you're working at the fairgrounds this year."

"Yes, sir."

"It's a good job if you've got the vigor. If I was twenty years younger, I'd sign up in a heartbeat, just for the fun of it."

Ruby turned around and smiled. "Have you been enjoying spending time with your family again?" Her hair was arranged with a braid wrapped around the crown, reminding him of Mary Bailey, the wife in *It's a Wonderful Life*.

Enjoying spending time with your family again? That sounded like a question for Dominick, not Tom. He wondered if cars in Haven were equipped with cameras and audio equipment, then decided it was best not to take any chances. "Yes, ma'am." Sometimes the less said, the better.

They pulled up in front of the house, and Ruby jumped out again, saying, "Let me get the door. It sticks." She pulled it open and then grabbed his hand, passing him a small, folded scrap of paper. Between her lips, came a slight sound. "Shh."

He discreetly tucked the paper into his pocket and said, "Thanks for the ride! I appreciate it."

"You're very welcome," Ruby said. "Say hello to your mother for me."

"I will."

Her husband called through the open window, "We'll see you at the fair this weekend."

He waved as they drove away, then opened the gate and headed up the walkway toward the house. When he reached the porch, Grandma's eyes suddenly clicked open. "Tom! You look quite a mess. What happened to you?"

"Just sweaty, Grandma." He ran his fingers through his matted hair. "From working at the fairgrounds all day." She didn't answer, so he added, "Can I get anything for you?"

"No, thank you. I'm right as rain."

No matter how many times he experienced it, the sight of her lips moving and the sound of Catherine Sedgwick's voice, rough from decades of smoking, always unnerved him. He nodded. "Well, if you change your mind, just let me know. I'm always happy to help."

Next to her, the dog, Beau, murmured a small whine, prompting Tom to pat his head. He was getting fond of the dog, who didn't require walking, feeding, or cleaning up after. Best of all, he seemed friendly and his mouth didn't move.

"Such a good grandson. You go on inside now. I know your folks have been waiting for you."

He did as he was told. Marion, who was concentrating on the edge of the staircase, a feather duster in hand, stopped when he came through the door. "Tom! How was your first day?" She seemed genuinely glad to see him.

"It went well." Upstairs, he heard a door open and close emphatically. Dorothy. It had to be. Ann was too gentle to close a door that hard.

"Your father is in the backyard, stringing up a clothesline for me. I saved dinner for you. It's on the stove." She added, "If you want some company, I'd love to hear about your day."

"Thanks, but I'm too worn out to talk. I think I'll eat, then wash up and get to bed early." He absentmindedly patted the pocket containing Ruby's note, the real reason he wanted some time to himself.

"That's a good idea," she said, sounding disappointed. "We can talk later."

Chapter Twenty-Two

So far, Felix Worthington had been true to his word. Ann's character hadn't been required to do much of anything. "Think of it as a walk-on part," he'd said. "Nothing too stressful at all." She knew it would probably entail more than that, but he was persuasive.

On her first day, she'd waved goodbye to the others and then settled down on the sofa to read an Agatha Christie novel, *Death in the Air.* With teaching full-time and attending to her family, she hadn't been able to settle into a good book for years and was pleased to see that Hercule Poirot still delivered the goods. So nice of Worthington to thoughtfully stock the bookcase with an assortment of novels from the era.

After lunch, Ann spent some time sitting in a rocker on the front porch next to Grandma winding yarn from skeins into balls (a suggested activity mentioned in her morning instructions). She found wrapping the soft strands around and around oddly hypnotic and soothing. Time passed more slowly in Haven, probably because she wasn't constantly fielding the pinging of notifications on her phone.

Her phone. If there was one thing she wished she had with her, it would be just that. She missed Aaron and the girls. The four of them were a tight-knit group. In giving birth to her two daughters, she'd created two good friends. She kept waiting for Emily to morph into a rebellious teen, mortified to be seen out with her parents and little sister, but so far it hadn't happened. Emily came home from school bursting to tell her about her day. She was kind to her younger sister too. Lauren had never seen signs of sibling rivalry between them, only affection all the way around.

As a family, they had inside jokes and enjoyed going on road trips together. Miles of teasing and laughing and singing along to the music. So different from her own childhood. Aaron had said she was giving Emily and Charlotte the childhood she wished she'd had, and in giving it some thought, she'd agreed. They weren't perfect parents, but there was always love in the house, and her girls would always have each other, even after their parents were gone. They'd never be alone.

Her arms and heart ached thinking about them, but she found comfort in knowing her ten-day absence was for the benefit of her family. She was going to secure their financial future. For one thing, her daughters would never have student loans, and she and Aaron could have a comfortable retirement with a wide margin for unexpected expenses. Her presence here also meant that the other four cast members had a shot at getting a big payout, although other than Meri, she didn't care much whether the others got their money. She normally didn't wish ill upon people, but with this group she couldn't seem to move beyond the past. The bad memories had stuck. She could forgive but would never forget.

A young mother pushing a pram waved from the sidewalk and called out cheerily, "Good afternoon."

"Lovely day today," Ann responded, raising her hand in greeting. "Enjoy your walk."

After the young woman went past, a voice nearby said, "Seems like we're due for rain."

Holy crap! Even knowing the animatronic Grandma Barlow could talk, it still startled her, making her jump and knocking the ball of yarn off her lap. Reaching over to pick it up, Ann said, "It doesn't look like rain." The ceiling-sky was bright blue, and the clouds were just wisps, drifting ever so slowly. The complete opposite of a rainy day.

"Sometimes things aren't what they seem." The head turned to look right at her, the eyes blinking before making contact with Ann's own. The effect was eerie. The lips moved and formed these words: "You know you've always been my favorite. Such a kind, sweet girl."

"Thank you, Grandma." Ann had the uneasy feeling that Grandma hadn't been programmed to speak after all, but instead was just a portal, a speaker through which someone, a real person, was actually talking. Or maybe her speech was activated by someone typing in the words? To test her theory, she said, "Grandma, I was hoping you can help me with something. I remember a time when Bud fell out of the tree, but Dorothy says I dreamed it."

Grandma's eyes blinked with a slight click, click, and her head nodded up and down. "Don't you listen to Dorothy. She doesn't have the sense God gave a grasshopper."

Ann set the ball of yarn in her lap and studied Grandma's face. "So you remember when he fell?"

"Just trust your own instincts." The old lady's voice had an old country twinge to it. "You were raised right, and you know what you know."

Not very helpful. Maybe it was a program after all.

Lauren remembered the moment when it had all changed for her. Working on the show had started off well enough. It wasn't her dream, but she liked being part of a family, even if it was all make-believe. Having an older sister gave her a sense of security and someone to look up to. She didn't mind being the tagalong and was honored when Amanda took her aside and shared a secret with her. "I really like Neal, but I think he's afraid to ask me out because I'm the star of the show." Amanda's plan had been to encourage Dominick's attentions in order to get Neal jealous, and Lauren's role in the whole thing was to interrupt Dominick and Amanda when they snuck off together before things got, as Amanda said, "too hot and heavy."

Lauren took her part seriously, and thought Amanda would be appreciative, but in front of the cast and crew she'd turned on her, screaming at her to stop spying on them. "Isn't someone supposed to be in charge of her?" she shouted, which brought Aunt Jackie running to admonish her. She tried to explain, but no one believed her. "She's lying," Amanda said. "That's what she does." Later Amanda and Dominick had called her names—pest, crybaby, wannabe—followed by mocking laughter.

Meri had been kind during all of this, once putting her arm around Lauren's shoulders and saying, "I know you want to hang out with the big kids, honey, but they really want their privacy." Even sweet Meri had believed them rather than Lauren, who was actually telling the truth.

At that point, it was apparent she was on her own. There were no adults who would defend her. Aunt Jackie only cared about Lauren's career—the money and the status. Meri, the consummate professional, was kind, but only in passing; Jeff was too wasted to care about anyone else; and Dominick and Amanda were mean and fickle. The rest of the cast and crew were too caught up in their own jobs to care about her well-being, and after Amanda had branded her as a busybody and a liar, no one wanted to be around her. Only Sean was there for her. She was a teenager and he was a child, but there was an old-soul wisdom behind his little-boy eyes. Acting wasn't his strength, and neither was reading, but he was smart and noticed everything. She began to seek him out, just to have someone to sit with during meals and the down times. For a short while, she did feel like she had a younger brother named Bud.

But then he was injured, and when she tried to tell the truth about what happened, she was called a liar again. After he left the show, she was alone once more.

Chapter
Twenty-Three

On Tuesday, Dorothy had opened the envelope with her name, pulled out a sheet of paper, and read: *Report to the soda fountain at Frederick's Pharmacy at 9:00 am to start your summer job.* A satisfied smile spread across her face. She had fond associations with the soda fountain at the pharmacy. So many of her scenes in the show had had her sitting at that very counter, gossiping with her best friend, Addie, or meeting up with other kids from school. She'd always gotten meatier dialogue when interacting with other teenagers. Dorothy was an obedient daughter at home but a sassy flirt when away from her family.

The message had included a small hand-drawn map with a star designating her end point, but she didn't really need to follow it. Milo had pointed out the street leading to the pharmacy when they'd first visited Haven, and she'd committed it to memory. She had excellent navigational skills, even without GPS. She wasn't crazy about heights, so going up was never a good idea, but any other direction was fine with her.

After breakfast, Tom headed off to the fairgrounds for his job, and Dorothy announced to the room, "I need to go to work too. I'm not sure how late I'll be at the soda fountain."

Her mother said, "Have a good time!" Ann said nothing, but Dorothy sensed her envy. It had to be difficult being stuck at home while everyone else ventured out having fun. Dorothy left early so she could have a leisurely stroll. Leaving the residential blocks, she turned toward Haven's downtown business area. As she walked on the sidewalk in front of the businesses, she caught sight of herself in the window of the barbershop and paused to smooth her hair, which attracted the attention of the men inside, one of whom let out a wolf whistle. In current times this would be sexual harassment, but 1940s Dorothy found she liked that vote of approval. What was it Grandma used to say? Oh yes: *Youth fades quickly; enjoy it while you can.*

She'd often heard people talk about being nervous when starting new jobs, but that had never been her experience, not even once. If they'd hired her, it meant she was the perfect person for the job, so what was there to be nervous about? Today, she entered the pharmacy with that same kind of confidence, walking to the back of the store to the soda fountain. Behind the counter, she recognized her old friend, Addie, wearing an apron and serving some kind of fizzy drink to a little boy and his mother. "Hey, Dorothy!" she called out, giving her a wave. "I'm so glad we get to work together today."

Addie had put on a good twenty pounds since the show aired, something that secretly gladdened Amanda, but the woman's face was unlined and she still had a dimple when she smiled. In all fairness, she looked pretty good. Addie handed her an apron, which Dorothy deftly put on over her dress. "I don't think you've worked on the new machine yet, have you?" Addie asked. Without waiting for an answer, she gave Dorothy an overview on the ins and outs of working the soda fountain.

Dorothy listened politely. She wasn't nervous about messing up. In this fictitious world, she was the centerpiece. If she put on the wrong topping or scooped too much ice cream, who would care? The storyline was the king. Everything else was incidental.

The two chatted about their families, with Addie talking about her mother's gout. "It's been bothering her something fierce, so I've had to do so much around the house, you wouldn't believe it. She's feeling better today, which I'm glad of, what with the fair coming up. I don't want to miss going to that."

The fair. Between George's request to accompany Ann and Addie mentioning it now, Dorothy got the impression it was central to this reunion story. How clever of Felix Worthington to come up with a large event that could involve all of them.

When the woman and her son left, Dorothy cleared their dishes away. Addie got to work setting them into soapy water to soak, while Dorothy wiped the counter with a damp cloth. While her focus was still on the chore, she heard a deep male voice say, "So this is where they keep all the pretty

146

girls in Haven!" She glanced up to see the new doctor in town, young Dr. Reed. Not actually all that young, maybe thirty-five or so? But younger than old Doc Tarter and an actual doctor in real life. Plus, he was certifiably hot, with chocolate-brown bedroom eyes and a smile that lit up the space around him.

"Dr. Reed, as I live and breathe," she said. "How lucky to be graced with your presence! Playing hooky from work?"

"Doc Tarter is holding down the fort. I just stopped by to purchase some medical supplies, and then I saw the two of you and suddenly I had a yearning for a root beer float." He flashed her a flirtatious grin as he eased himself onto the stool.

"A root beer float?" Addie said. "Coming right up."

While Addie busied herself scooping out the ice cream, Dorothy got to work, chatting up the good doctor. She asked about his patients, and he told her about little Jimmy Curtiss, who'd come into the office with his mother yesterday with the complaint of a mysterious rash. "Turns out his mother had tried a new laundry detergent that just might be the culprit."

"You're like a real-life Sherlock Holmes!" she exclaimed.

He nodded. "It did take a fair amount of questioning to figure out the source of the problem." Leaning forward, he added, "In the meantime, I gave him some cream to help with the itching."

Addie set the glass in front of him, along with a long-handled spoon. "This should keep you busy for a while."

Dr. Reed took a sip through the straw, then stirred it with the spoon. "Are you girls going to the fair later in the week?"

His question was to both of them, but his eyes were on Dorothy.

"Maybe," she said. "Why? Are you thinking of going?"

"I just might." He grinned amiably at her, the flash of perfect white teeth making him look even more handsome. "It depends."

"Depends on what, exactly?"

"Only if you're going to be there." This time he wasn't even pretending to include Addie.

Dorothy felt a fluttering from inside her chest. Who needed George Bonner when she had a doctor seeking her out and flirting with her? "I might be there." She traced a spiral onto the counter with her fingertip. "I don't believe I ever caught your first name, Doctor."

"It's Nathan. Nathan Reed." He set the spoon down and extended his hand.

They shook, and she felt a shiver of delight at the feeling of his hand wrapped around hers. So foolish of her to have this kind of reaction. It was just a scene. Even so, she couldn't help but think ahead to what could potentially happen when her time here came to an end. He was a doctor, and she'd be a millionaire. If they did become a couple, it would be easy for her to relocate to wherever he lived. But maybe it would be best to keep her options open and not fall for the first hot guy who crossed her path. Money would buy her time. When you had both, there were lots of options. "Dorothy Barlow," she said.

"Oh, I know who you are," he said. "Everyone knows Dorothy Barlow." He leaned forward so Addie wouldn't hear. "The prettiest girl in town."

She felt her face flush red, and it wasn't acting this time. "I'll make a point to be at the fair."

"Well, then so will I."

"I'll count on seeing you there. Nathan."

When he left, she watched his backside and decided he looked good from every angle. She no longer cared about George Bonner. Ann could have him. Seemed as if Felix Worthington had given her a much more interesting story-line.

Dr. Nathan Reed had left a handful of coins on the counter. When she tried to split the tip with Addie, she waved it away, saying, "Go ahead and keep it. It's clear he meant it for you."

Without arguing, Dorothy slipped the money into her pocket. It might come in handy at the fair.

Chapter Twenty-Four

Gerald loved his job. He enjoyed getting ready at home, putting on a button-up dress shirt, pressed trousers, and a tie, along with a snappy-looking suit coat. A briefcase and a fedora worthy of a private investigator in a black-and-white movie completed the look, putting him right into character. It seemed that all of Haven came through the bank's doors, stopping by to see him. They trusted Gerald Barlow and poured out their hearts, telling him about their lives, both the good and the bad. The double doors to his office were always open so he could see everything that went on in the bank.

He had a secretary, a stout, congenial woman named Mrs. Williams, who seemed to find everything he said absolutely brilliant. The lenses of her glasses magnified her eyes, making her resemble an anime character. She laughed at all his jokes and answered nearly every request with, "Yes, sir! I'll take care of that right away." It occurred to him to tell her she didn't have to call him *sir*, but he liked hearing it, and she seemed to enjoy saying it, so he let it go. Mrs. Williams took care of everything, including bringing him coffee and checking to see if he wanted the tabletop fan on the corner of his desk repositioned.

He had little contact with the two tellers, young ladies named Helene and Ruth, who were positioned behind a counter and separated from their customers by grillwork, presumably to protect them from bank robbers. Judging from their smiles and chipper voices, they enjoyed their work, something that set the tone for the whole bank.

Mrs. Williams and the assistant bank manager, a wiry, twitchy man named Mr. Muncie, had desks in the outer area of the bank, while he had his own office with a mahogany desk, large picture window, and two framed watercolors of sailboats floating on a placid lake. A rotary dial phone, intercom, and oscillating fan graced his desk. He was a man of stature.

Life in Haven was turning out to be a big improvement.

He quickly summed things up—at work he was a respected boss, fawned over at every turn, and at home, even better, there was Marion. How wonderful to be in her presence, to finally say the words he'd wanted to speak for so many years. She was still a bit standoffish, but he sensed the beginning of a thaw. Already she'd begun giving him a kiss goodbye and taking an interest in everything he had to say. At night he listened to her breathing, wishing he could reach over and touch her, but knowing it was too soon. He imagined all the progress he could make, given another week or so.

Having adult kids warmed his heart as well. As Jeff, he'd been a failure at marriage, which wasn't all that uncommon in the acting world. As a consolation, he thought of each divorce as having provided a learning experience. At the very least, he'd discovered what not to do in a relationship. His only regret was never having been a father. From what he could tell, having kids enhanced a person's life, especially as the parents headed toward old age.

It wasn't that he hadn't wanted kids. He'd always envisioned himself as a father, but when his first wife had failed to get pregnant and insisted he be tested for fertility, he'd been reluctant. It was an embarrassing test, both in what was required to provide the sample and also in knowing his semen was going to be examined, but the medical professionals had already ruled out any problems on her end, so finally he'd agreed to it.

When the results came in, he learned more than he'd ever wanted to know about sperm count and motility. He found himself skimming the report and not really listening as the doctor explained the specifics. It all came down to one thing, as far as he could tell: he was sterile. A failure at providing the one thing men contributed to the baby-making process. "You're not alone," the doctor said. "Having an extremely low sperm count is more common than people realize." His wife had wanted to explore other options, but adoption was the only one that had any appeal to him. So they filled out mountains of paperwork and went through psych evaluations and a home study, got their references in order. Eventually they'd been approved and put on a waiting list to adopt a baby, but the marriage had ended before it ever went any further.

With his next wife, he'd made it clear that there would be no kids, and she seemed fine with that. Until she wasn't. Oh well, it's not like they got along all that well anyway. She was the superficial type, consumed with liposuction and high-end spa treatments. When she left him for her life coach, he wasn't surprised.

As Jeff, he was a jobless single man with no children. In Haven, he had an important position at the bank, a lovely wife, and a family. The whole package. Between his old life and this new state of being it was clear: Gerald Barlow outshone Jeff Greer in every area.

And the work was easy. Every morning he opened the bank safe, a refrigerator-sized structure fronted by a circular dial the size of a dinner plate, the combination of which he found in the back of the ledger in his desk drawer. He'd start his shift by opening the safe and pulling out the cash drawers for the two tellers. The first day he'd had trouble opening the damn thing, but his assistant, Mr. Muncie, had come to his rescue, opening it for him. With his head bent over the wheel, Gerald got a good view of his neatly parted glossy black hair. He'd only had it open for a moment when he shut it and insisted Gerald do it himself. "You spins the wheel and you gets the prize," Mr. Muncie said with a chuckle as he talked Gerald through it. Following his directions, Gerald spun it around twice until it landed on number 32, then turned it left and stopped on 18, and finally he rotated it to the right, halting on number 7.

"There you go!" Mr. Muncie had exclaimed when he'd successfully opened it. "Easy peasey, eggs and cheesy." With an exaggerated bow, he'd returned to his desk.

Muncie was a quirky man with a tendency to use comical expressions, like, "Okey dokey, that's no jokey." His work hours were spent sitting in a far corner opposite the tellers, poring over bank documents while wearing an eyeshade constructed with green celluloid. He reminded Gerald of an updated Bob Cratchit, and like Bob Cratchit he was so quiet that Gerald sometimes forgot he was there.

Magically, the cash drawers with the correct amount of money were always inside the safe each morning, and also magically, during the night his ledger was updated with the deposits and withdrawals for the previous day. Stacks of banded cash were neatly stacked on the lower shelves of the safe, but there'd been no need to touch them so far. He imagined they were there for show. The way the bank job was set up, he was left with little to do during the workday, except visit with various townsfolk, read the paper, and go out to lunch.

The first day there was some excitement when a customer brought in a counterfeit bill, but the second day was more mundane. By then he was used to the routine and was able to open the safe without any help from Mr. Muncie. Spinning the dial made him feel part sea captain, part game show host, and at the end when the tumblers lined up with a satisfying click, he squelched the urge to cheer. Maybe his biggest problem had been being born in the wrong era. Clearly, he would have excelled as a businessman during the 1940s.

At five o'clock on Tuesday, when the bank closed, Mr. Muncie said, "I'll take care of the cash drawers, Mr. Barlow."

He'd done it the previous day as well, so Gerald's best guess was that this was his job. He nodded and said, "Very good, Mr. Muncie."

"Glad to help, and that's no lie."

Gerald bid a good evening to Mrs. Williams and the two young lady tellers before putting on his brown fedora, the hat that marked him as a man of business.

As he was heading to the door, Mrs. Williams called out, "Mr. Barlow!"

His hand paused on the knob. "Yes, Mrs. Williams?"

"Don't forget that the bank examiner is coming tomorrow." She stood with her hands clasped in front of her like a child singing in a grade school assembly. "He has an appointment to see you at eleven!" She gave him a wide smile.

Gerald nodded. "Of course. I'll be here." She didn't say anything else, so he added, "Until then," and made his way outside to the parking lot. Getting behind the wheel of the Buick, he wondered what *that* was all about. Felix seemed to love giving them surprising twists, what with the counterfeit bill, Tom and Dorothy having jobs, the upcoming fair, and Meri becoming an angel of mercy for their neighbor. This bank examiner angle could be something troubling, or the man could wind up being a long-lost cousin or a high school buddy.

He started up the engine and backed out of his parking space. No point in ruminating on it. Tomorrow he'd see how the situation played out.

Chapter Twenty-Five

On Tuesday evening, Tom went into the bathroom and shut the door. Assured he was away from the spying eyes of the cameras, he fished Ruby's note out of his pants pocket. The paper was the size of those found in fortune cookies, and the print was tiny. He leaned against the sink and read: *Don't let Dorothy go on the Ferris wheel.*

Huh. He assumed that the Ferris wheel would be one of the rides at the fair, but he hadn't seen any signs of it on his first day of work. What was it that Ruby knew? Was the Ferris wheel unsafe? He couldn't imagine that Felix Worthington would spend a fortune to create a whole town from nothing only to neglect safety issues. The billionaire was a self-proclaimed superfan. In theory, that made him predisposed to keeping them alive. Tom shook his head before shredding the note and flushing it down the toilet. So confusing.

He had no trouble with advising Dorothy not to go on the ride, but he didn't think it would even come up because she was terrified of heights. She'd once told him that she'd fallen off a ladder as a little girl and for years afterward had heart-pounding nightmares of falling off cliffs. On the show, she'd once had to climb a tree and had begun hyperventilating. Once it was clear she couldn't do it, Lauren stepped in to take her place. Years later, she'd told him she'd worked on her fears with her therapist and made some great strides in that area. Still, a Ferris wheel didn't seem like something she'd willingly seek out.

On Wednesday, his second day on the job, Tom returned to the fairgrounds. His muscles were sore from the physical effort of the previous day, but for the first time in years he was eager to work.

"Barlow!" Herman bellowed out his name as a greeting. "You're going to be with Tex's group this morning."

He pointed, and Tom trotted over to where a group of men stood in a circle, all of them having a smoke before starting their workday. Without even asking, a lanky man wearing muddy workpants and a sweat-stained T-shirt handed Tom a cigarette and a book of matches.

"Thanks." Tom lit the match and cupped his fingers around the cigarette in his mouth. After he inhaled and the end glowed red, he dropped the match and stomped it out with his toe. He imagined how Worthington would work the cigarette and beer angle into the show. Most likely, Gerald Barlow would somehow find out his son Tom had been drinking beer and smoking cigarettes and give him a fatherly talk about the dangers of overindulging at such a young age. The speech would be followed by a clap on the back, with his father saying, "Let's just keep this to ourselves, shall we, son? There's no need for your mother to find out."

One cigarette was all he had time for before work officially started, which turned out to be enough to take the edge off. He finished it while Tex explained the group would be assembling and raising the Ferris wheel that morning.

The Ferris wheel. Tom didn't know what it meant to have it mentioned twice in less than a day, but the words definitely caught his attention.

Tex said, "Should be able to finish in a few hours, if we do it right. And we're gonna do it right. No one gets hurt on my watch."

Tom had never given much thought to what went into putting rides together for a fair, but he learned by doing, the other men instructing him as he helped unload sections off the back of a large truck. First, they built what they called the tower, and from there they assembled and hung each section, one by one, bolting everything together as they went. He was drenched with sweat by the time they were finished. The finished ride was impressive, even if it was on the small side for a Ferris wheel—only twelve cars total, each featuring a bench that seated two riders.

The men took a break to size up what they'd done. "Well done, boys," Herman said, after coming over to inspect their work. "There's another group gonna take care of the mechanicals, so this is it for today."

"The mechanicals?" Tom asked.

Herman grinned. "The motor that makes this beauty turn. You're going to be an expert at how it works, seeing how you're going to be the one operating the ride on Friday and Saturday."

"Me?" Tom couldn't keep the doubt from creeping into his voice. "I've never done that before."

Herman said, "No matter. Mr. Dineen has you on the schedule for all day Friday and Saturday."

"I hope someone is going to train me."

"I could teach a baby how to operate this ride," Tex said, whooping with laughter, his one gold canine tooth glinting in the light. "Even with a diaper full they could do it. The whole thing is just two levers. One starts it turning. Partway is slow, all the way is full speed. The other one controls the lock wheel. You wait until everyone is on before you start it, and you stop it one at a time when you're letting the riders get off. Think you can manage it, Barlow?"

Tom nodded. "Yes, sir."

Herman clapped him on the shoulder. "Don't you worry too much. You and Otis will both be running the ride. It'll be his first time too."

Oh great. There would be two of them who were clueless. Small consolation.

When the men broke out the beer this time, there was no more razzing Tom about his age. They'd moved past that, apparently, or maybe he'd proved his mettle. The beer was icy cold, and along with another cigarette, it hit the spot. He was too tired to contribute to the conversation, but he liked listening to them banter about jobs they'd had in the past and brag about their exploits with women. It didn't really fit the family vibe on *A Little Slice of Haven*, but he couldn't help but think that with all their bravado they would make outstanding guests on his radio show.

Chapter Twenty-Six

On Wednesday, after Tom and Dorothy went off to work, Ann parked herself on the porch, leaving her mother inside to do some housework. The front porch had become Ann's favorite spot to people-watch and talk to Grandma Barlow.

Grandma had some reassuring expressions, saying things like, "Don't you worry, your time will come," and "It's always the darkest before the dawn." Occasionally, Grandma would use her name and give her compliments, like, "Ann, you look very pretty today," or ask her to give Beau fresh water. To keep up her end of things, Ann discussed the weather and told her what she knew about the fair that was going to be in town on Friday and Saturday. After telling her about the fair, Grandma had said, "I don't think my old bones are up to that much excitement, but I want to hear all about it when you get back."

Ann could never decide if someone was behind the voice or if the AI was particularly astute, but either way, once you got over how creepy she was, Grandma was a reliably pleasant conversationalist.

 Sitting on the porch and watching the folks in the neighborhood gave her the sense she was inside a movie. Not a particularly compelling film, but mildly of interest and a good way to pass the time until she could leave Haven and go home. Each day there were different pedestrians who passed by the house—young mothers pushing babies in prams, women with little ones heading to the market, children riding their bikes or roller skating. On one occasion, a little girl's skate had come off and she'd fallen on the sidewalk right in front of the house. Immediately, Ann had bounded off the porch to help. Luckily, the child, whose name was Betty, wasn't hurt. Also fortunate, she had the skate key hanging around her neck on a string. Ann had been able to position the child's foot in the skate and use the key to tighten it until it was snug. When finished, she helped the girl to her feet, and Betty was off, calling out her thanks as she skated away.

Right before lunchtime, Marion popped her head out the door. "Anyone want to walk up to the pharmacy to visit Dorothy at the soda fountain?"

Ann, who'd been petting Beau, lifted her head. "Can I get a hot fudge sundae?"

"You can get anything you want, sweetie." Marion turned to address Grandma. "Mother Barlow, would you like to join us?"

Grandma's mouth opened with a slight click. She lifted her chin, turned her head, and said, "Thank you, dear, but I think I'll stay home and hold down the fort. Today's just not a good day for me."

"Oh no. I'm sorry to hear that." Marion did sound sorry. "Anything I can do to help?"

"Thank you, but I think not. Best thing for me is to sit a spell and rest my eyes. That's the only cure when my knees are giving me grief."

After Marion went to get her pocketbook, she and Ann were off, just the two of them, waving back to Grandma as they left. As they walked down the sidewalk, Marion said, "I don't know about you, but I was getting a little stir-crazy being at home. It feels good to get out."

Ann nodded, even though she felt the exact opposite. Going somewhere meant having to interact with other people, which required her to mentally put on her Ann suit. If she were being honest, she found it a little nerve-racking to have to say and do everything in the style of the younger Barlow daughter. But if she *had* to leave the house, and it seemed she did, she was glad to be in Marion's easy company.

As they turned the corner and went down the block, they could see George Bonner off in the distance. He wore a shopkeeper's apron over a button-down shirt and trousers and was sweeping the sidewalk in front of Bonner's Sewing Store. When they approached, his face lit into a smile. "Mrs. Barlow, Ann, how nice to see you." He leaned against the broom.

"Nice to see you too, George," Marion replied.

He turned to Ann. "Did you ask your father if you can go to the fair with me?"

Ann pressed her lips together and shook her head. "I told you, George. I'm not interested in going to the fair with you."

"What's this all about?" Marion asked, looking back and forth between the two.

George straightened up. "I'd like permission to accompany Ann to the fair this weekend. Friday and Saturday. Or just one of the days would be fine too." He spoke rapidly, as if wanting to get the words out before being interrupted. "We'd just go as friends." He stopped, and when the pause wasn't filled, he added, "If that would be fine with you and Mr. Barlow, of course."

Marion shook her head. "It seems Ann has already given you her answer. If she wants to go to the fair, she can go with her sister or with her father and me. I don't appreciate you pursuing this knowing she's not interested."

"Geez," he said. "I didn't mean anything by it. I just really like Ann."

"You'll have to like someone else." Ann folded her arms. "I'm not interested."

"Okay, then." He gave his attention to the broom. "Have a nice day."

As they walked away, Marion spoke to her daughter. "Good for you, sticking up for yourself."

"He's such a pain."

They went the rest of the way not talking, the lack of conversation making Ann even more aware of the sounds of cars driving by and the birds in the trees. A slight breeze brought the smell of exhaust. Overhead, puffy clouds drifted slowly across the bright blue of the sky. Funny how quickly she'd come to accept the ceiling as the sky. Whoever had designed it had done an incredible job.

The jingling of the bell on the pharmacy door announced their entrance. Marion led the way to the back of the store, where they found Dorothy and her friend Addie behind the counter, talking to one lone customer, Dr. Reed, the new physician in town. "Mother! Ann!" Dorothy called out. Her tone was friendly, but her expression looked less than pleased. "What brings you here?"

"Just came by for a treat," Marion said.

Ann slid onto the stool next to her mother. "I'd like a hot fudge sundae, please, with extra nuts."

Dr. Reed greeted them. "Ladies, nice to see you." Then he turned his attention to Dorothy. "I guess I'll be seeing everyone at the fair on Friday." He stood, leaving a handful of coins alongside an empty glass. He tipped his hat before placing it on his head. "Good day."

After he'd walked away, Marion ordered. "I'd like a double scoop of vanilla ice cream, please. And a glass of water, if it's not too much trouble."

"Not too much trouble at all," Addie said, getting out the glassware and lifting the ice cream scoop out of the water.

While Addie was working to fill the order, Marion said, "The fair is on Friday and Saturday. Don't you girls have to work the counter on those days?"

Dorothy idly wiped the counter in front of them. "Mr. Frederick is closing the soda fountain on those two days. He said there's no point in keeping it open, since the whole town will be down at the fairgrounds anyway."

"He's probably right." Marion accepted her ice cream dish and a spoon from Addie. "Thank you, Addie. This looks delicious."

Addie set the sundae down in front of Ann and handed her a spoon. "Just the way you wanted it." With a mischievous glint in her eye, she said, "Did Dorothy tell you that Dr. Reed is sweet on her?"

"Oh, he is not!" Dorothy protested.

"Yes he is! Can you imagine that? He's handsome, smart, and a doctor too. I think I hear wedding bells." Addie cupped her hand around her ear.

"Nathan just asked if I was going to the fair," Dorothy said, a blush creeping over her cheeks. "He was asking both of us, really. Just being polite."

"Nathan?" her mother asked. "Calling him by his first name is very personal." Her brow creased in disapproval.

"His idea."

"He seems like a nice man, but he's way too old for you, Dorothy."

"I know that, Mother. I never said I was interested in him."

And in that moment, Ann recognized the same flippant tone she sometimes heard from her own teenage daughter. Silently, she admired the acting going on before her. *Well played.* She concentrated on her sundae, leisurely stirring the hot fudge into the ice cream, letting the other three women take care of the dialogue. Once they were finished with their ice cream, Marion snapped open her pocketbook and pulled out some money to pay before they said their goodbyes.

Outside, Marion said, "Just one more stop before we head for home." She strode purposefully down the sidewalk.

Ann kept in step with her, only moving aside when a man with a cane approached from the opposite direction. After he went by, she asked, "Where are we going?"

"Stopping to see your father at the bank. A little surprise."

Chapter Twenty-Seven

Meanwhile, at the bank, Gerald was experiencing a completely different kind of day. He'd thought it would be similar to the day before, since that morning's sealed envelope had contained a short, simple directive: *Another day at the bank. Enjoy!*

He pulled his car into his parking space alongside the building, stopping for a moment to admire the words "Reserved for Bank Manager Gerald Barlow" stenciled on the brick wall in front of him, then grabbed his briefcase, left the vehicle, and sauntered toward the bank. If he'd been able to whistle, he'd have done it just then, because it would have made a nice accompaniment to the visual, but he'd never mastered the art. Instead, he swung his briefcase back and forth, giving the impression of a happy man heading off to a job he enjoyed. Exactly the kind of thing fans of the show loved.

Going through the bank's doors, he greeted Mrs. Williams and the two tellers, Ruth and Helene, then headed straight to his office. He congratulated himself on the fact that it was day three and already he had a familiar routine, hanging his suit coat over the back of the chair and setting his hat on the ledge by the window.

His morning was outstanding. All of Haven's friendliest residents came to see him, either popping their heads in the door to say hello or stopping in to visit, coming into his office one at a time and sitting in the comfortable chair opposite his desk like they were old friends. Phyllis Jones, who'd stopped in to cash a check, actually brought him a basket of muffins. "Blueberry, right out of the oven," she said, putting the basket on the desk in front of him. "Your favorite!"

Gerald lifted the linen napkin to see golden muffins bursting with blueberries. He hadn't been aware that he had a favorite, but maybe it had come up before? Lately, he was discovering all kinds of things about himself. "They look delicious," he said. "Thank you so much."

She hadn't been out the door for more than a minute before he'd broken one in half, taking in the fresh-baked smell. Without giving it much thought, he ate two in short order. When the ever-devoted Mrs. Williams came in to top up his coffee cup, he sent the basket back with her. "Please share these with the others," he said, "or I'll eat them all myself before lunchtime."

"The girls were just saying they were getting hungry. And Helene will be especially delighted," Mrs. Williams said with a smile. "She loves Phyllis's blueberry muffins!"

Maybe Phyllis Jones had confused him with Helene. Either way, there was no denying the woman had a knack for baking.

After that, he had a long conversation with Harry Aden, who'd come in to make his last loan payment on his business. Appearing in the doorway, he said, "Just had to tell you the good news. Aden's Garage is now mine, free and clear. I can't thank you enough, Mr. Barlow. If you hadn't approved the loan, I never could have started my own shop. You changed my life." He shook Gerald's hand.

"Glad I could help." A person couldn't hear these sentiments of gratitude and not get a warm feeling. Gerald suggested he sit down for a talk, but Harry regretfully said he had to head back to work.

"So much to do," he said with a shake of his head. "Business has been so good, I had to hire another mechanic. Not that I'm complaining!"

The rest of the morning went quickly. Gerald barely had time to do the crossword puzzle in the newspaper, what with all the neighbors and friends popping in to say hello. He'd completely forgotten he had an appointment until Mrs. Williams came to the door and said, "Mr. Barlow? Edmund Brown, the bank examiner, is here to begin the audit."

The audit? Gerald grinned. She sounded so serious, which made it seem official. "Of course, show him in."

Mr. Brown strode in, a briefcase in one hand. His white hair and matching, neatly trimmed mustache made him look as if he'd been at the job for a long time. He waved off Gerald's offer of coffee and got right down to business. "I'll need to examine all of your ledgers and documents, and make sure that the money in the drawers and the safe matches the listed assets."

"Of course. Whatever you need," Gerald said smoothly.

"I'll also need a list of all account holders. Checking, savings, and those who have loans with the bank."

"I'm sure Mrs. Williams can help you with that. She keeps excellent records." At least he thought she kept good records. If her diligence with the coffee pot was any indication, she was generally on top of everything. He called out, "Mrs. Williams!"

She arrived so quickly that she must have been right outside the door. "Yes?"

"Can you supply Mr. Brown with whatever paperwork he needs?"

"Of course." She stepped into the room and handed the bank examiner a stack of papers. "I prepared this ahead of time."

Gerald reflected on how easy it was to be a bank manager when gifted with a secretary like Mrs. Williams. He reflected on the fact that a person's quality of life was determined by the people around them.

"Excellent," Mr. Brown said, scanning the top page. "Since you've listed the total cash assets of the bank right here on top, let's take care of that first."

Mrs. Williams nodded and said, "If you need anything else, just let me know." She left as silently as she'd arrived.

"Do you need me for this?" Gerald asked Mr. Brown.

Mr. Brown's forehead furrowed. "Of course. We'll be going over this together." He beckoned for Gerald to follow him, then led the way to the safe. "If you would open it, please."

"Certainly." Gerald concentrated as he spun the wheel right, then left, then right again. He exhaled in relief when he heard the tumblers click into place. "Voila!" he said, pulling the door open. He stepped aside to let Mr. Brown go ahead and do whatever came next.

Mr. Brown stood motionless, then blinked. "Is this some kind of joke?" He gave Gerald a cold look. "If it is, I don't think it's very funny."

"A joke?"

"Where's the money?"

Gerald took a step closer and saw what the bank examiner was referring to—a completely empty safe. Not a dollar inside. "There were stacks of money here just yesterday." Confusion came over him like a sudden fog descending over a clear day. "Mrs. Williams?" he called out. "Can you come over here?"

"Yes?" She joined the men. "You needed me?"

Gerald gestured to the safe. "We seem to be short some money. Did you or Mr. Muncie move it out of the safe?" He glanced over to the corner of the bank, to the spot that just yesterday had housed Mr. Muncie's desk, but there was no Mr. Muncie and no desk either. Instead, there was a filing cabinet topped with a large fern. "Where's Mr. Muncie?"

"Who?" she asked, looking at him over her glasses.

"Mr. Muncie, the assistant bank manager!"

"I'm sorry." Mrs. Williams shook her head. "I don't know anyone by that name. And we haven't had an assistant bank manager in years."

This had to be some kind of a test, or a prank. A prank, that was it. They were pulling one over on him, trying to get him rattled. Perhaps this would be April 1st on the show, making this an April Fool's Day prank. Gerald took a deep breath. "Mr. Muncie. A skinny man, wearing a green eyeshade. Always has some wisecrack." He pointed. "He's been sitting at his desk in the corner for the last two days."

Mrs. Williams held out empty hands. "I don't know what you're talking about, Mr. Barlow. It's always been just you, me, and Ruth and Helene."

"He sat in the corner. That corner." He could hear his voice getting louder, but he didn't hold back. "Didn't say much, but when he did it was some quip. He was the one who showed me how to open the safe."

"You let someone else open the safe?" Mr. Brown asked incredulously. "That goes against bank policy."

At any moment, one of them would break and start laughing. "I know you're pulling my leg," he said. "And I agree that it's funny, but I think we've squeezed as much humor as we can out of the situation." He glanced around the bank. "Mr. Muncie? You can come out from wherever you're hiding and tell us where you put the money." Both tellers and a customer, a plump older lady wearing a housedress, stopped talking and turned to watch.

When Gerald got no response, he addressed the young ladies who worked at the bank. "Ruth? Helene? You remember Mr. Muncie, don't you? The assistant bank manager who sat at the desk in the corner?" He pointed a finger at the filing cabinet.

They both shook their heads and said, nearly in unison, "No, sir."

Helene said, "Sir, we don't have an assistant bank manager."

Gerald sighed and folded his arms. "Okay, I get it. You're all in on it. The joke's on me. I give up."

"I assure you, this is no laughing matter." Mr. Brown's voice was tinged with anger. "If you don't know where the money is, then this is a criminal matter. If you can't come up with the money, the board of directors will be pressing charges."

Gerald's mind whirred with all the possibilities. They weren't playing it off as a joke. What else could it be? Maybe this was an opportunity for the townspeople of Haven to rally around him, contributing all their money to save him in his lowest hour. Shades of *It's a Wonderful Life*. He thought that was a distinct possibility. All he had to do was play along and wallow in depression. Then, when a miraculous solution came to save him, there would be a triumphant ending.

"Let's go through this step by step," Mr. Brown said. "Besides you, Barlow, who has the combination to the safe?"

Mrs. Williams piped up. "Only Mr. Barlow has the combination to the safe." She was starting to seem less efficient and more of a pain in the ass.

Gerald ignored what she'd just said and replied, "Just me—and the assistant bank manager, Mr. Muncie."

"So you gave the combination to the safe to this Mr. Muncie? You know that goes against bank policy?"

"I didn't *give* the combination to Mr. Muncie. He gave it to *me*. And he coached me on how to open the safe. I wouldn't have been able to do it without him." A young couple came in through the bank doors, the husband letting his wife go first, a protective hand resting on her back. "Look, can we discuss this in my office?" Without waiting for a response, he turned and left the main area, followed by Mr. Brown. When Gerald saw that Mrs. Williams had trailed along and was now standing in the doorway, he said, "That will be all for now, Mrs. Williams."

When it was just the two men sitting across from each other, Gerald's desk between them, he felt his heart slow down. He hadn't realized how riled up he'd been until that moment. It was ridiculous, of course, but experiencing the actual emotional reaction made acting unnecessary. "Now," he said, tenting his fingers on the desk, "let's start over. To begin with, I can promise you that I did not take that money. When I left last night, it was in the safe. What happened after that would be up to whoever put the drawers back in the safe." It was Mr. Muncie, but saying his name again didn't seem to be the best idea. "I never touched any of the cash in the safe. I've always left it banded and sitting right on the shelf."

"Interesting." The way he said it made it sound like he didn't find it interesting at all. "If you've never touched it, how do you prepare the cash drawers each morning?"

"That's not me. Those things are already done by the time I arrive."

"But you handle reconciling the cash drawers at the end of closing, is that correct?"

"No," Gerald admitted. "That's taken care of as well. Usually, I leave and go home before the drawers are counted."

"Let me guess—the drawers are always counted and the money put away by the mysterious Mr. Muncie, who no one has seen except for you?"

"That's right." Gerald had a sudden wish for twenty-first-century technology. A security camera would come in handy right now. "So, you can see that I couldn't possibly have taken the money."

"I don't see that at all," Mr. Brown said. "What I see is missing money that only you have access to. And your lame attempt at blaming the theft on someone else is laughable." He leaned forward in his chair and pointed a finger at Gerald. "You, sir, are a liar and a thief."

"I'm telling you the truth!"

"You can say what you want, but the fact remains that the money is missing, and as bank manager you're responsible for it."

"I understand that it's my responsibility, but what I'm telling you is that I don't know anything, so I can't help you."

"I'll be back tomorrow." He stood up. "If the money isn't in the safe, we'll be taking further action. It's in your best interests to see it restored by the time I return." He left the office abruptly, and Gerald followed in his tracks.

"Believe me, if I had the money, I would return it."

Mr. Brown stopped and turned. "So you've already spent it?"

"No, sir. I have no idea where it is. The last time I saw it was when Mr. Muncie was with me."

"Enough of the lying. We're done here."

Something about the accusation threw him off-balance. He knew this whole scenario was all for show, and yet it felt—how did it feel? He had to think of the word. *Personal.* It felt personal. He watched as Mr. Brown stormed off in a huff and impulsively yelled, "I'm not lying!" He'd wanted to come off as strong, but the tremble in his voice made him sound guilty.

The door to the bank opened, and in walked Marion and Ann. His wife gave him a smile that normally would have warmed his heart. "Surprise!" she said, as Mr. Brown slipped past them and out the door. "We were in the neighborhood and thought we'd stop in to see you at work."

"Not now, Marion," he said, frowning. "This is not a good time."

Chapter Twenty-Eight

Felix Worthington sat in the home theater of his Montana ranch, remote in hand, watching bits of the previous two days in Haven. Milo had offered to handle the remote, but Felix had said, "No, I'll do it. I'm looking for specific behaviors."

Specific behaviors. Milo nodded as if he understood, but actually he didn't understand the reference at all. No matter. It was Felix's show, and he was the boss. Milo watched as Felix fast-forwarded over much of what had been filmed the previous two days, stopping to watch Tom working on the fairgrounds and bonding with the crew over a shared beer and a smoke. Another point of interest for him seemed to be Dorothy's flirtation with the doctor at the soda counter. Gerald's encounter with the bank examiner was another scene Felix played over and over again. Stopping it at one point, he turned to Milo and asked, "Does he seem worried to you?"

"Definitely rattled," Milo said. "His acting is superb."

Felix continued, letting the scene play out until Gerald yelled, "I'm not lying!" right before Mr. Brown left the bank.

"Gerald seems to be in a really bad place," Milo said. "How is it going to go from here? Is someone else going to come forth at the eleventh hour and admit they took the money?"

"Probably not."

"Why don't the others in the bank know about Mr. Muncie? Is it part of a dream sequence?" He'd been thinking about this for a while, and that was the only reasonable option he'd come up with. But it seemed unlikely. They'd never had dream sequences on the show before.

"You'll just have to wait and see," Felix said, a slow smile crossing his face. "I have all kinds of surprises lined up." He rewound the tape and checked all three scenes again, Dorothy and Tom at their respective jobs and Gerald interacting with Mr. Brown.

His boss glossed over the scenes with Marion and Ann, even though the two women had been charming and stayed in character the entire time. The only commonality between the scenes he'd found absorbing involved jobs. A theme or just coincidence? He was clearly searching for something, but what? Milo asked, "Are you thinking Dominick went out of character by drinking and smoking? When I saw that, I wondered if it would disqualify him from getting the money."

Felix, eyes still on the screen, shook his head. "Teenagers drink and smoke, especially in a work environment when it's offered. And in the 1940s, the attitude toward cigarettes was completely different. Still, the way he's taken to it isn't in character. I would expect a newer smoker to cough or sputter." He turned down the sound and watched the bank scene again.

"Has anything about all of this surprised you so far?" Milo asked.

Felix clicked on the remote, and the screen went dark. Automatically, the overhead lights went on, faintly at first and getting brighter until the room was fully illuminated. "Surprised me?" he repeated, drawing out the words. "In what way?"

"Have the actors done anything you haven't anticipated?"

"Yes, actually." Felix set the remote on the arm of the chair. "I've been surprised by how Tom has taken to his job. I would have thought Dominick would hate the physical labor, but he seems to be thriving."

"I noticed that too."

"Too bad." Felix sighed, then got up and said, "Get some sleep, Milo. Tomorrow is another day."

Chapter Twenty-Nine

If Gerald thought Wednesday was bad, Thursday turned out to be even worse. He was greeted at the bank by Mr. Brown and three members of the board of directors, all middle-aged men dressed in suits and wearing glasses. *Nondescript* was how he'd have described them. Average weight and height. Not handsome, but not ugly either. None of them stood out in any way. They'd have made perfect extras, but he couldn't see any of them in a starring role.

Mr. Brown introduced the three men. "Mr. Barlow, I'd like you to meet Misters Wilhelm, Fogleman, and McGrath. I've explained about the stolen money, and they've come with me today to conduct a thorough investigation."

Looking past them, Gerald saw that Mr. Muncie and his desk hadn't returned. The filing cabinet that had replaced him was still there, a mocking reminder that he'd once had an assistant. Beyond that, Helene and Ruth were already at their places standing behind the teller windows, while Mrs. Williams sat in her usual spot, tapping a pencil against her desk blotter. He caught sight of their faces and sighed. Each one gave him a disapproving glare. So different from the fawning and lighthearted banter he'd experienced initially.

He'd thought that Marion might have something to say about the matter, but she'd been noncommittal. She'd been miffed at how rude he'd been during her surprise visit to the bank. "I'm sorry you were busy, dear, but the way you spoke to me and Ann was appalling." She didn't seem to understand how much pressure he was under.

"He actually accused me of stealing from the bank!" he'd explained soon after arriving home. "Unbelievable. How long have I worked there?" He didn't honestly know and doubted she did either. He continued, irate. "All those years, and they suspect me of being a thief. He actually called me a liar." In retrospect, he realized that was what hurt the most. Gerald Barlow was an upright citizen, a man of his word. No one would ever accuse him of being dishonest.

Marion had barely seemed to register the enormity of the situation, and when she did speak it was to say, "I'm sure you'll work it out somehow. You always do."

Where was the outrage on his behalf? He wanted to shake her, but that would be out of character for him. The kids didn't seem to care either. Tom and Dorothy had gone up to their rooms after eating dinner, and Ann had slipped outside to sit with Grandma on the porch. When he followed her out to tell his mother what had happened at the bank, she had said, "Confession is good for the soul, son." Her words, accompanied by the clicking of the mouth opening and closing, were downright annoying. And maybe it was his imagination, but Ann, who hadn't said a word, looked as if she was holding back a smirk of amusement.

"I have nothing to confess," he'd said, throwing up his hands. "I didn't take the money." Seeing the futility of the conversation, he'd turned on his heel and gone back inside.

Now he stood across from four men who clearly thought he had stolen the money. What a disaster. This storyline had taken an ugly turn, but he knew that when it came to plot points, it was always darkest before the dawn. The hero had to experience a whiff of death in order for the audience to feel the release of joy upon his escape. He had to believe that this was just a catalyst that would ultimately lead to his triumph.

Mr. Brown broke into his thoughts, saying, "Let's continue the discussion in the meeting room."

Gerald didn't even know the bank had a meeting room, but he mutely followed them down a side hall. Across from the bathrooms, a door that had previously had a sign on it saying it was a janitor's closet was no longer identified as such. The door, now open, revealed a table surrounded by six high-backed chairs. Bookcases lined one side of the room, and pictures of previous bank presidents hung in a row on the opposite wall. When Mr. Brown gestured to a chair and told him to have a seat, he slid into place.

Gerald said, "I appreciate you coming here today, gentlemen, but I told Mr. Brown everything I knew yesterday. I intend to fully cooperate. I'll start out by saying I don't know how the cash vanished from the safe, but I assure you it wasn't me. I think once we get past that, we can start searching for the real culprit." They exchanged uncertain glances, and he took advantage of the silence to continue. "I think my impeccable record as manager of this bank speaks for itself."

The man he thought was Mr. McGrath cleared his throat. "We will certainly take that into account before we file a report with the police."

"There won't be a need for that," Gerald said. "I'm confident we can resolve this quickly."

But it wasn't resolved quickly. In fact, it wasn't resolved at all. For several hours, they grilled him. They asked about his whereabouts for the last three days and had questions about his family.

"How are you planning on paying for Tom's college tuition?"

"Marion and I have money set aside for our children's education." It seemed like something Gerald and Marion would do. They were a responsible couple.

"Is it true that you often foist work off on your employees, work you should be doing yourself?"

This was somewhat true. "I don't foist anything on my employees," he said, clarifying. "But I like to allow them to help as a reward for taking the initiative."

"Why did you allow a friend to open the bank safe?"

"He wasn't a friend. Mr. Muncie presented himself as the assistant bank manager. The other employees accepted his authority, and he already knew the combination to the safe. I had no reason to believe otherwise."

The questions kept coming, so fast and hard, like playing tennis against four other people, all of whom were volleying balls in his direction.

"Have you ever taken something that doesn't belong to you?"

"What would you do if you found a hundred-dollar bill on the sidewalk outside?"

"If you suddenly came into possession of a hundred thousand dollars, how would you spend it?"

"Do you consider yourself an honest person?"

"Have you ever lost a job due to theft?"

"Why should we believe you didn't take the money?"

"Are you lying to us?"

"Do you have a habit of stealing?"

"Where is the money?"

The questions continued rapid-fire, and he tried to respond just as quickly. After a while, he wasn't even sure if his words made sense anymore. *This is how they get you*, he realized. *They wear you down.*

They stared at him across the table, their expressions both challenging and disapproving. He could feel the animosity pouring off them. His eyes were tired, making him nostalgic for the eye drops in Jeff Greer's medicine cabinet back home.

In the midst of all of this, Mrs. Williams came into the room, carrying a tray of glasses and a metal pitcher of water. She deftly poured a glass for each man in the room and walked around the table, setting a drink in front of each one of them.

"Thank you, Mrs. Williams," Mr. Brown said. "That will be all." As if she was his secretary instead of Gerald's.

Gerald took a handkerchief out of his pocket and dabbed his face and the back of his neck. Was the furnace running?

The room's temperature seemed to be rising. From what he could tell, they'd been interrogating him for four or five hours, and nothing had been resolved. Time for him to take charge. He pushed back from the table. "Gentlemen, it's been a pleasure speaking with you, but we're done now. You have no evidence of wrongdoing, and I'm not feeling well. I'm going to go home."

With some satisfaction, he noticed the surprise on their faces.

"We aren't finished here," Mr. Brown said.

"I'm finished," Gerald said, standing. He'd been right—a nearby vent was blowing warm air right on the spot where he'd been seated. He'd seen enough crime shows to know they'd tried to force a false confession out of him. "Good day."

All four of them stood at once, and the one who'd been identified as Mr. Wilhelm said, "Mr. Barlow, we'll give you until next week Monday to return the money. After that, we'll have to get the police involved."

Gerald nodded. On Tuesday, the experiment would be over and he'd be leaving Haven. Between now and then, something miraculous was sure to happen to get him out of this mess. "Do what you need to do. I'm going home to my family."

Chapter Thirty

On Friday, while Marion and the kids planned to go to the Fair, Gerald's instructions said he was due back at the bank for another day of work. "Are you sure you can't come along?" Marion asked, handing him his briefcase. "Play hooky, just for one day?"

"I wish I could, my dear, but I simply have too much to do at the bank." He'd had a sleepless night wondering how the missing money dilemma was going to play out. Originally, he'd have bet anything that his family and community would have rallied around him, but there were no signs of that happening. "They called me a liar," he'd said over dinner the night before. They'd sat down to eat at a later hour to accommodate Tom's work schedule, so all five of them were present when he told the story of his inquisition at the bank. He was sure they'd be outraged on his behalf. Instead, they'd responded with bored stares and useless advice.

"I know it's upsetting, dear." Marion patted his arm.

Tom said, "I wouldn't worry about it, Dad. I'm sure it will be fine."

Dorothy nodded in agreement. "I lose things all the time, and then they turn up when I least expect them."

"If you know you didn't lie, why do you care that they called you a liar?" Ann asked.

This was, as they said in the twenty-first century, a teachable moment. "There's much more at stake than a simple label," he told her. "By calling my honesty into question, they're besmirching my character."

"And that upsets you," she stated flatly.

"Yes, it upsets me very much." It cut to the core, if he was being honest, going way beyond acting out a part. Gerald and Jeff Greer had become intermixed, and it was starting to be difficult to know where one ended and the other began.

"Huh," Ann said, spearing a chunk of beef roast with her fork. "Interesting."

By the next morning at breakfast, all of them seemed to have forgotten his problems. The fair took precedence over everything else. "I heard there's going to be a fortune-teller," Dorothy said, "and a cotton candy truck."

"There'll be a lot of food stands," Tom said. "You won't have to make dinner tonight, Mother."

"That will be a nice change," she said lightly.

As Gerald walked out onto the porch, briefcase in hand, Grandma Barlow piped up. "Hope your day is better than yesterday, son."

He muttered, "That makes two of us."

At the bank, neither Mrs. Williams nor the tellers greeted him. Ruth and Helene were chatting with each other when he came through the door, while his secretary was at her desk, head down, reading over some typed pages. Well, no matter. They were minor actors, just a step above being extras, while he was the patriarch of the Barlow family and one of the stars of the show. He went straight into his office, and just like the day before, he put his suit coat on the back of his chair and set his hat on the window ledge.

Sitting at his desk, he noticed a folder labeled "Theft Investigation Report – Gerald Barlow Interview." He was expected to read it, that much was certain, or it wouldn't be there. He needed to bring an appropriate emotional response to it. Should he get angry or cry? He'd always been good at tearing up on cue, and viewers loved to see it, especially women. The female fans loved a vulnerable man, as long as he didn't overdo it. He softly read the words on the cover, "Theft Investigation Report – Gerald Barlow Interview," and sighed. Flipping it open, he read over the three sheets of paper inside. They were held in place with metal brads, making the report resemble a very thin book. Most of it was blather. Mr. Brown explaining how, in a routine visit, he'd asked Mr. Barlow to open the safe only to discover that the safe was empty. The report covered their discussion about Mr. Muncie, calling him "a friend of Mr. Barlow's" and making it sound as if he'd just given out the combination to a non-employee. There was an account of Mr. Brown's discussion with the three board members prior to their visit to the bank.

Gerald scanned the rest of it and noted that the missing amount was listed as being just over $100,000, which explained why they'd asked him how he would spend that amount, given the chance.

A hundred thousand dollars in cash seemed like an excessive amount for one bank to have on hand in the 1940s, but what did he know? He shrugged and kept reading.

The last page summarized their findings. *The investigative committee found Mr. Barlow to be confrontational and uncooperative. His story of a fictitious assistant bank manager named Mr. Muncie was clearly devised to divert suspicion to another party. It is this committee's opinion that Mr. Barlow is lying.*

There it was again. His honesty called into question. Did they never watch the show? Jeff Greer may have prevaricated on occasion, but Gerald Barlow was a paragon of virtue.

Mrs. Williams interrupted his thoughts, bringing in a cup of coffee and coming around to his side to set it on the desk in front of him.

He gave her a smile and said, "Thank you," but only got a nod in response. As she left the room, he felt compelled to call out, "That will be all, Mrs. Williams. Carry on."

As he picked up his cup, one of the desk drawers, slightly open, caught his eye. Had it been open before? He didn't think so, but couldn't say for certain. He tried to close it, but something had jammed it up, so he pulled it all the way out to take in the sight of a half-filled bottle of liquor wedged between a stapler and a stack of ledgers. Bourbon, his favorite. Like a sucker punch to the gut, seeing the bottle sucked the breath out of his chest.

Gerald Barlow imbibed periodically, but always at home or at a restaurant, and usually for an occasion. Never at work. On set, the liquor was actually lukewarm tea. He lifted the bottle and gave the cap a sniff, but he couldn't determine any smell. Still, something told him it was the real deal. Did they want him to drink on the job and get fired? Was this intended to be a story of a downfall and redemption?

Jeff Greer's former reputation as a drinker and his resulting stint at rehab were public knowledge. If this was part of the storyline, he wasn't playing. He'd signed up to be Gerald Barlow, and Gerald Barlow was a good man, the kind of man who wouldn't drink on the job.

He set the bottle on his desk, noticing how the sun streaming through the window backlit the glass, making the amber liquid glow. Such a beautiful sight for something so destructive. He knew that even unscrewing the cap would unlock some muscle memory that would lead to pouring it into his cup, then drinking it. Drinking even one sip would have him drinking all of it, then after that he'd search for more to drink, which would start something that would never end. He'd drink ad infinitum until he'd destroyed everything good in his life. He wasn't going to give in to temptation, not as Gerald or Jeff.

He grabbed the neck of the bottle and carried it out into the main area of the bank. Helene was counting out singles for a young man leaning forward on the counter. "Seventeen, eighteen, nineteen, and twenty. Will there be anything else, Mr. Rathman?"

"No thank you." He stacked up the bills and slipped them into his wallet. "Now I'm off to spend it!"

"Have fun at the fair," she said as he walked away.

Gerald marched over to Mrs. Williams and dropped the bottle in the wastebasket next to her desk. "I'm not sure how this got in my desk drawer. If it was a joke, it's not a very funny one."

She blinked, surprised. "I see, Mr. Barlow." Her answer was noncommittal, but he thought he spotted a flash of approval in her eyes.

Next Tuesday couldn't come fast enough.

Chapter
Thirty-One

For Tom, the previous few days of work had been preparation for the fair. In his mind, they were the rehearsal for the event, so Friday, the first day of the fair, became showtime. He liked how Felix Worthington had made the storylines intersect, with his sisters and mother coming to the fair as attendees while he'd be there working the Ferris wheel.

He couldn't even guess what their instructions for the day were, and he didn't particularly care because he was focused on his directive, the best one yet. It had said: *Today's a good day, so keep a positive attitude! Today Tom Barlow will meet the love of his life. She'll be wearing a cherry-red dress, with beige buttons down the front and a fabric belt. A blonde. Keep your eyes open and your lips ready!*

Finally, a storyline befitting Tom Barlow. He'd seen Tom's transformation with having a job and interacting with the other men on the crew. A coming-of-age plotline. It would make compelling viewing, but it all had a very masculine energy. Adding in a love interest would balance things nicely, and personally, he'd always had a thing for blondes. This was going to be fun.

Maybe once this was over, he could leave the radio business and resurrect his acting career. He knew he wasn't a leading man, but he had definite comedic chops and a likeability factor women found endearing. This might be the jumping-off point he needed.

Tom was already stationed at the ride when Marion, Ann, and Dorothy arrived. He spotted them from afar, but couldn't leave his post to greet them. He'd been paired with Otis, who was also new to the Ferris wheel. The rules were simple. Never let a rider turn around and get back on. Everyone goes to the back of the line and has to pay with a ticket. Make sure each passenger is buckled and that the safety bar is engaged.

They'd been told that one of them would man the lever, while the other helped riders onto the seats, making sure they were strapped in and the crossbar snapped securely in place. When the ride was over and the people were ready to disembark, the routine was the opposite—unsnapping the bar, instructing them to unbuckle, and making sure they got off safely. He and Otis, a teenager with bad skin, periodically traded off roles to make it fair.

During all of this, he scanned the crowd hoping to spot his mystery woman. Wearing a cherry-red dress meant she'd stand out, so he wasn't worried about identifying her, and since the note said they'd meet at the Ferris wheel, presumably she'd come to him.

He was still looking for her when his mother and sisters came to the front of the line, ready to fill the last available seat on the ride. Dorothy stepped to one side, while Marion handed Otis two tickets. "You're working with my son, Tom Barlow," she said to Otis, pride in her voice.

"Yes, ma'am," Otis said. "Is the other young lady with you?"

"I'm not riding this time around," Dorothy assured him. "Just watching."

Tom helped Marion and Ann onto the ride, then made sure they were safely ensconced. He glanced back at Dorothy, who stood near Otis, watching her brother at work. "Enjoy the ride," Tom said, his own catchphrase. Otis preferred "Enjoy the view," but honestly, it didn't matter either way. They'd already paid and were strapped in. It was going to happen whether they enjoyed it or not.

Now that the twelve seats were filled, Otis started it up and Tom came over to make introductions. "This is my younger sister, Dorothy," he said. "She won't ride, because she doesn't like heights."

"I used to be afraid of heights when I was a kid," she said, correcting him. "But I think I might get on the Ferris wheel yet."

Ruby's warning came back to him: *Don't let Dorothy go on the Ferris wheel.* Tom spoke quickly. "That might be a good idea *someday*, but I'm not so sure you want to start overcoming your fear with a Ferris wheel." As the wheel revolved, Ann and his mother came past, calling out his name and waving. From their smiles, it looked like they were having fun.

Otis scoffed. "This one's not even a big deal. We get little kids on here." He shielded his forehead with the flat of his hand and glanced upward. "The top isn't much higher than standing on a second-story balcony."

"I've been thinking of trying it," Dorothy said. "If I was with the right person, I think I could do it."

"There are other rides," Tom said, pointing out the baby roller coaster, the swings, and the carousel. "Not as high."

"We'll see," she said, with a lilt in her voice. "Would you tell Mother and Ann that I went to talk to some friends and that I'll catch up with them later?" Not waiting for him to respond, she sauntered off, disappearing through the crowd.

Dorothy found Dr. Nathan Reed kneeling in front of the dart-throwing booth, attending to a teenage boy who sat on the ground with a gash on his forehead. A small crowd gathered around them, but despite the blood pooling from the wound, the doctor was calmly assuring the fairgoers all was fine. "Just a minor dart injury. A superficial cut," he said, pressing a white handkerchief against the patient's forehead. "Nothing to worry about."

He guided the boy's hand up to the cloth. "Hold this steady so we can stop the bleeding. My car is parked nearby. I think you should come back to my office so I can treat this properly. Can you walk?"

"I think so." The kid seemed a little dazed. In shock, maybe? Dorothy had to remind herself that none of this was real. Being immersed in Haven was doing a number on her brain.

When the boy got up, the crowd clapped. Dr. Reed guided him away from the booth. People stepped aside to clear a path for them. When the doctor spotted Dorothy, he smiled and said, "Dorothy! How good to see you." He stopped, and the boy, still holding the cloth to his forehead, halted as well.

"You're leaving?"

"Yes, unfortunately." He tilted his head apologetically. "Duty calls! Will you be here tomorrow?"

"I don't know. Should I be?" A slow smile stretched across her face.

"I think it would be best. Myself, I'll be at the entrance at noon."

"Then I'll be there too."

He grinned. "Until later, Miss Barlow."

When did men stop talking like that? The innuendo of something happening later, combined with being called Miss Barlow, seemed innocent enough, almost respectful, but she found the subtext flirtatious. "Looking forward to it, Nathan," Dorothy said.

As they walked away, she overheard the kid say, "I gotta let my ma know what happened."

The doctor responded, "Of course. You can call her from my office."

She wasn't surprised that he had to leave. It had been in her directive. Now all she had to do was reconnect with Marion and Ann and enjoy the rest of the day. Tomorrow, she was spending time with the sexy Dr. Reed. As it turned out, Dorothy Barlow had grown up quite a bit since the show ended. She had to hand it to Felix Worthington. He really knew how to weave a narrative.

By the end of the morning, the novelty of working the Ferris wheel was getting a little thin, so Tom was glad when Tex came by to relieve him. "Barlow!" he shouted as he approached. "I'm taking over for ya. Forty-five-minutes is all the break you're getting. If I were you, I'd find myself something to eat."

He didn't need to hear it twice. "Yes, sir."

"I'm not kidding when I say forty-five minutes is alls you get. Not forty-six or forty-seven. If you're late, I'm sending Otis here to hunt you down, and believe me, you don't want that." He clapped a hand against Otis's back. "He's not a big fellow, but this boy is made of muscle. I hear tell he once killed a man."

"I never killed anyone," Otis said sheepishly.

"I'll be back in time." Tom glanced at his watch. "I promise."

Leaving his place at the Ferris wheel, he headed over to the food stands, keeping an eye out for a blonde in a red dress. He got in line at the hot dog stand and, when it was his turn at the counter, ordered a hot dog and a Coke. "You're Tom Barlow, right?" the lady behind the counter said, tugging on her hairnet.

"That's right."

"I know your mother. Tell her Gretchen says hello."

"I will. Thanks."

The hot dog came in a paper food tray with a dollop of potato salad. When Gretchen handed him his drink, she set a fork down on the counter on top of a paper napkin. "Don't forget to return the cutlery when you're finished." She gestured to a water-filled bin on a table off to one side.

"I won't forget." Tom carried his lunch over to an empty picnic table, and as he ate, he mulled over the day so far. A beautiful blonde was somewhere on the horizon, soon to connect with him. The food was delicious, the weather was perfect, and his drink was chilled. Life was good.

Off in the distance, he heard the music of the carousel. On the opposite side of the fairgrounds, a polka band played. He couldn't see it from where he sat, but he knew there was a dance floor in front of the bandstand because he'd helped to set it up.

He was spearing a chunk of potato when he became aware of someone standing across the table. His eyes registered the red dress first, then his gaze traveled upward, appreciating her fine hourglass figure. When he got to her face, his jaw dropped open in recognition, and for a split second he forgot he was Tom Barlow. "Jaime?" He sputtered out the word in shock. The last time he'd seen her, she'd bitched him out for not spending more time with their son. At the time, her blonde hair had been pulled up in a messy topknot, and she'd worn yoga pants and a shapeless T-shirt. Her appearance today was a complete transformation, closer to the actress she'd been when they first met.

"Is this seat taken?" she asked smoothly, pointing to the opposite side of the table.

He recovered quickly. "No. Please join me."

"I think I will." She smiled seductively, then reached over to grasp his bottle of Coke. "Do you mind?"

Of course he minded. She'd made him so miserable he didn't want to give her one penny or one sip more than she was entitled to, but this was a scene that had to be played out, so he smiled and said, "Of course not. Help yourself." Jaime being cast as his love interest was the worst. Felix Worthington was either clueless or a complete asshole.

She took her time sipping from *his* bottle, then set it down in front of him, running a finger along the rim, and then she sighed. "So refreshing." She held out a hand. "I don't think we've met. I'm Elizabeth Ness."

He shook her hand. "Tom Barlow."

"I know what you're thinking," she said. "Any relation to Eliot Ness? The answer is no, but just like him, I'm known to be persistent. But not untouchable." She laughed at her own joke, making him want to gag. "So, Tom, what do you do for fun in this town?"

"You're not from Haven?"

"No, I'm staying wtih my great-aunt Bertha. She's such a dear. She wasn't feeling well enough to come to the fair but gave me some money and encouraged me to come and enjoy myself. I saw you, and I thought, *That is one good-looking young man, and he's all by himself.* You looked like you needed a friend."

At least the conversation was going in the right direction. "So you think I'm good-looking?" He raised an eyebrow.

She laughed. "Exceptionally good-looking, but I'm sure you have a mirror and know that already."

"So what caught your eye?"

She tilted her head, keeping her eyes on his face. "It wasn't one thing—it was everything. Those big brown eyes, the curly hair, a great physique, and a winning smile. You've got it all."

The words were echoes of things she'd said when they'd first met. He softened a bit, realizing that she had no choice in the matter—the setup required her to speak nicely to him. Maybe this wouldn't be a complete disaster after all. He glanced at his watch. "I have to go back to work in twenty minutes, but would you ride the Ferris wheel with me? I hear the view from up top is pretty spectacular."

"I believe I'd enjoy that."

Tom got up from the table, leaving the remains of his lunch behind. There were people to take care of that. He walked around to her side of the table and offered her the crook of his elbow. She slipped her hand around his arm, and off they walked, toward the Ferris wheel.

Chapter Thirty-Two

When they got home from the fair, the girls headed into the house, while Marion lingered on the front porch, ostensibly to talk to Grandma Barlow. She pulled her rocking chair over so the two were close together, and then she chattered about the day's events, telling her mother-in-law all about the rides, the music, and the neighbors they'd encountered. When she ran out of things to say, she ended with, "I hope you had a pleasant day while we were gone."

"Indeed," Grandma said, her head swiveling in Marion's direction. The eyes blinked three times. "Beau and I had a lovely day, didn't we, boy?" In response, the dog gave a short yip of approval. "Are you and Gerald planning on going tomorrow?"

Marion laughed nervously, not knowing what tomorrow's directions would bring. "We'd like to, but you never know. I guess we'll see how we feel after breakfast."

"Probably a good idea." Grandma's chair kept steadily rocking, her feet tapping the porch with each forward movement.

"I'm heading inside. Do you need anything?"

"No, dear. I'm right as rain. But thank you for asking."

Marion got up and went over to give Grandma an embrace. During the hug, she made a point of patting the old lady's pocket, to reassure herself that the hidden cell phone was still there. Her breath caught in her chest when she realized it was gone. Her fingers scrambled against the fabric, checking if it might have slipped, but no, the pocket was flat against Grandma's thigh, no rectangular outline to be found. Grandma's voice became the faintest whisper in her ear, "Looking for something, Marion?"

She went cold, the words hitting her like a throat punch. Trying to maintain her cool, Marion forced out a response. "No, everything's fine." She straightened up. "Give a shout if you need anything." She walked into the house without looking back.

Inwardly, she reeled at the realization that her lifeline to the rest of the world was gone. Even worse, someone had taken the phone, which meant Worthington most likely knew she'd left it there in the first place. Would this disqualify her from getting the money? Of course it would. The thought made her physically ill. She choked down the bile she could taste in her mouth.

That night, the missing phone was all she could think about. One of the production staff had clearly taken it while all of them were gone. Had they seen her leave it on the initial walk-through of Haven? That had been prior to the actual start of the ten days, so she might be able to make a case for herself that way. She hadn't used it either. Maybe Felix Worthington would take pity on her. She hoped so, because otherwise this was all for nothing.

Gerald apparently had his own problems. He tried to follow her into the bathroom, saying, "We can brush our teeth at the same time. Save on water." Marion knew it was a strategy to talk to her without the prying eyes of the cameras, but she wasn't going for it. Holding out a firm hand, she said, "Nothing doing, buster. A lady likes to be alone in the bathroom." *Buster* hadn't been a nickname she'd used for him on the show, but it seemed appropriate here. He looked crestfallen at her refusal, but so be it. He wasn't the only one who was going through something.

Besides, her bathroom time was sacred, the only part of the day when she knew she wasn't being recorded or filmed. She did a few dozen sit-ups and push-ups, hoping to offset the muscle atrophy that came from living Marion's life. From rock climber to oven door opener. The contrast was vast. After changing, washing her face, and brushing her teeth, she opened the door to see Gerald standing there, his pajamas in hand. "Your turn," she said brightly, stepping aside to let him in.

Once they were in bed under the covers, he elaborated on his day, telling her what the investigative report had said. "It ended by saying, 'It is this committee's opinion that Mr. Barlow is *lying*.'"

Her directive that morning had told her she shouldn't be overly sympathetic or helpful concerning Gerald's problems at the bank, which was good because she wasn't up to assuaging his feelings over fictitious accusations. "That must have hurt," she said.

"Darn right it hurt. And then some prankster left a bottle of bourbon in my desk drawer."

"Really."

"Yes, really. I stormed out of my office and dropped it into Mrs. Williams's wastebasket. I told her I wasn't sure how it got in my desk drawer, but I didn't think it was a very funny joke."

"It sounds like you handled it well."

"Well enough," he said. "I just don't understand why all of this is happening. I'm an honest man, trying to do the right thing. Why is everyone turning on me?" He got up on one elbow and leaned in closer to her. "Do you think if you and the children told all the townspeople about my problem that they'd come to my defense? I've done so much for Haven and have so many friends in the community. I'm sure they'd be here for me in my time of need."

Marion could feel the warmth of his breath on her cheek and heard the anguish in his voice. Hearing his vulnerability went a long way toward softening her attitude toward him. She thought about all the things they could discuss later on, once they were back to being Jeff and Meri. For now, she said, "Dear, I wouldn't worry about it. I'm sure it will all get sorted out on its own."

"Why in God's name would you think that?" He sounded exasperated. "Things don't just get sorted out on their own. If we're waiting for people to step up unsolicited to vouch for me, it's never going to happen. I don't think you understand how serious this is. I'm in a really bad place, Marion."

If it were up to her, she'd have been happy to come up with a plan to help him, but her directive was clear. This was a problem he needed to solve on his own. She turned over to face the wall. "Gerald, it's late. Can we talk about this tomorrow? I'm really tired."

He sighed heavily. "I'm tired too. At least tomorrow is Saturday." He lay back down, pulling on the covers.

"Things will look better in the morning," she said, making her voice sound sleepy. This, she remembered, was a line Marion had used several times over the years. Marion, the cockeyed optimist, always bolstering the family. Dear, sweet, cheerful Marion. "Try to get some sleep, dear."

"I'll try," he grumbled.

Meanwhile, Ann lay in bed, not quite ready to fall asleep. She could hear the distant sound of cars driving past the house and the muted voices of her parents from down the hall. On the other side of the room, Dorothy tossed and turned, punching her pillow into shape and shifting around as if not able to get comfortable.

Ann smiled in the dark. The first part of her stay in Haven had gone faster than she'd anticipated. She was halfway to home now. In the last few days, she'd thought of her girls often and wondered how they were faring without her. She'd never been away from them for this long. Sometimes at night, half-asleep, she reached out to reassure herself that

Aaron was next to her. It was jarring to realize she was alone in a twin bed in Haven.

She still missed her family and thought of them constantly but had to admit she was starting to enjoy herself. So many times she wished for her phone, not just to hear her family's voices but also to take pictures to show them later. The girls would love seeing her in the Barlow house, wearing formfitting dresses every day. The dress she wore today had a ten-inch zipper that ran up the side. It was like being sealed inside a dress that hugged every curve. So 1940s. Since she couldn't take photos, she made a point to make mental images, willing herself to remember every detail so she could tell them about it once she made it home.

Going on the rides and eating herself full at the fair had actually been fun. Without realizing it, she'd lapsed into vacation mode, not worrying about everyday things like the downfall of junk food and the possibility of weight gain. At the fair, she and Marion had indulged their every whim, including the best blueberry pie à la mode she'd ever had the pleasure to eat. Dorothy had ditched them early on, going off to find friends, which had enabled Ann to have Marion all to herself.

She had to admit that Marion played the part of the mother quite well. Ann had the experience of mothering her own daughters but had never been the recipient of that kind of love, at least not that she recalled. As a child, she could only remember Aunt Jackie and her grandparents, none of whom had been nurturing.

Marion, on the other hand was the definition of nurturing. She was taller than Ann by eight inches, and maternal by nature, draping an arm around Ann's shoulders and checking to see if she wanted to take a break in the shade after they'd gone on several rides.

After the TV show had ended and her stint playing Ann was over, Lauren had been so angry at everything that had transpired that her bitter feelings seeped out and covered the rest of the cast. Guilt by association. Ann saw now that Marion hadn't really done anything wrong. She just hadn't stood up for Bud.

Ann thought back to her resistance to this project, but now she was grateful to have accepted the invitation. She was starting to see all the puzzle pieces come together in a very satisfying way. And the denouement? It was going to be a doozy.

Finally, she'd get some measure of closure.

From the other side of the room, Dorothy shifted again, making so much noise she had to be making a point. She yawned loudly, then said, "Ann?"

"What?"

"Did you have fun at the fair today?"

"Sure." Ann tapped her fingertips together.

"Did you see George Bonner?"

"No. I don't think he was there."

"Can you keep a secret?" Dorothy whispered into the night. "Just between us sisters. You can't tell Mother or Father."

Ann's interest was piqued. "What is it?"

"You have to promise not to tell."

"I promise." She made a cross-your-heart gesture just in case the cameras could see in the dark. "Tell me."

"My secret is that I have a date with Nathan Reed. Dr. Reed." Her voice trembled with excitement, the words coming out in a rush. "I know our parents wouldn't approve, but it's all very innocent. I think he just wants someone to go on the rides with, and he's new in town and all, so he doesn't know that many people. We were talking at the soda fountain and really hit it off. He wants me to ride the Ferris wheel with him."

From outside came the muffled sound of a car horn. Ann didn't respond, so Dorothy continued. "I think it's so romantic. We'll be sitting side by side, taking in the view. I decided that if he tries to kiss me, I'm going to let him."

"So you don't like George anymore?"

"George?" she said dismissively. "He's just a Haven boy who works in a shop. Nathan's a doctor, and he's been out in the world. He's even traveled to London, England! I asked if he saw the king, and he said no, but he did see the changing of the guard at Buckingham Palace."

"I'd love to see that someday," Ann said.

"Me too." There was a long silence, and then Dorothy asked, "So could you do me a favor? When you're at the fair with Mother and Father tomorrow, if you see me with Nathan, could you distract them?"

"You want me to cover for you? I don't know . . ."

"Don't be a fuddy-duddy, Ann. Just help me out, and I'll owe you a favor. I know you probably won't be able to keep them away for the whole day, but if I can even get a little bit of time with Nathan, that would be wonderful. This is more important to me than anything."

"I thought you didn't like heights."

"If I'm with Nathan, I'm sure I'll be fine," she said impatiently. "What do you say, Ann, are you going to help me out or not?"

"All right, I'll do it."

"Oh, thank you! I'll do something special for you one day, just you wait and see."

Chapter Thirty-Three

On Saturday morning at six a.m., Tom's eyes snapped open. One thought came to the forefront of his brain: *It's show-time!* He sat up on the bed, stretched, and grinned. The day before, he'd been shocked to encounter his ex-wife in Haven, but his consternation had turned to glee when he realized her role had been custom-made to provide him with a great storyline. And he had to give Jaime credit—her acting had never been better. At some point she'd stopped being Jaime in spirit and had committed wholeheartedly to being Elizabeth.

When they rode the Ferris wheel, she'd gazed adoringly at him for about thirty seconds before leaning in for a passionate kiss that had turned into a full-on make-out session, the kind he hadn't had since he was a much younger man. A tantalizing, teasing kiss, bodies pressed against each other, the implied promise of more to come later. He was lucky that the ride ended when it did, just short of the point of no return. Seemed like Jaime in her new incarnation as

Elizabeth Ness was just his type of woman. And the best part? They'd be meeting up again today, after his shift ended.

Unlike most people, he'd never had an opinion of Felix Worthington either way, but now with things shaping up in his favor, he decided Felix was a god among men.

Early morning with the family was the usual. They exchanged pleasantries, had breakfast, and opened their individual envelopes with their directives. He always read his first thing, committed the words to memory, then tucked the piece of paper into his pocket to dispose of elsewhere. He wasn't sure what everyone else did with their scraps of paper, but he'd yet to come across one anywhere in the house.

His instructions for today said: *Enjoy your day at the fair! Stay until you get official word that it's time to leave. Ignore what you see happening to the other members of the family. This is all about you. Each one of you has your own path.*

Little did he know that all of them had received the same directive that day.

Once he'd arrived at the fairgrounds, he greeted all his new friends as he strode from the front entrance toward the Ferris wheel. The place wasn't open to customers yet, so it was just the workers, most of them smoking or tossing back a cold drink as they set up stands and rides.

"Tom!" He turned to see Gretchen calling from behind the counter of her booth. "Want a cold Coke?" She held out a bottle.

He stopped, then backtracked. "Don't mind if I do." Although they'd exchanged pleasantries the previous day, they weren't friends, exactly. Of course, he was a Barlow, which made him memorable.

She cracked open the soda with a bottle opener and handed it to him. "Going to be a busy day."

Tom took a swig. "How much do I owe you?"

"For you? No charge. It's on the house."

"Thanks, Gretchen. See you later!" Walking away, he clutched the cold bottle and felt a surge of happiness fill his heart. It just felt so damn good to be here, much better than he'd anticipated. When he'd imagined this new version of Haven, he'd assumed he'd have to re-create Tom verbatim, reliving all of his teenage dramas, which included sitting in his room at night, waiting for Gerald to knock on the door, coming to dispense some fatherly wisdom. Instead, his character had evolved and now had a job and adult friends. This fair idea was particularly brilliant. The event might be fake, but the fun that people were having was definitely authentic. He saw the faces of the kids on his ride and knew they weren't acting. They were having the time of their lives, and he was part of it. A big part of it, since none of it would be happening without him and Otis.

Living in Haven meant perfect weather, working outdoors (sort of), no bills, and nobody complaining to him. He had little in the way of responsibilities, and every day was an unexpected adventure. Honestly, if it weren't for the lack of sex, he could live this life forever.

When he got to the ride, Otis was already there, wiping down the seats with a wet rag in preparation for the day. As he cranked on the lever a quick up and down, it turned the wheel in motion just long enough for the next seat to come his way. When he spotted Tom, he paused and gave him a grin. "Here's the man of the hour."

"Am I late?" Glancing at his watch, he noted it was nine o'clock. If the watch was keeping good time, he'd reported for work at just the right moment.

"No, I got here early, so I started without you. Want to help?" He handed Tom the rag and stepped back. While Otis manned the controls, Tom wiped down the seats. Good mindless work. The best kind. Otis said, "Mr. Dineen stopped by right before you got here. He said you only have to work until lunchtime."

Tom stood up. "How come?"

Otis shrugged. "His nephew showed up and needs the work, is what I gathered. It's not a problem, is it? I figured you'd want to spend some time with your lady friend."

"No, I don't mind," Tom said, turning back to his work. Interesting that Mr. Dineen was often referenced but never seen. He had a lot of power for someone with an off-screen part. Good work if you could get it.

The morning hours went quickly, with a steady flow of customers eager to ride the Ferris wheel. He and Otis had an unmistakable rhythm, each one working in sync with the other. Help the customers on, one seat at a time. Then once the seats were full and riders secured, they let the wheel rotate six times before slowing it down and having the passengers disembark. After that, they wished everyone a good day and started over again, repeating the whole routine with a new group.

Despite the sameness of the process, working the Ferris wheel energized him, made him feel upbeat. Keeping busy made the time go faster. Over the course of the morning, the sun rose in the sky and the noon hour snuck up on him.

Tom was showing Mr. Dineen's nephew, Ned, how to work the lever when Elizabeth walked up and gave his biceps a squeeze. Today her hair was parted on one side and came down in soft golden waves past her shoulders. She wore a bright-blue dress with the tiniest yellow flowers on the collar and around the waistband. The innocence of a floral print coupled with the figure-hugging style was something a man could appreciate.

"Hello, Tom." Her voice was nearly a purr. "Any chance you want to spend some time with me?" Her lips parted, revealing gorgeous white teeth.

He reached out a hand and winked. "I'm all yours."

Chapter Thirty-Four

Dorothy found walking around the fairgrounds with Ann and their parents to be a total slog. She'd selected her most flattering dress, a crimson-colored crepe number that complimented her dark hair, and she'd spent a lot of bathroom time on her hair and makeup. She had a clear objective, and it wasn't to be filmed as a dutiful daughter.

In the car, she'd been relegated to the back seat with Ann, making her feel like the teenager she was playing. Gerald's driving made her insane. So freakin' slow. And why did he have to wave to everyone as they went by? If he thought his friendly overtures would make it into the final show, he was wrong. Dorothy had a much better scene coming up. Anything with Marion and Gerald would just be framework. This reunion was the younger generation's turn to shine.

When they arrived at the fair, they moved in a group, making her itchy to be free. Soon after, Marion suggested that the two girls might want to go off on their own. Dorothy was ready to accept the invitation, but Ann ruined things by saying, "Don't be silly, Mother. We like spending time with you." Such a suck-up.

If she'd left to go off on her own at that point, it would have looked bad to the Haven fans, so onward she trudged, going on the swings with Ann, accepting Gerald's offer of ice-cream cones, and making small talk with George Bonner and his mother. And walking. Endless walking around the fairgrounds, admiring the polka dancers and watching young men at the dart-throwing booth trying to impress their girlfriends. In their small group, she sensed some tension between Marion and Gerald and guessed it was because his storyline had gone south and none of them had responded appropriately. Good grief, if he hadn't figured out that all of this was pretend he was an even bigger idiot than she'd thought.

Frankly, she'd liked him better as a drunk. Not a politically correct opinion, so she knew better than to ever voice that aloud, but it was true. Back when he was drinking, he was aggravating as hell—but way more interesting. Now, he was such a ball of knots that even standing next to him made her nervous.

She'd noticed, too, that Ann and Marion had formed some kind of weird alliance, which was unexpected, because on the show Ann had been more of a background player, the kid actor who rounded out the cast but never had her own storyline. Of course, Marion had been a static character herself, so maybe that was the commonality.

All she had to do was get through the morning, break away from the other three at the right time, and meet up with Nathan Reed. In the meantime, she hoped her hair held up.

Right before noon, she diplomatically said, "Does anyone mind if I go off to find my friends?" When no one objected, she gave them a little wave and headed for the front entrance.

All morning, Gerald played the role of doting family man. He accompanied Marion and the girls through the fairgrounds, fished out his wallet to pay for ice-cream cones, and made appropriate small talk as they went. That morning's directive had instructed him to stay until he had official word that it was time to leave. The ambiguity of the statement made him uneasy. He couldn't imagine they'd have to stay until ten o'clock that night when the fair closed. And what constituted official? The not knowing made him nervous.

Of course, Gerald was anxious in general. Having the storm cloud of the missing money hanging over him was a source of misery. Walking around the fair, he carried an agitated, uncomfortable feeling in his gut, a sense that he was waiting for *something* to happen. He just didn't know what that something could be. He scanned the crowd, waiting for the bank examiner to seek him out, come running up to tell him that Mr. Muncie had been located trying to leave town with a suitcase full of stolen money and that the other employees had only denied knowing the assistant bank manager because they'd been threatened with their lives if they talked. Gerald would be vindicated then, and his family and coworkers would rejoice. There might even be a celebratory scene of them lifting a glass to toast him, which would be a nice wrap-up to a reunion movie.

Or alternately, perhaps he'd run into a few of Haven's wealthiest denizens. He imagined encountering two couples, all of them dressed to the nines, the men in three-piece suits, their wives in serious dresses, seeking him out at the fair.

When they met up, they'd announce that they'd heard about the trouble at the bank and were willing to cover the deficit while they worked tirelessly to prove him innocent. He imagined one of the men saying, "Frankly, I'm appalled that anyone could ever suspect Gerald Barlow of any wrong-doing!" His wife would clutch her pearls and nod in agreement. Then the other gentleman would pull a checkbook out of his inside jacket pocket and say, "I'm willing to write a check right now to make this problem go away. To think that they'd accuse Mr. Barlow of theft!" He'd shake his head, outraged. And then there'd be a scene wherein the board of directors and Mr. Brown would apologize for having mistreated him. Gerald, being the bigger man, would forgive them.

Placed in the hands of savvy writers, this plot conundrum could be resolved quite easily.

The day did improve after Dorothy left to find her friends. He sensed some thinly veiled animosity between her and Ann. Nothing he could put his finger on. A sort of impatience on Dorothy's part? Sisters. It was always something. Once Dorothy was out of the equation, the dynamics of the group felt lighter, as if the fourth person had been an unnecessary drag.

After getting food, they sat down to have lunch at a nearby wooden picnic table. They'd found one they could have to themselves, and best yet, it was in the shade.

Gerald chewed on an ear of sweet corn dripping with butter and dusted with salt, and when he was through, he finished off his meal with a delicious piece of fried chicken. His Coke was outstanding too, sweet and refreshing. Marion and Ann had opted for hot dogs and lemonade. He watched them take delicate bites while he chowed down, making a bit of a mess, not that he cared. When he returned his silverware to the water bin, he got his fingers a bit wet and wiped them with a napkin. Good as new. "I think that's the best fried chicken I've ever had," he announced when he returned to the table.

Marion, who was now eating some potato salad, said, "Mine was good too." She took a sip from her drink.

"Fair food is always the best," Ann added.

He felt better then, both physically and emotionally. Hunger had been the root of much of his moodiness, he could see that now. Once back home, he'd miss this time in Haven, he was sure of it.

The three of them did another lap around the grounds. This time, Marion let him hold her hand. Near the ax-throwing booth, he stopped. "I'd like to give this a go." When it was his turn, his girls cheered him on. He managed to hit the target four out of five times, one of them hitting the bull's-eye squarely in the middle with a satisfying thwack. Marion and Ann clapped when the blade of the ax made perfect contact.

"Well done, Father," Ann said.

After he'd completed his throws, the carnie called out, "We have a winner!"

For his efforts, Gerald pored over the prizes, eventually selecting a new hairbrush in a clear cellophane package. He bowed as he presented it to Marion. "For you, m'lady."

She curtsied. "Thank you, sir." She tucked it into her pocketbook, and they continued on.

The crowd had gotten thicker. The polka band that had been playing earlier was replaced by a barbershop quartet, four men in banded flat-topped hats, vests, and sleeve garters who were singing about a bicycle built for two. At the other end of the park, the music from the carousel filled the air. When they got close enough to see the revolving horses, Ann wanted to stop and watch. Gerald recognized the calliope music and began humming along. He froze suddenly upon spotting a familiar face in the mass of people ahead.

The music faded into the background as his vision locked in on one man. He took in the guy's overall appearance, recognizing the wiry build and the jerkiness of his movements. He'd have known him anywhere. Mr. Muncie. He wasn't wearing bank attire but was dressed in a short-sleeve shirt with suspenders and work pants. A straw hat was tipped back on his head, revealing his distinctive glossy dark hair.

"Muncie," he said, the word coming out between his teeth in a hiss. Even as he spoke, Muncie was on the move, quickly heading away from where they stood.

"What?" Marion asked, touching his arm.

Gerald brushed her off and strode forward, his heart pounding. He pushed through a group of people, one man saying, "Hey!" but still he kept going, zigzagging through the crowd, until he got Muncie in his sights again. Seeing him was no coincidence. The entire bank crisis had led up to this, and he was going to act his heart out.

When he was an arm's length away from the man, he reached out and grabbed at his suspenders, yanking him backward. "Now I've got you." He couldn't keep the glee out of his voice.

The man spun around, forcing Gerald to let go. When they were face-to-face, the guy said, "Whaddya think you're doing?"

With a shock, Gerald realized it wasn't Muncie at all. This man was a close match, as if someone had drawn Muncie's face from memory but hadn't quite captured the sharp angles and pronounced chin. The eyes and shiny black hair were the same though, as was his approximate height and build. "I'm sorry," Gerald said, the words coming out in a stammer. "I thought you were someone else."

Marion and Ann caught up to him, closing in on either side.

"Next time, check first before you go grabbing someone," the man said angrily. He adjusted the hat on his head.

"What's going on, Father?" Ann asked.

"I thought he was Mr. Muncie. From work," Gerald responded weakly. "From the back, he looked just like him." His mind still went back and forth between the man he saw before him and Mr. Muncie. The resemblance was strong, and he'd been so sure . . .

Marion said, "You thought Lewis was Mr. Muncie?"

"You know him?"

"Of course, from the market. It's Lewis McAvoy. I know I've mentioned him."

Lewis tipped his hat to her. "Good afternoon, Miz Barlow. Are you enjoying the fair?"

Not only did they know each other, but from his manner of speaking, this man held her in high regard. Everyone liked Marion, Gerald thought. He'd always thought he was likeable as well, but he saw now that he was mistaken. She was the one people gravitated to, the one who remembered the names of everyone on set, including the interns. He could never be bothered.

"We're having the best time." Marion nudged Ann. "Aren't we?"

"Yes, we are," their daughter answered. "So much fun."

Gerald said, "Sorry for the mix-up. I honestly thought you were someone else."

Lewis nodded. "No harm done. You folks have a lovely afternoon."

"We will," Marion said, her voice cheery. "Give our regards to Loretta!"

After Lewis walked off, Ann said, "Mother and I are going on the Ferris wheel. What do you think, Father? Are you up to taking in the view?"

"I don't think so," he said. "Why don't you two go on ahead? I think I need to just sit in the shade for a while." In his mind's eye, he saw himself at the beer tent, clutching a mug filled with amber-colored liquid topped with foam. The beer called to him. He could imagine the feeling of it sliding down his throat and warming his blood, taking the sharp edges off the last few days.

"If you're sure?" Marion tilted her head, a concerned look on her face. "We could sit with you."

"No, you two have fun. I just need to rest these old bones for a bit. I'll catch up with you later." He watched from behind as they walked off, arms linked. Even from this angle, he could tell they were chatting and laughing like girlfriends. Were they like this before? He didn't think so, but it had been a long time ago.

Heading to the beer tent, he wondered if he would really do it. On an intellectual level, he knew that breaking his sobriety was a death sentence, but part of him didn't care. He had no money, no significant other, no children, and no job prospects. He wasn't suicidal and he didn't have a death wish, but life and all its trappings didn't seem like such a great deal either.

In the beer tent he found that the drinks were sold in cans and bottles, rather than the mug he'd envisioned. So he wouldn't be getting a head of foam, but the end result was the same. He paid for a can of Schlitz and watched as the bartender opened the flat top with a church key, punching an opening through both sides for even flow. Holding the can steady, he left the tent and went to find a place to sit down. His heart thumped with every step, the can in his hands feeling both precious and as lethal as a time bomb.

He found a good spot in the shade, took a seat, and was about to lift the can to his lips when Ruby Sapp appeared, a bottle of ginger ale in hand. "Hello, Mr. Barlow! Mind if I join you?" Without waiting for a response, she sat next to him, and in one swift move, she reached over and took the beer out of his hand, replacing it with her bottle of soda.

"You think you want this, but trust me, you really don't," she said, holding up the beer. "The soda will be so much better for you today."

He looked at her in stunned disbelief and gestured to the beer. "I really did want that."

She stood up and gave him a thin-lipped smile. "I know. Just try to get through the day. Besides, the ginger ale is good. I think you'll like it."

When Ruby was gone from view, he ran a finger over the condensation covering the sides of the bottle. He looked back at the tent, his brow furrowed, and considered buying another beer, but the decision felt like it had already been made, so instead he stayed put and took a long sip of soda. It wasn't what he'd been craving, but it wasn't the worst thing he'd ever had either.

Chapter Thirty-Five

Tom decided that an afternoon with Elizabeth Ness was his reward for everything he'd endured for the last several years of having to deal with Jaime. As Elizabeth, she was charming and sweet, laughing at his jokes and hanging on his every word. He knew it was all playacting, but he didn't really care.

They walked the grounds until they got hungry, then took a break for lunch. He bought two plates of fried chicken and two bottles of root beer, and they sat under a tree in the shade. When he presented her with the plate and soda, she said, "Such a gentleman. Thank you, Tom."

"My pleasure." He settled down next to her, his back against the tree, legs extended.

"I haven't had a picnic in ages," she said, nibbling at a drumstick. "And it's such a gorgeous day."

"Perfect weather," he agreed.

She talked about her job working as a secretary in a law firm in Haven. "They specialize in real estate transactions and wills and trusts. It's been busy lately, and I can barely keep up with the workload," she said. "When I get home from work, my fingers are sore from so much typing."

She held out her hand to show him; he took hold of her fingers and pulled them to his lips. "Poor thing."

Elizabeth laughed. "You don't have to feel sorry for me. I'm living the life! I'm out with a handsome fellow, eating delicious food on a beautiful summer day."

He grinned. "I feel like I'm the lucky one."

She tilted her head to one side, giving it a thought. "Maybe so."

When they were finished, he insisted on taking care of the cleanup. When dropping off their garbage and utensils back near the food stand, he spotted Gerald off in the distance, sitting on the ground in the shade near the beer tent. He had a beverage in one hand and was taking small sips. He looked alone, very alone, as if he didn't have a friend in the world. Tom wondered where Marion and the girls had gone to, but it was just a fleeting thought. He wasn't really all that interested.

That morning's directive had been clear that today was all about him as an individual. He had no obligation to interact with any of the rest of them and would be staying until he received the official word that it was time to go, whatever that meant. Until that point, he was going to have as much fun as possible.

He returned to find Elizabeth looking at her reflection in a small silver compact and dabbing her nose with a powder puff. "Oh, there you are," she said, snapping it shut. "I was just thinking it might be fun to cut a rug. I hear that this afternoon's band is pretty good."

Tom shook his head and hedged. "I'm not much of a dancer."

"Oh, come on!" She pulled on his arm. "Just give it a go. It might be that you're more of a hoofer than you think."

"I highly doubt that," he said, but she was already guiding him in that direction, grinning as they went, so it didn't appear he had much say in the matter.

The band was only halfway decent, but the Frank Sinatra wannabe at the microphone had a smooth, pleasant voice. Elizabeth led him to the dance floor where half a dozen couples swayed to the music.

"I'm not so sure about this." He stood in place, letting her guide his hand to her waist. He'd learned over the years that despite his love of music, he personally had no sense of rhythm, so he avoided anything requiring synchronized movement. Even at his own weddings, he'd done the obligatory dance with the bride, then begged off soon afterward. He feared stepping on his partner's feet or going in the wrong direction and looking like an idiot. And in this instance, knowing he was being filmed, there was the possibility his shortcomings were being recorded for all time. Most often he'd have begged off, but now her lips were convincingly up against his ear.

She took his hand and whispered, "Just go from side to side. Back and forth. Nothing fancy, just move in time with the music."

That he could do. Tom took a deep breath and shifted from foot to foot, eventually relaxing. "I think I've got it."

"See? I told you so."

With her body against his and the anonymity of being in the center of a cluster of dancers, he felt the tension leave his body. Revisiting Haven had opened his world in a big way. He could do this. Dancing had only been daunting in his own mind. He was never going to be a professional dancer, but maybe at the next wedding he'd break out a few moves.

They were at the end of the next song when he felt a hand roughly grab his shoulder and yank him away from Elizabeth. It happened so fast that his breath couldn't catch up to his lungs. He staggered backward and found himself facing a solid mountain of a man—a head taller than Tom, with a thick neck, wide shoulders, and massive arms. The guy growled, "What are you doing with my girlfriend?" The other dancers and Elizabeth stepped back, widening a circle around them. The music stopped and the singer trailed off, eventually going silent. All eyes were on the two men as they faced each other. The quiet was so all-enveloping, he could hear the blood pumping in his ears.

"Your girlfriend?" Tom said, glancing toward Elizabeth, who just shrugged.

"Damn right she's my girlfriend." The big man gave him a shove, nearly knocking him off his feet.

Reeling from the force of the blow, Tom stumbled, then regained his balance and held his hands up in surrender. "I didn't know she was anyone's girlfriend. I swear." He shot a look toward Elizabeth, hoping she'd come to his defense, but she was no longer there. Vanished.

The man leaned over and clamped his massive hand on Tom's shoulder, fingers pressing all the way to the bone. He leaned so close that Tom could see the blood vessels in the whites of his eyes. "You leave her alone, you hear? If I see you anywhere near Elizabeth, I will *kill you.*"

Tom reminded himself that this was acting, but the man's viselike grip was causing very real pain. That damn Jaime. She was the one who'd insisted on dancing, so she had to have known about this. She'd set him up. "I'll leave her alone. I promise." He hated the way his voice sounded, shrill and desperate.

Now the giant had his hands on both of Tom's shoulders, clamped so tightly Tom could have lifted his legs and been suspended in the air. The man roared, "I have half a mind to beat you senseless."

"You don't need to do that." Tom found himself begging, and he wasn't acting. "It was an honest mistake. I swear I won't have anything to do with Elizabeth from now on. I wish the two of you the best."

The man held his gaze for way too long, then shook Tom back and forth with such force his teeth chattered. "Don't forget. I'll be watching you." His voice was still menacing.

"I know. I won't forget."

The big man threw Tom down with one swift move, like a kid tossing a dodgeball. Tom felt his back bump against a bystander before he fell backward onto the ground. From his place on the ground, he watched Elizabeth's boyfriend storm off. An older gentleman stepped forward and offered Tom his hand, but embarrassed, he waved it off and rose to his feet. "I'm all right," he said, even though he wasn't all right at all. His face was flushed red with humiliation and his tailbone hurt like a mother.

The singer said, "Let's all give Tom Barlow a big round of applause. Sorry it didn't work out with the girl, Tom."

Sheepishly, he acknowledged the crowd's clapping with a wave, but inwardly he wanted to melt into the ground. What the hell kind of storyline was this? Tom was supposed to be the hero. Not saying he had to win the fight, but he could have at least talked some sense into the guy and come out looking like the voice of reason here. The way it had played out, he just looked like a pansy-ass. There was no way this footage would ever see the light of day. Not if he had anything to say about it.

What a load of crap.

He staggered off the dance floor and walked away.

Chapter Thirty-Six

When Dorothy reached the entrance to the park, Dr. Nathan Reed was there waiting for her, leaning against the front gate. "Am I late?" she asked him.

"No, I was early. Eager to get here, I guess." He flashed her a wide smile. "It's been quite a morning. I left the office as soon as the last patient was seen." He gestured for her to walk with him.

"Did you have more patients than usual?" She walked alongside him, close enough to touch, but still leaving the smallest bit of space for propriety's sake.

He nodded. "Dr. Tarter and I had our hands full. Most of our patients had fair-related ailments. I saw a number of sick tummies from overeating. One older gentleman had muscle cramps in his legs from walking more than usual. Oh, and one young lady had a bad case of vertigo. Turned out she was just dizzy from being dehydrated, so we prescribed drinking water." He chuckled.

They went past two teenage girls, one of whom said, "Hi, Dorothy! Having fun?"

"Yes, thanks." She raised a hand in acknowledgment, even though she'd never seen that girl before in her life.

The girl shouted after her, "I'll call you next week so we can go over the new sewing patterns!"

Dorothy said, "Sounds lovely. We'll talk then."

Farther down, she spotted George Bonner standing with two other men. One by one, all three guys called out to her.

"Hey, Dorothy!"

"Lookin' good, Dorothy!"

"Dorothy Barlow!"

She nodded and kept walking.

"Seems like you have many admirers," Nathan said.

"Not really. I just know a lot of people here."

"Of course. You grew up in Haven." They were getting closer to the heart of the fair now, the stands, booths, and rides. The calliope provided the background music to their conversation. He cleared his throat and said, "I'm surprised you agreed to meet me. In fact, while I was waiting at the entrance, I kept thinking you might stand me up."

She stopped and turned to him, a quizzical look on her face. "Why in the world would you think that?"

"I thought your parents might not approve of us spending time together."

Dorothy put a hand on her hip. "I'm over eighteen. Old enough to make my own decisions. Besides," she said, reaching for his hand, "I can't imagine anyone not approving of you." Her eyes darted around, looking to see if the cameras had caught this bold move on her part. Look at how her character had evolved! High school girl Dorothy was now a grown woman and not a demure little miss anymore.

Her assertiveness struck the right chord with him. Clasping her hand, he said, "I'm glad to hear it, because I've been looking forward to getting to know you."

As they were walking together, she spotted a tent with a sign in front: *Madam Serena Tells Your Fortune, 50¢*. "I know it's silly," she said with a sheepish smile, "but I've always wanted to have my fortune told."

Nathan said, "Then that's what we'll do."

He led her to the tent entrance. Looking inside, they saw a woman wearing a crown of flowers and flowing robes, sitting cross legged on the ground in front of a low table that held a crystal ball. "Madam Serena?" Dorothy asked.

"Why yes, my child. Come in, come in." The woman beckoned for them to join her. "I've been waiting for you."

It was cooler inside the tent, and darker too, but Dorothy's eyes quickly adjusted. She and Nathan took a seat on some cushions opposite the fortune-teller. Close up she saw that the woman was older than she appeared at first glance. Her light-colored hair was actually white, and her face showed the lines of a woman who was at least sixty. A stack of silver bracelets adorned each wrist. Judging by the fragrance, the flowers in the wreath around her head were real. She lifted her arms as if to give glory and said, "First, you pay. Am I telling both your fortunes or just one?"

"One fortune, please," Nathan said. "For the lady." He fished the right change, two quarters, out of his pocket, then set them down. In a flash, Madam Serena slid the quarters across the table and dropped them into a metal box on the ground next to her. They landed with a clank.

She turned back to them and said, "Now we begin." Closing her eyes, she placed her hands over the crystal ball.

Dorothy had been expecting something more mystical. Incense or crystals or dozens of lit candles, maybe. A puff of smoke for ambiance would have been a nice touch. Instead, the psychic was just a lady caressing what looked like a clear glass ball sitting on a wooden pedestal.

Finally, Madam Serena opened her eyes and spoke. "I see you are in good health, and I'm happy to report that you will retain that health for the foreseeable future."

"That's good," Dorothy said, nodding in response. Clearly, this woman was starting with the obvious. Dorothy looked fit and had walked in on two legs, so good health was a reasonable assumption.

"So you don't need to worry about becoming ill."

"I understand."

"I see something different in your aura. It's like there are two sides to you. The side you present to the world and the one that you keep private, hidden. Do you understand this?"

"Yes."

The fortune-teller gazed into the crystal ball. "I see that you live life with gusto. You were born to be loved and adored. I see a throng of admirers hanging on your every word. People want to take pictures of you. They want to be with you. Everyone knows your name."

"I was just commenting on that very thing," Nathan said, giving her a nudge.

Dorothy leaned over the table. "What about money? Will I ever be rich?"

"I see that in the years ahead, you will want for nothing."

"That's good." She sat back, satisfied.

Madam Serena's brow furrowed. "Now I see something most unusual. It has to do with Haven. As much as you'd like to leave this town, I see that it's pulling you back. Haven will be very important in your future. It's no longer just your childhood home. As of late, it has gained a greater importance." She stared straight at Dorothy. "Do you understand the meaning of that?"

"I think so." A greater importance? Two million dollars greater. Dorothy shifted on her cushion. "What about my love life? Do you see any romance in my future?" She shot a glance at Nathan, who grinned and covered her hand with his own.

Madam Serena gazed into the ball and frowned. Shaking her head, she said, "You will have no shortage of male attention, but nothing lasting, I'm sorry to say." She met Dorothy's gaze. "But not to worry. The crystal ball tells of things to come as seen at the moment, but you have choices and you have free will. Everything you say and do has the potential to change the future. Nothing is set in stone."

So it might happen, or it might not. A convenient philosophy for predicting the future. "I see."

"It's up to you to decide. A dalliance or a casual date could turn into the love story of a lifetime. It's all up to you."

Nathan chimed in. "What about the near future? What do you see happening today?" He gave her fingers a gentle squeeze. "I've got a pretty good idea, but I'd love to know for sure."

She returned her gaze to the ball, fingertips lightly tapping the glass. "Today, today . . ." The fortune-teller sighed. "I see you will be making a visit to the hospital later today. A loved one is not well."

"Is it my father?" Dorothy asked. It was clear he'd gained a chunk of weight in the last twenty-five years. That combined with his history of drinking put him at risk for all kinds of things. Or maybe it was Grandma Barlow. In either case, a medical emergency would be a dramatic plot twist.

Madam Serena shook her head. "I can't see clearly, so I don't know for sure." She stared straight into Dorothy's eyes. "All I can tell you is that it will be a shock. I'm so sorry to be giving you this bad news." A strong breeze caused the open tent flap to billow. As if this was a cue to wrap things up, she said, "Is there anything else you wish to know?"

"Could it be that I'm the one who's going to be at the hospital?" Nathan asked. "I'm a doctor, you see. I'm there all the time."

"No, it's definitely Miss Barlow," the fortune-teller said, giving a quick finger point for emphasis. "Any other questions?"

"No," Dorothy said, disappointed. "I think that covers it."

Chapter Thirty-Seven

When Milo had described the control room monitoring Haven to his mother, he'd said, "You know how they depict NASA's Mission Control Center in movies? That's exactly what it looks like." Technically, Haven was a top-secret project, but keeping quiet about it had nearly killed him. He had to tell *someone.* None of his friends could be trusted, but he knew his mother wouldn't breathe a word.

He'd gone on to relate how there were two rows of staff manning twenty computer monitors, with a large screen in the front of the room for those times when Felix wanted to watch what he called "the primary scene" in detail. At night, they had fewer people stationed at the monitors, each of them focused on their assigned Barlow family member, just in case something relevant happened during that time. So far there hadn't been any sleepwalking or attempts to do anything else besides sleep or go to the bathroom, but you never knew.

"I wish I could see it," his mother had said wistfully.

"When it's all over, I'll ask Felix if you can come out," he'd promised. His mother and Felix Worthington had met several times. The three of them even had dinner together on occasion. They seemed fond of each other. He had a feeling his boss would allow her to visit.

The second day of the fair, Felix had arrived at the control room first thing in the morning and hadn't left his spot except for a quick trip to the restroom. When Nathan and Dorothy entered the fortune-teller's tent, he excitedly said, "Get this up on the big screen!"

They all watched as Madam Serena spoke to Dorothy and Nathan. When the couple left the tent, Milo asked his boss, "Did you know Dorothy would want to get her fortune told?"

"I was certain of it." Felix's eyes were still on the screen, watching the pair as they walked up to one of the food stands.

"How did you know?" Milo had worked for Felix for eight years and never stopped marveling over his intellect. His early investments in bitcoin had been the jumping-off point for his wealth. He'd parlayed that into an investment in real estate, amassing an even greater fortune. From there he'd dabbled in stocks and private deals backing tech developers. Somehow, he always managed to get in early, and he always seemed to sell at the most opportune time. His instincts were uncanny in their precision.

Felix glanced up at Milo. "I've been watching her. In her job at the news station, she did a week-long series on the paranormal—interviewing ghost hunters, mediums, faith healers, psychics, that kind of thing. She seemed fairly enamored of the topic. Even knowing that the fortune-teller is just an actor at work, I knew she wouldn't be able to resist."

Milo took a moment to consider this, then said, "I know what's going to happen next in the storyline. I just don't understand why." Felix had a knack for compartmentalizing, so Milo was always kept somewhat in the dark. All of the Worthington employees knew something, but no one knew everything, and that's the way Felix liked it.

"Hmm." His gaze was back on the screen.

"All of it, building the town, bringing the cast here—all of it was all designed to lead up to the hospital scene, wasn't it? I can see that clearly. I just don't understand the point."

Felix leaned back and reached out his arms in a stretch. "I guess you'll just have to wait and see."

Chapter
Thirty-Eight

Nathan, a true gentleman, paid for everything. After buying Dorothy lunch, he took a turn at the darts booth, winning a pearl necklace, which he gallantly looped over her head. "For you, dear Miss Barlow," he said.

The necklace was a cheap imitation, the pearls clearly plastic, but she was still tickled, emotionally buoyed by the pleasure of his company and the energy of the fair. When he suggested going on the Ferris wheel, she set her concerns aside and agreed. "I'd love to see the view from up there."

As they walked, she imagined how the camera would capture the two of them on the ride. It would give him an opportunity to gaze at her in adoration, while she'd be able to rest her head on his shoulder. If she became afraid, he'd comfort her. That would make an awesome scene as well.

They arrived at the Ferris wheel, arm in arm. Dorothy no longer cared who saw her on a date with the doctor, not even her parents. Actually, if she did run into Gerald and Marion, she could make an impassioned plea that would play out well for the viewers. It was her story arc, and she was going to own it. Getting to the front of the line, she asked the skinny teenage boy, "Isn't my brother Tom working here today?"

"Tom?" The kid pushed his brimmed hat up and wiped his forehead. "Nah. He only worked the morning, then he took off. Had a date. Saw him walking around with some blonde cookie. They looked like they were close, if you know what I mean."

Nathan handed over two tickets, and they were directed to the last empty seat. Dorothy took the inside spot, and Nathan settled in right next to her. Thigh to thigh. Shoulder to shoulder. The attendant leaned in to adjust the belt, but Nathan said, "I've got it." He crossed it over their laps, clicking it onto a loop on the armrest next to him. The attendant swung the bar and secured it into place.

Dorothy and Nathan exchanged smiles. She had a feeling this would play out well on film, so she leaned in, coming so close their faces nearly met, and said, "Pretty soon the two of us will be on top of the world."

The teenage attendant, the one who'd said Tom had left earlier, pulled on a lever and called out, "Enjoy the view!" The motor whirred, and they began to slowly move backward. In the distance, Dorothy heard a commotion—a woman in the crowd shrieking, "Get out of my way. There's an emergency!" Just as their seat began to rise, the woman, dressed in white, with a nurse's cap pinned to her head, pushed through to the front of the line and shouted, "Dr. Reed, you're needed at the hospital right away! There's been an accident. No time to waste."

Nathan detached the seat belt and pulled the security bar up, then hopped down, saying, "Sorry, Dorothy. Duty calls." He took off running.

"Wait! Don't go. Don't leave me." She stretched out an arm, but he was out of reach, and now she was too high up to jump down herself. She watched as he wove his way through the crowd. As the ride rose higher, she became aware of the bar bouncing loose and the strap dangling down past her feet. Petrified, she was able to click the bar into place, and with trembling hands she drew the lap belt hand over hand until finally she was able to grab the metal clip and reconnect it. But no matter how hard she tried, she couldn't tighten it. The lap belt was just as loose as if it were around two people.

The ride carried her higher, and suddenly her fear of heights kicked in. She gripped the rail, even as her heart pounded in her chest. Tears welled up in her eyes. With Nathan at her side, she could have held his hand and rested her head on his shoulder. It still might have been scary, but it would have been the right kind of scary. Now she was alone and loose on a seat that suddenly seemed to be rocking back and forth on its own. Glancing down, she held tight, sensing that she could drop quite easily.

Her sense of panic intensified, consuming her.

"I need to get off the ride," she screamed. "Get me off!" She couldn't control her breathing anymore, gulping mouthfuls of air as she sobbed. Her palms were slick with sweat, and she felt a surge of nausea.

When the ride had gone all the way around and reached the bottom, she thought about jumping off, but the wheel spun too quickly. If she'd gotten off her seat at that point, she'd have been hit by the next set of passengers. Still, she took the opportunity to address the two kids operating the ride as she went past. She yelled, "Stop the ride! Let me off." She couldn't see them very well through her tears, but the ride did slow as she went back around, coming to a halt when she was at the very top.

The ride had stopped.

"Hey!" shouted one of the riders.

"What's the big idea?" This came from someone at the bottom.

"Come on! Start it up again."

The whole ride shuddered, making her seat swing back and forth. Dorothy's stomach churned, and she felt like vomiting. She looked skyward and said, "Please get me down, please get me down, please get me down." Her pleas were punctuated by jagged, shallow breaths. She didn't have the energy to shout anymore, but she only had to be loud enough to reach the microphones and cameras she knew were overhead, hopefully zooming in on her right at that moment. Someone had to be noticing her distress. This couldn't be part of the show.

Below her, the other riders were getting restless.

"What's the problem?"

"Turn on the ride!"

"What happened? Why won't it go?"

One of the ride attendants shouted, "Sorry, folks. Seems that the ride is broken. We're working on getting it going as soon as possible!"

A little boy shouted, "Hurry up. I got to go to the bathroom." His statement elicited laughter from some of the fairgoers on the ground.

This was like a cruel joke. How could the Ferris wheel be broken, endangering the riders? It had been running all day.

She wiped her eyes with the back of her hand, and taking a deep breath, she cautiously leaned over and looked down. The drop was greater than she'd anticipated. Could anyone survive a fall like that? A renewed surge of fear jerked her upright. She was barely aware when she started screaming again. "Someone help me. Please. I need to get down from here!" She was hysterical, chest heaving with her sobs. But she had no control and no longer cared how she looked to the cameras.

She had to get down. Now. Because as scared as she was of falling, she also felt an irrational impulse to hurl herself over the side. She could picture herself falling to her death, her ruined body sprawled bloody on the ground. The idea of it made her woozy. An image of what would happen if she fainted rose from the floor of her brain. Her shriek was involuntary, the words shot like gunfire from her mouth. "Help me, dammit! Someone help me! Get me off this thing!"

From the ground she heard someone call up, "Amanda, hang on. I'm coming up. Give me a few minutes." She couldn't look over the edge again, it was just too much, but she knew the voice. It was Marion—or rather, Meri—and suddenly she knew everything would turn out fine. Meri had that effect on people. She was a comforting presence, invariably knowing the right thing to do in any situation.

"Okay," Dorothy called out, her voice hoarse from shouting. "Hurry!" She closed her eyes and waited for Meri to make everything okay.

Chapter Thirty-Nine

They'd heard the commotion before they got there. Marion and Ann had been heading toward the Ferris wheel, planning on going on the ride themselves, when they heard what sounded like a woman crying out for help. Getting closer, Marion saw Dorothy at the top of the ride, the wheel stuck in place, her seat swinging slightly. "Oh my word," Marion said, shielding her eyes with the flat of her hand.

Next to her, Ann said, "What's happening?"

"I don't know."

They pushed their way through the crowd to the front, where they found two employees, both looking no older than high school students, examining a metal control box. Marion said, "That's my daughter up there. What happened?"

The boy crouched next to the box looked up and said, "The lever just broke off. We're trying to fix it."

The other one, a stocky kid, held the lever and said, "We're trying to see if we can push it back in place."

In a second, Marion summed up the situation—these two were such babies, children trying to figure out the mechanicals of a machine they didn't understand. Clearly in over their heads. She took over. "So there are two levers. What do they do?"

"This one"—he held up the one in his hand—"is for the drive belt."

"It makes it stop and go?"

"Yep," the kid said. "The other one"—he pointed to the one still attached—"is called the lock wheel. It keeps each car in place when we load and unload."

"Is it locked now?"

He nodded. "The people on the bottom got tired of waiting and wanted to get off, so we locked it in place."

Over the sound of the nearby calliope music, Dorothy screamed for help in a way that tore at Marion's maternal heart. Meanwhile, the crowd shouted out suggestions and questions.

"Get a mechanic!"

"Can you get a big ladder?"

"Someone help that poor woman!"

"What's happening?"

Marion took a step back and aimed her gaze skyward, sizing up the way the ride had been constructed to see if it could be climbed. Mentally, she mapped out each hand- and foothold, and the distance between each one. Scaling it would be fairly easy. The support beam that ran from the ground to the middle was already structured like a ladder. Getting from there to the top would be a little trickier, but there were enough structural struts placed close together that it was doable. She'd definitely done more difficult climbs. Usually with the right shoes and equipment, though, and never in a dress.

From above, Amanda screamed, "Help me. Someone help me!" The tremor in her voice made Marion's heart ache for her. And in that second, she was no longer Amanda, the actor, or Dorothy, the character, but someone's child, the stand-in for Meri's own daughter, Hailey. She'd known Amanda as a teenager during her boy-crazy stage, and sometimes, even though they were now both adults, their positions as peers fell away and she felt a surge of motherly love for her. For all of the Barlow kids, really. She hadn't thought those two years on the show had counted for much, but time hadn't erased the bond they'd created just by showing up, day after day, supporting each other and seeing each other at their worst, and their best. Forced together, they'd merged fiction and real life, coming out less than family but more than coworkers.

To the kids trying to reattach the lever, she said, "Keep the ride locked, because I'm going up. While I do that, one of you needs to go get your boss and let him know the ride is broken." With her head tipped back, she called out, "Amanda, hang on. I'm coming up. Give me a few minutes."

As she began her climb, she heard Amanda call back to hurry, but Meri knew hurrying was the last thing she wanted to do when taking this kind of risk. Going higher, she acknowledged the fear that surged through her body, and knew it was good. Her mentor and instructor had told her that those with no fear were the ones who got injured. Fear kept you alert and alive.

Below, the crowd was abuzz, watching the crazy lady climb the Ferris wheel. She heard Ann shout out, "Be careful, Mom."

Bless her heart for staying in character. Meri knew she herself had probably blown her chances of getting the $2 million. Someone knew of the hidden cell phone, which was the first count against her. Add that to the fact that Marion didn't have the skills to climb an amusement park ride, and she'd clearly broken character.

When she reached the halfway point, the crowd on the ground clapped and began to shout encouragement.

"Keep going, lady!"

"Well done, Mrs. Barlow!"

"Woo-hoo! Look at her go!"

This was accompanied by some commenting that she was crazy and about to fall to her death. Why did people have to be so negative? She put the naysaying out of her mind, and at each moment she focused on her next move. She waited a moment between each one, assessing and resting, then reaching out for her next point of contact. This was not her preferred type of climb, but it did feel good when her foot found a solid place to land. Her muscle memory for climbing was still intact, and she felt strong and capable.

When she reached the top, she didn't lose her focus. Too many climbers became overly confident when close to their goals. Often, that didn't end well. She caught sight of Amanda. While she'd stopped shrieking, her face was pale, and her body trembled. This was not acting, but real fear.

"Move the bar," Meri called out when she was closer. She stood on one of the struts, her head level with Amanda's shoulders. "I want to climb up onto the seat next to you." For a second she thought Amanda might refuse, but then she nodded and lifted the bar, which allowed Meri to grab hold of the seat and hoist herself up and into a kneeling position, facing toward the back of the seat. Slowly, she turned her body around inch by inch until she was sitting. Once she was in place, Amanda lowered the bar and locked it in.

The people below erupted into applause and cheers. Lauren's voice rose above the din. "Well done, Mom!"

Yes, Lauren was definitely getting the $2 million.

Amanda glanced over, eyes filled with tears. "I can't believe you came for me."

"Oh, honey, of course I did." Meri put her arm around Amanda's shoulder, steadying her. "I wouldn't leave you up here all alone."

Amanda gulped and whispered, "I think I'm having a heart attack."

"More likely you're having a panic attack. It feels like that sometimes. Close your eyes and rest your head on my shoulder." Meri stroked her hair. "Just breathe, slow and steady. I'm here now, and I'm not going to let anything bad happen to you."

"How are we going to get down?" Amanda's voice had gentled, the fear subsiding.

"They're working on that now. It won't be long." Meri made the shushing noise that had always comforted Hailey as a little girl. "It's okay to relax. You're safe. Everything's going to be fine."

Chapter Forty

Ann had watched her mother climb the ride with bated breath, then exhaled in relief when she finally saw her seated next to Dorothy, the security bar clicked into place. She felt a surge of admiration for Meri.

Marion Barlow might have been the winner when it came to being domestic and sweet, but Meri Wetzel was a total badass.

Her take-charge action was inspiring.

One of the teenage boys who worked the ride had run off to find their boss, and the one remaining seemed at a loss. Ann decided he needed some direction, so she started things out with an introduction. "I don't think we've met. My name is Ann. What's your name?"

The question appeared to take him by surprise. "It's Otis, ma'am." He nervously bounced on his heels. "Otis Greene."

"You worked with my brother, Tom Barlow, right?"

"Yeah." He nodded. "Tom's a good fellow."

She pointed to the one functioning lever still attached to the metal box. "Did you say that this one is called the lock wheel?"

In answer, his head bobbed up and down. "Yes, ma'am."

"And right now it's in the locked position?"

"Yep."

She put her fist to her mouth, thinking. "So if we unlocked it, we could turn the wheel, right?"

"Usually that's how it works, but right now the lever that works the motor isn't on."

"But we could move it manually."

He scratched his nose. "I don't get your meaning."

"Grab hold of it and turn it by pulling."

"Won't work." He shook his head. "It's too heavy."

She reached over and moved the lever to disengage the lock, then turned to the crowd. "Can I get some help here? Someone strong?"

"I don't think you should be doing that." Despite his words, Otis didn't try to stop her, just clasped his hands and looked nervously off in the distance, a frown creasing his forehead. "The boss should be here anytime now."

Several men stepped forward, two guys about her age and three teenagers. "What do you need?" one of the older men asked, adjusting the brim of his hat.

"The ride is unlocked now, so in theory we can rotate it if we have enough muscle power." She turned back to Otis. "It goes clockwise?"

"Yes." He stepped back and folded his arms to watch. It was her show now.

Stepping forward, one of the men said, "Let's give it a try."

Working together, they pulled the seat above them until it reached ground level. When the two girls in the seat released their lap belts, Ann cautioned them to wait. "I have to lock it first."

"I'll do it," Otis said, sounding almost begrudging.

She helped the two girls off, and the crowd roared in approval and clapped. Ann wouldn't have thought this would be such a big deal, but apparently in Haven world, a stuck ride was an exciting event, especially when the Barlows were involved. Once the two passengers were a safe distance away, the group of helpers repeated their efforts to turn the wheel.

They cranked on the ride, pulling down the riders one by one, with Ann yelling out orders. "Keep going," and "That's enough," and "Stop!" They continued until Dorothy and Marion were at the bottom, finally able to disembark.

"Thank you," Dorothy said. "Thank you so much. I thought I'd be stuck up there forever."

Ann had never seen her so visibly shaken. "You're welcome," she said, then turned back to get the rest of the passengers down.

Marion led Dorothy away from the platform, and they waited off to the side. Ann and her team of men kept going, releasing the next set of riders, a woman and her young son, a boy of six or so. "I have to pee so bad," he said as he hopped off, and his mother answered, "Can you hold it until we get to the restrooms?"

Once the last set of passengers had disembarked, the ride was officially emptied and Ann's job was done. She turned to see Gerald and Tom standing next to Marion and Dorothy, all of them regarding her with wide-eyed approval. "Well done, sis," Tom said. It was the nicest thing he'd ever said to her that wasn't in a script.

She gave his arm a light punch. "You could have helped."

"I thought of it, but you seemed to have it in hand. I didn't want to gum up the works."

A man's voice in the crowd yelled, "Let's hear it for Ann and Marion Barlow! The heroes of the day!"

Spontaneously, what sounded like every person at the fair joined in. "Hip, hip, hooray! Hip, hip, hooray! Hip, hip, hooray!" The sound came from all around, swelling and then reverberating.

Ann sheepishly waved, then leaned over and spoke to Marion. "You inspired me to take charge."

As the family stood together in a cluster, Ruby Sapp made her way through the crowd to face them, out of breath and red-faced. "Thank God I found you." She took hold of Gerald's arm and said, "I have a message for the whole family. You need to go to the hospital right this minute. There's been a terrible accident."

Chapter Forty-One

At the hospital entrance, they were met by a grim-faced nurse holding a clipboard. "You're the Barlows?" she asked. Her uniform was an impeccable white, as was her winged nurse's cap, pinned in place on either side of her glossy red hair. Her name tag identified her as Nurse Carol.

Gerald answered for all of them. "I'm Gerald Barlow, and this is my family. Can you tell us what this is all about?" They'd all speculated on the ride over. Was it Grandma or one of the neighbors? Tom tried to recall what he knew of the Barlow relatives. On the show there'd been an episode involving Marion's brother, John, his wife, Missy Ann, and their two kids. The Shephard family. The story was that they were visiting from out of state. The two cousins were spoiled and rude, but after a week with their Barlow cousins, they'd come to appreciate small-town life and had learned some manners as well. That family had only appeared on one episode, and he hadn't seen any of them since. It was unlikely to be the Shephards, but who knew what was in store for them today? After being betrayed by his love interest and threatened with bodily harm, Tom had given up trying to guess what was coming next.

Ruby Sapp, the only one who seemed to know anything, wouldn't or couldn't answer any questions about the identity of the patient, just hurriedly walked them straight to their car, all the while urging them to hurry. Funny that she knew exactly where their vehicle was parked but hadn't a clue as to who was in the hospital.

The nurse, instead of answering Gerald's question, just said, "Come with me." She turned and walked down a long hall, her white rubber-soled shoes squeaking as she moved. The smell of disinfectant filled the air, so strong it made Tom wrinkle his nose. When they reached the end of the hallway, she turned a corner. They followed like obedient ducklings, ending up at an open doorway. "If you'll wait here," she said, ushering them inside. "The doctor will be with you soon."

She went down the hall, leaving them in a waiting room. Two freestanding ashtrays stood on either side of a couch, and matching chairs were arranged along the other walls. Tom took a seat, noticing that the ashtrays were filled with snubbed-out cigarettes, some of them lined with lipstick. Hopefully, they wouldn't be waiting in this room for long.

Everyone but Marion took a seat. She paced around the room, as if not able to decide where to sit. Gerald reached out as she walked past. "Sit here, honey," he said, motioning to the spot next to him on the couch.

She shook her head and crossed her arms. "I don't like this." Her forehead furrowed. "I'm worried something is terribly wrong."

Gerald got up from his spot to reassure her. "The nurse said the doctor will be with us soon. Let's just wait and see what he has to say before we start worrying." He embraced her in a hug.

When the doctor arrived, she pushed him away. "Doc Tarter? They told us there was some kind of accident?"

"Have a seat, Marion," he said gruffly.

Reluctantly, she sat next to Gerald, who put his arm around her shoulders.

Tom couldn't believe how they were prolonging the drama, but he supposed if it was too torturous to watch they'd shorten it during editing.

"I have very bad news," he said, making eye contact with each one of them. The doctor had been known as Gerald's good friend from school, as well as the family doctor and a fellow churchgoer. They'd managed to cast the same actor from the show, and surprisingly, he didn't look too different, even after all these years. Whoever did the work on his face had done an outstanding job. Tom had seen the guy in guest roles on various TV shows over the years and knew he'd also done voice work for video games and cartoons. Today he was once again old Doc Tarter, the same guy who'd delivered all three of them as babies, extracted a fishhook from the back of Bud's hand, and treated Tom's poison ivy rash. Obstetrician, internist, and dermatologist all rolled up into one. Sort of an all-purpose physician.

Marion said, "What's going on, Doctor?"

He sighed, tenting his fingers together. "I'm sorry to be the one to tell you this, Marion and Gerald, but your son, Bud, has been in a terrible accident. He fell out of a tree at your home two hours ago, hitting the ground hard. He was seriously injured. Multiple broken bones and a severe blow to the head. We've given him something so he's not in pain, but I'm afraid there's not much else we can do for him."

The entire family sat in stunned silence. Tom couldn't believe they were rehashing this incident. He'd put it behind him a long time ago. A kid fell out of a tree. So what? This kind of thing happened all the time. He himself had an old scar on his leg from a skateboarding incident. Things happened.

Ann spoke up in a quiet voice. "But he's going to be fine, right?"

Tears came to the old doctor's eyes. "I'm afraid not, Ann. He has internal injuries that we can't fix."

Ann stood up. "But you have to fix him! Can't you do surgery?" She wiped her eyes with the back of her hand. "He's my little brother. You have to help him!"

The doctor rested a hand on her elbow and leaned in to whisper, "I'm so, so sorry, Ann. Believe me, we've done everything we can."

"Maybe we could take him to a different hospital?" Dorothy said, clearly not remembering that there was no other hospital. "One in a bigger city that's better equipped?"

"No." He shook his head sadly. "Transporting him would be impossible at this point. It's my professional opinion he wouldn't survive the trip."

Marion's voice broke through. "I want to see him."

"Of course." Doc Tarter nodded. "I wanted to prepare you ahead of time that his injuries are fatal. It will be difficult for you to see him like this, but remember, he's not in any pain."

All of them traipsed down the hall and climbed the stairs to the second floor. This, Tom thought, was where the real work took place. As they went down the corridor, through open doors they saw patients in beds, nurses attending to them. An orderly pushed a cart with trays of domed plates. On the right, they passed a room where a small child cried for their mother. Farther down a woman sobbed, saying, "Help me. I'm in so much pain."

So depressing, and not like the usual fare on *A Little Slice of Haven*. Unless this was a setup in which Bud miraculously got better? That was the only scenario he could imagine working for the Haven fans.

Bud's room was all the way at the end of the hall on the left. Doc Tarter ushered them in, then stepped away. They entered the room to see Dr. Reed leaning over the patient, holding a stethoscope against his chest. The animatronic Grandma Barlow sat in a chair in the corner, her usual expression on her face. Walking in, Tom noticed the bruising on the little boy's cheek and the way his torso rose and fell with shallow breaths. *My God,* thought Tom. They'd done a good job choosing the actor. This kid was a dead ringer for the boy who'd played Bud Barlow.

Once he got past the similarity in appearance, shock set in. Why would they choose to include Bud in this? The kid hadn't even been part of the family for that long, and the fans almost never mentioned him. Bringing up the fall from the tree was a low blow. Were they trying to rattle him? He cleared his throat in order to get Dorothy's attention, but her shocked gaze never wavered from the little boy in the bed.

As they entered, they quietly formed a ring around the patient. Dr. Reed stood up and gave Dorothy a nod. "I'm sorry, Dorothy. I know how much you love your brother." He turned to their parents. "I'm just heartsick for all of you."

"Thank you," Marion murmured.

"How did this happen?" Gerald asked. "Who brought Bud here?"

"I believe your mother heard your son fall and telephoned for help." Dr. Reed looked over at Grandma Barlow, who nodded her head in agreement.

"Is he in pain?" Marion asked, her face showing concern.

"No," the doctor assured her. "He's been heavily medicated. Bud is not in any pain."

Marion nodded. "I'm glad of that."

"I'll let you have some time with your son," he said, easing out of the room. "If you need anything, just press the call button."

"Thank you, Doctor," Ann said.

If Tom wanted to be any part of this, he had to participate. Stepping forward, he rested a hand on Bud's shoulder, then drew back in shock. This was no actor. The body in the bed was an animatronic creation, just like Grandma. If anything, the likeness was even better than they'd done with Grandma. A twin of young Bud, right down to the elfin face. He had long eyelashes for a boy and small ears. His brown hair stuck out in wisps under the head wrapping, some of it plastered to his neck by perspiration. It was uncanny how well they'd modeled the robot after the actual kid.

Tom glanced over at Dorothy, who was visibly affected, her face twisted with emotion. He tried to send her a mental message: *Don't let this mess with your head. It's not real.*

Grandma's voice broke in, startling all of them. "Bud told me he climbed the tree because two big kids dared him to, but then the kids ran off and left him all alone." Her voice had a reedy, raspy sound. "He called for help, but no one heard him. He tried to get someone's attention by throwing his watch at the window, but no one came, and he felt like no one cared. He was so afraid. Trying to climb down, he slipped and fell. Poor little guy was in so much pain. Broke three bones in his legs, you know, two on one side and one of the other. Broke some ribs too. His head was smashed against a rock." Her mouth closed and Tom thought she was done, but then she started up again. "I suppose you think this is funny, Dorothy and Tom."

"I don't think it's funny. I don't think it's funny at all," Dorothy said, her voice strong. "I think it's a damn tragedy." She turned and strode out of the room. They heard her footsteps receding, going faster and faster until it sounded as if she was running.

Chapter Forty-Two

When the doctor had initially hit them with the news of Bud's injuries, all of them took it fairly well, but actually seeing the boy in the bed shook them to the core. Ann's gaze darted around the room, taking in the reactions of the other family members. Despite their acting training, a genuine glimmer of emotion managed to sneak through. Tom's face showed annoyance, Dorothy's expression registered guilt, and Gerald and Marion appeared startled and confused. Grandma's speech then struck a nerve with each of them, amplifying every feeling.

Even Ann, who'd only been a child herself and had done nothing wrong, felt a sense of remorse and guilt at seeing Bud in bed, bandages wrapped around his head. *Poor little guy.* He never really had anyone to look out for him.

The electronic figure was a work of art, so lifelike that Ann could imagine he really was breathing in and out. His eyelids fluttered on occasion, as if he were struggling toward consciousness. Or maybe fighting off pain? Regardless, the effect made her uneasy.

When Dorothy left the room, all of them exchanged a look, not knowing whether to go after her. Finally, Gerald said, "It's a lot to take in. Maybe we should give her some breathing room." Self-consciously he looked up at the ceiling, as if asking God or Felix Worthington or the cameras for answers.

Ann was having none of it. "I'll go check on her," she said, but outside the door the corridor was empty. Walking its length, she turned at the corner and encountered a nurse holding a clipboard. Their eyes locked, and using the clipboard to cover her hand, the nurse pointed to a waiting room across the hall.

Dorothy sat in one of the chairs, her head in her hands, her back rising and falling as she sobbed.

Ann knocked on the doorframe. "May I come in?"

Dorothy glanced up, but only long enough to nod permission. She sniffed, tucking a strand of hair behind her ear with a trembling hand. This was either an Academy Award–winning performance or she was genuinely distressed.

Ann sat next to her. She rested her hands on her knees and just let her presence in the room be enough. It was strange seeing this side of Dorothy. She'd always been the older sister, full of confidence, a smile on her face. She'd had a good life, on both sides, real life and television. Parents who loved her. Boys who adored her. Things came easily, something that didn't surprise her. Personally, she'd always struck Ann as superficial and egocentric, but that was just a perception. It was hard to really know someone even if you cared about them, and Ann hadn't cared about Dorothy. Still, seeing someone in pain activated her mothering instincts. Ann spoke quietly. "Is there something I can do to help?"

"No, but thank you." Dorothy straightened up, and now Ann could see that the front of her dress was rumpled. "I just couldn't stand being in that room and seeing him like that. He looked so little under those sheets, you know?" She wiped her eyes with the back of her hand and gulped in a mouthful of air.

Ann nodded. She knew. Seeing Bud through adult eyes put it all in perspective. He was such a little guy, and so much had been expected of him.

Who expected a seven-year-old to work a job? And not just any job, but the kind of job that put a kid under enormous pressure to perform well, even on the days they were tired or cranky or just didn't feel like it. Adults chose to act in television. Most of them yearned to get in front of a camera, had dreamed of an acting career for years and were fully prepared for it.

Children fell into a different category. Some kids loved it. Others were *told* they loved it.

"I know. It's hard."

"It's harder for me than you," Dorothy said. "I'm the oldest sister. I was supposed to protect him." She sniffed.

"None of us were there."

"I could have been there."

That begged the question, *Why wasn't Bud at the fair?* She knew the answer, of course. The actor hadn't come back, and they hadn't hired someone else to replace him. The animatronic figure was all that was necessary. Bud's value had been in this very scene and how it all played out.

The boxy speaker in the upper corner of the room blared with a woman's voice. "Dr. Reed, you're wanted at the front desk."

"Come on, let's go back to the room," Ann said. "We should be together as a family."

"Grandma blames me." Dorothy spat out the words. "I can tell. I'm not sure I can face her." Her lips set in a grim line.

"No one blames you. You're just being hard on yourself." Ann said the lines for the benefit of the camera. "Come on. We'll go together. I think it's important for us to be there." She stood and gestured to the door.

To her surprise, Dorothy nodded and got to her feet.

Chapter
Forty-Three

Hailey was seated in front of her desktop computer at home on a Zoom call with her boss when her phone pinged, so she ignored the text until the meeting was over.

Once they'd finished the conversation and she turned her attention to her phone screen, a cold chill ran down her back in seeing that the text was from Meri. The ten days weren't over, and her mother had explicitly told her there would be no communication except in the case of an extreme emergency. Something was wrong.

Terribly wrong.

Yet the message was casual. Friendly.

I miss you. Anything new?

The wording was precisely the kind of text she'd get from her mother. It was the timing that was confusing. She picked up the phone and tapped out an answer, saying she hadn't thought she'd hear from her. Asking if there were any problems.

Sorry, I didn't mean to worry you! No problem at all.

They went back and forth, with Meri telling her the time had gone quickly and she thought of her every day. Living in Haven was quite the experience! She'd tell her everything once she was home. In the meantime, she was asking a favor of Hailey, the details of which she spelled out over the course of several texts, complete with emojis. (Meri loved peppering her texts with emojis, although she only had six that she used on a regular basis.)

She ended by asking her daughter: **What do you think? Are you in?**

Hailey held the phone loosely in her hand, a slow grin spreading across her face. Was she in? Hell yeah! With sure fingers she tapped out: **Wouldn't miss it for the world.**

Chapter Forty-Four

Felix had known that the day at the fair would be pivotal, but the results were beyond anything he could have imagined. In anticipation of watching what he'd known would be a critical day, he'd parked himself in front of a monitor and viewed the events as they played out in real time, zooming in when things got interesting. Except for quick bathroom breaks, he never stepped away, not even for meals. Instead, everything he needed was brought to him.

Ever since Milo had compared the room used to monitor Haven to the Mission Control Center at NASA, Felix found it impossible to get that image out of his head. There were similarities in the setup and in the emotional investment as well. Personally, he was as keyed up as if the participants were on a life-threatening mission. No one was going to die, of course. At least, that had never been his intent, but if pressed he would have admitted that this particular day had not gone as expected. His heart hammered in his chest when Marion began to climb the Ferris wheel. So foolish.

She could have fallen to her death. As scary as it was, it was also enormously compelling viewing, so he didn't try to stop her. Once she'd successfully made it, he breathed a sigh of relief, and mentally gave her credit for courage and resourcefulness. Of course, she'd broken character to calm her television daughter, but that was her decision.

Taking a sip of his drink, he popped another pill, the updated version of the stimulant he'd started using as a teenager for his ADD. He'd had so many problems as a child, both behaviorally and with learning, and it all stemmed from the way his brain was wired. His reading problems, his squirminess, the daydreaming that made him look as if he were simpleminded. It wasn't so much that he couldn't focus, it was that he couldn't do so on command.

Oddly enough, he could hyperfocus when the topic was of interest, and when that happened, step aside, because he only knew one speed and that was full throttle. That ability was what had enabled him to turn a million dollars into billions. Without much effort on his part, his brain generated patterns, anticipated trends, and saw with crystal clarity where best his money would grow. He was almost never wrong. Most people assumed his wealth came as a result of his early entry into bitcoin, and yes, that did account for a big chunk, but that was only part of the story. His company also backed inventors who needed money to develop tech projects; once the product went to market, both sides reaped the rewards. The real estate he bought and then sold at a great profit was another source of financial gains.

With success came opportunities and more success. His instincts were sharp, and he meticulously monitored all of his investments. And if he'd learned one thing about negotiating, it was this: the one who was willing to walk away had the upper hand.

And he was always willing to walk away, because there was always more out there, just waiting for him to find it.

Re-creating Haven was a passion project, the sole objective of which was just to exist. Any movie or limited series that came about as a result of these ten days would be a bonus he wasn't counting on. Money was never the goal. He'd made and populated Haven for his own personal curiosity. He'd watched the YouTube videos over and over again, wondering what had happened to all of them, until finally he'd decided to settle the question once and for all.

Now he sat back and watched the hospital room on the big screen, pleased at how it was coming out. Milo had been in charge of the team that had moved Grandma from the front porch to the hospital. They'd positioned her in the front seat of a taxi, then wheeled her into the hospital building in a wheelchair before getting her set up in the corner of Bud's room. "I felt kind of bad leaving Beau behind at the house," Milo had said.

It had taken a second for Felix to remember that Beau was the dog. "But you really couldn't take a dog with you to the hospital," he'd answered. It had been difficult enough moving the Grandma figure and then getting her hooked up again after being relocated. Besides, dogs weren't allowed at the hospital.

"I know that," Milo had responded. "He just looked lonely on the porch by himself. The other guys agreed. As we were backing down the driveway, Beau gave a yelp like he wanted us to come back. It was pitiful."

Hearing this made Felix grin. A lot of time and money had been spent by the robotics team. Knowing that the staff had assigned emotions to the animatronic figures confirmed he'd done it right.

Now he watched as Marion, Gerald, and Tom gathered around Bud's bed. They spoke in hushed voices, then stopped altogether when a male orderly wearing a white shirt and equally white trousers walked in carrying a stack of wooden folding chairs. As he set them up around the bed, Marion said, "Thank you. That's very kind."

"You're welcome, ma'am." He gestured to Bud with a nod of his head. "I'm sorry for your family's troubles. I'll keep all of you in my prayers."

When Dorothy and Ann came back, the others were already seated. Without saying a word, they took the empty seats next to Marion and across from the two guys.

Felix was pleased with the tableau. He'd designed the room himself, taking care with every detail. It was a little larger than most hospital rooms of that era, especially for a single patient. The extra-wide door had been standard even then, but he'd made this one a foot wider. A wall-mounted clock hung above the door. The linoleum squares that made up the floor were a mossy green, as were the curtains, but the rest of the room was blindingly white, including the metal bed rails. Next to the bed was a nightstand with a small lamp, but he'd specified that the overhead lights be on for the whole scene for maximum illumination. Even if they wanted to, the Barlows wouldn't have been able to adjust the lights.

Other details had been added solely for emotional impact. The radiator under the window supported a shelf holding a large vase of cut daisies, the very flowers that Bud had given Marion as a gift on one of the shows. The joke was that he'd picked them from the neighbor's garden. Marion would surely remember the significance. On the wall above the headboard, framed artwork showed children about Bud's age as frolicking angels in heaven. In the context of the situation, the images were heartbreaking.

After Dorothy and Ann returned and all of them had been sitting in awkward silence for five minutes, Felix gave the cue for the next entrance, and within seconds Dr. Reed strode through the door. Nathan Reed, an actual physician who'd worked in community theater all during his high school and undergrad days, had been quite a find. Tall and good-looking, with a voice that could melt butter, he fit the role perfectly. Better yet, he never questioned his part, and played it to perfection.

He strode in and gently said, "I'm sorry to interrupt, but I wanted to check on Bud." Gerald got up and moved his chair aside to allow Dr. Reed to pass. They all watched glumly as he stepped next to the bed, then leaned over to place a stethoscope on the little boy's chest. Felix noted that while Ann and Gerald appeared solemn, both Dorothy and Marion looked to be on the verge of tears. Only Tom's face was impassive.

Dr. Reed straightened up, then addressed the room. "First of all, I want to tell all of you that everyone here at Haven Memorial has your family in our thoughts and prayers. Bud is a special boy, and we can't even imagine how difficult this is for you."

Ann said, "Thank you, Doctor."

He continued. "Your vigil will almost certainly be over by morning, so I'd suggest using the time you have in a meaningful way." He clasped his hands, and his voice got quieter. "Bud has been medicated, so he's not in any pain, but he can hear you. Talk to him. Tell him how you feel. It will bring comfort to him, and to all of you as well."

Tom looked as if he was suppressing a smile. That guy, Felix thought with derision, was born with a smirk on his face. The rest of them were properly mournful. The women in particular looked pretty shaken.

"Do you have any questions?" Dr. Reed asked gently.

Each person shook their head, but from the corner, Grandma spoke up. "How much time do we have with him?"

Dr. Reed held out his hands. "My best guess is no more than a few hours."

"But miracles happen, right?" Ann asked hopefully.

The doctor nodded. "Sometimes they do." He rested his hand on the doorframe. "I'll give your family some privacy. Push the call button if you need anything." And then he was gone.

Ann stood up. "I'll go first." She rested her hand on Bud's shoulder, then leaned over to kiss his cheek. "Bud, you were the best brother anyone could have. I love you more than I can say, and I will never forget you." The boy in the bed gave a small sigh. She stood for a few more minutes, stroking the side of his face with the backs of her curved fingers.

Felix put a hand to his cheek, imagining the feel of the caress.

Milo interrupted the moment. "Are you all right, sir?"

"Just fine."

On the screen, Ann stepped back to take her seat, and Gerald stood, clasping his hands awkwardly in front of him. He cleared his throat and said, "Oh, little Bud. We weren't there for you when we should have been. I love you, son. I'm so sorry." His eyes filled with tears, and he turned away from the camera, shoulders shaking, until finally he was audibly sobbing. Tom handed him a handkerchief, which he put to immediate use.

Felix waited for Marion to comfort Gerald, but instead she got up and sat on the edge of the hospital bed. "Poor sweet baby," she said quietly, then she leaned in to whisper in his ear, speaking so softly that the microphones in the room couldn't pick up the words. Somehow, this made the scene all the more poignant. Marion stayed there for the longest time, almost as if she couldn't bear to be away from him. The room was quiet except for the ticking of the wall clock.

When Marion reluctantly went back to her seat, Tom got up quickly, as if he'd been waiting to take his turn. "Hey, little buddy." He awkwardly patted his brother's shoulder. "I'm sorry for what happened. I hope you're feeling better soon." Having fulfilled his part, he reseated himself, then gave Dorothy a pointed look as if to say, *Your turn*.

She rose unhurriedly to her feet, then took a deep breath before stepping over to the side of the bed. Leaning over, she said, "I'm so sorry I wasn't there when you needed me. I've thought about it so many times and wish I had stayed.

Or gone back to check on you. You're so little. Such a baby. I forgot how little you were." And then she began to sob, leaning over with her hands on her knees. Felix found himself oddly touched. He hadn't anticipated this kind of reaction and took a grim satisfaction in seeing her sad face.

Dorothy stumbled back to her chair, then covered her face with her hands. She was quiet now, but seeing her like this clearly pained all of them. If they'd been acting before, somehow the line had been crossed from a created reaction to a deeply felt emotion. Marion reached over and rubbed small, comforting circles on her oldest daughter's back.

Milo spoke up. "How long should we leave them like this?" He gestured to the screen. "It's so sad."

"Very sad," Felix agreed, "but their misery is somehow beautiful, don't you think? Let's keep it going for a while."

275

Chapter Forty-Five

Gerald found sitting in the hospital room strangely exhausting. All of their collective pain in one spot wore him down, the load made heavier by the fact that so much of it had been carried for more than two decades. He hadn't even realized how much the show had affected him. How was it that this group of people, thrown together by fate, and apart for so many years, could still be so intertwined?

Over the years, he'd occasionally thought about the little boy actor, Sean, and wondered what had become of him after he left the show. He never knew, and now part of him wondered if the kid actually *had* died as a result of his on-set injuries. If so, was this Felix Worthington's way of paying homage to him? Would the boy's name and dates wind up being posted on the screen under the words "In Memory of"?

Dorothy continued to cry silently, while Marion kept a reassuring hand resting on her back. She was a natural at being a mother. Gerald had no paternal instincts, but he was a hell of an actor and could at least play the part of a father.

"I'd like to say a prayer," he said, gesturing for them to stand. No one said a word, but they all rose, shuffled closer to the bed, then clasped their hands together and bowed their heads. The words came easily to him. "Merciful Lord, we ask for your love and guidance on this day as we watch over our youngest family member, Bud Barlow. Bud is a sweet boy, and we've been blessed to have him for seven years. We ask for a miracle healing, if it's your will. Guide us with the strength to move forward on the path you've laid out for us. We pray for strength and compassion and vow to do better in the future. Amen."

"Amen!" Every person in the room, including Grandma, echoed the word.

And then there was nothing to do but wait. Gerald resisted the urge to look at the clock. The doctor had said their vigil could last until the morning. They'd all left Bud behind in his darkest hour—the least they could do was to be there for him now.

When Ann spoke, the sound of her voice broke through the quiet, startling him. "Bud's favorite treat after doing his lessons was always chocolate chip cookies."

"With milk," Marion added. "A coffee mug full of milk."

Tom rested his chin on his fist. "He'd always dunk the cookies in the milk until they were nearly soggy."

Dorothy nodded. "That made him so happy. He could eat a whole sleeve of Chips Ahoy in one sitting." A ghost of a smile crossed her face.

Gerald had his own memory. "The cowlick on the top of his head stood up no matter how much you tried to slick it down."

"Yeah, and he hated having his shirt buttoned up to the top. Said he felt like it was choking him." This from Tom.

Dorothy said, "He didn't say *choking*. He said it was *strangling* him. I always thought that was a funny word for a little kid to use. He could be a little dramatic, but it was cute."

"He hated that you called him Squiggles," Ann said. Her comment was aimed at Tom, but there was no malice in her voice.

"I shouldn't have done that," Tom said, running his fingers through his hair. "I was pretty immature. I thought it was funny because he couldn't sit still for like more than ten seconds."

"He was a sweet boy," Marion said. Gerald felt a pang at hearing the past tense. "Used to run up and give me hugs for no reason."

Ann said, "He hated it when people thought he was stupid, because it wasn't true. He was actually very bright and creative. Sometimes he made up poems in his head. He used to recite them to me."

The boy in the bed made a murmuring noise, and Marion got up and stood over him. "I think he looks a little better." Her voice was hopeful. Gerald knew she was angling for a miracle. "His coloring has improved." She rested her hand against his cheek. "Hang in there, Bud. We love you."

Grandma said, "I always say, hope for the best, expect the worst." Did her character say that on the show? Gerald thought she did.

Felix watched as Marion scooted her chair closer to the bed and began to hum something to her son. He didn't recognize the song, but it had a soothing sound. This seemed like a good time for a transition. He turned suddenly to Milo and said, "It's time to end the scene. Cue the actor."

"Are you sure? All this reminiscing is pure TV gold. The Barlows are really broken up. *I* feel like crying, so I know the fans are going to love it."

"The scene is over." Felix tapped on the desk with one finger. "End it."

Milo sighed, then sat down at his monitor and tapped into the keyboard. Within a few minutes, a nurse walked briskly down the hall and into Bud's hospital room.

The nurse walked in and sidled in sideways alongside to the bed until her backside faced Gerald. They all froze, and Marion stopped humming. The nurse didn't acknowledge any of them, just focused her attention on Bud, who now lay completely still. She pressed her fingertips to his throat, then took a stethoscope out of her pocket to check his heart. Leaning over the patient to listen, an alarmed look crossed her face, and Ann had a sinking feeling that this was it. The end of their vigil. The nurse addressed the room. "I need to get the doctor." She scurried out as quickly as she'd arrived, her white shoes squeaking down the corridor. From the shocked looks on everyone's faces, they'd all come to the same realization.

The clock's ticking became louder as they waited. Ann felt tears well up in her eyes. The waiting had been interminable, but even knowing the child in the bed wasn't real, the end was still painful. There was something so raw and finite about death, even a metaphorical one.

Dr. Reed came in, followed by Doc Tarter. Mutely, the family moved their chairs away from the bed and then stood watching wide-eyed as Doc Tarter did an examination of Bud, the littlest Barlow, the one who'd never really had a chance. He checked for a pulse by pressing his fingertips against the boy's neck, then listened to his heart, first with a stethoscope, then by pressing an ear to his chest. Ann found this gesture to be both old-fashioned and dear.

Once he'd straightened, Doc Tarter addressed all of them with a sad shake of his head. "We did everything we could for him, but it just wasn't enough. I'm so sorry to tell you that your sweet boy is gone." He exhaled audibly before pulling the sheet over Bud's face. "He's left this world and is in a better place."

Dr. Reed said, "My condolences on the loss of your son and brother."

Doc Tarter nodded in his direction. "Time of death is 3:14 a.m."

From the corner, Grandma spoke, her voice raspy but clear. "Losing a child is unnatural. Just wrong. If anything, I should have been the one to die." No one contradicted her, and when they ultimately decided to go home, she said, "I think I'd like to stay here for a while, praying over my grandson. All of you go on ahead. I'll get a ride from someone here."

They drifted out of the room as if disoriented. Ann observed them as an outsider might. It seemed as if one weight had been lifted, while another had been thrust upon them. They'd lost something they'd forgotten they'd even had, and now felt it keenly, all the while trying to convince themselves it wasn't real. The problem was that the truth had been interwoven into the hospital scene, and parsing out the real from the fake was proving to be difficult.

Stepping out the front door of the hospital, they blinked at the dark night sky. As if on cue, a burst of lightning was followed by a low growl of thunder, and scattered raindrops began to fall, cold on their skin. By the time they got to the car, their clothes were soaked. They drove home in a downpour, their windshield wipers flicking back and forth with the precision of a metronome. No one said a word.

Chapter Forty-Six

Sunday and Monday went by in a sleep-deprived blur. When they'd returned from the hospital Saturday night, Gerald had patted Beau's head on their way into the house, and then they'd all trooped upstairs to their respective bedrooms. Gerald found it hard to fall asleep. Lying in the dark, he could tell his wife was also wide awake. Getting up on one elbow, he whispered into the dark, "Marion?"

"Yes?"

"I can't help but think that Bud's death was my fault. Maybe if I'd been a better father, he never would have fallen out of that tree." He was having trouble keeping his voice steady. "I should have been there to help get him down or catch him."

She didn't answer for the longest time, and when she did, he didn't get the reassuring words he'd hoped for. Instead, she said, "Try not to dwell on it. Nothing can be changed at this point." She shifted and pulled the covers closer. "Good night, Gerald."

He couldn't let it go. "Do you think I'm a terrible father?"

She sighed. "I don't think you're anything. Try to get some sleep."

Good advice, but he didn't get much sleep at all, and not for lack of trying. Sunday turned out to be a sunny day, the storm from the previous night having passed quickly. They woke up to find Grandma back in her rocking chair on the porch, wearing a black dress with a crocheted collar. She was the first one to greet the visitors who came that day, a steady stream stopping by to bring flowers, food, and prayer cards. News spread fast in Haven, and it seemed everyone in town had heard about Bud's death.

The Barlows walked around in a daze, glad to follow the prompts of the other townspeople. One of their neighbors, Francine Rathman, came with her little boy, Teddy, to collect their funeral clothes, which she offered to iron to perfection. "You all have enough to think about. Let me do this." Francine went upstairs with Ann, and soon Gerald saw the two women come down the stairs with clothing draped over their arms, while Teddy carried a cloth bag filled with their dress shoes.

"Teddy does a right fine job polishing shoes," Francine said, tousling his hair with her free hand. "And I can iron a crease that could cut paper. We'll get to work and bring everything back the night before the funeral, all ready to go."

Gerald accompanied Ann, Francine, and Teddy to the door and inwardly groaned when he recognized the bank examiner coming up the walkway.

Edmund Brown approached Gerald, hat in hand, ready to pay his respects. "I was so sorry to hear about your little boy," he said, holding Gerald's gaze.

"Thank you."

"I also wanted to assure you that we aren't going to take any action regarding the discrepancy at the bank for another two weeks, out of deference to your family's tragedy."

Gerald nodded. "I appreciate it, sir." Truthfully, though, he'd forgotten all about the bank crisis. In two weeks, he'd be long gone from Haven, back in the world as Jeff Greer, and none of it would be his problem anymore. The two men shook hands, and Mr. Brown turned and left. "Good riddance, asshole," Gerald muttered under his breath.

More folks dropped by to give their condolences. Every one of them had a remembrance of Bud, something sweet he'd done or said, all of which gave Gerald an uncomfortable feeling. He hadn't paid much attention to the child at all, but to the viewers and townspeople he wasn't just one of the Barlows. Bud was his own person. Bud's first grade teacher, Mrs. Sands, brought some of his papers from school, including an essay titled, "How I Know My Parents Love Me." After the teacher left, Marion sat down to read it, then burst into tears. Was she acting? He couldn't tell anymore. She handed the page to Gerald before she fled to the bathroom, but he couldn't bring himself to read it, so he shoved it into a drawer in the credenza. His heart was heavy.

On Monday morning, Marion's ladies' society from church arrived as a group to take Gerald and Marion to the funeral home to plan Tuesday's service. Gloria Youngbauer, now on crutches, along with Lydia Zagon, Virginia Moore, Susan Campton, and Rose McGrath showed up at the house. They sat in the parlor. Rose had an actual list of things to do: music to choose, photos to assemble, a death notice to write.

Marion and Gerald were exhausted and unsure of how to proceed, so they were glad of the help.

"Too bad the church is still under construction," Lydia said. "But we can still have a lovely gathering at the funeral home. You'll see. Tuesday's service will be perfect."

Tuesday's service. In mulling it over, Gerald realized the ten days were ending with a funeral. Not what he would have expected, but he was glad the whole experience would be over soon. He was ready to go back to his own apartment and slide into his old life. It may have been a sad, lonely one, but at least it was authentically his own. Marion had said it best: *I don't think you're anything.* A dismissive statement, hurtful in its truth. Did his whole life of more than sixty years add up to nothing? He was starting to think that might be the case.

Carrying the family photo albums Dorothy had found, he and Marion accompanied the women's group to the Haven Funeral Home to make the arrangements for the next day's service for their son. At the funeral home, they discovered Reverend Malone was out of town, but during a phone conversation he promised he would be back in time to conduct the memorial service. "I don't think we need to do anything at the cemetery. Just a service will suffice."

That was a relief. Gerald didn't know if he had it in him to be a pallbearer and stand graveside.

Reverend Malone continued. "I'll work on my speech tonight," he said. "We'll make it the perfect tribute for your little boy, a most beautiful soul."

From there it was time to go over the details of the memorial service with the funeral director. By the time they'd finished making all the decisions, Gerald was emotionally and physically drained. Marion must have felt the same way, because she was uncharacteristically affectionate, taking his hand and resting her head on his shoulder. That night, when they were in bed together, she said, "I'm sorry for the way I answered your question last night. I was so distraught I wasn't thinking straight. I don't think you're a terrible father. You're a good man, Gerald. Don't be too hard on yourself. All of us make mistakes."

"Not you. I don't know of any mistakes you've ever made. I think you're perfect."

She snorted softly. "If you only knew. I've made so many mistakes that I've lost count. Big ones. The unforgiveable kind. I'm as flawed as anyone."

"I don't believe that."

"Well." She turned on her side to face him in the dark. "I love that you don't believe that. Good night, Gerald."

"Good night." The fact that she thought she was capable of making unforgiveable mistakes made him love her all the more.

Chapter Forty-Seven

Hailey had never wanted to be an actor like her mother, but now, waiting for her turn to make an entrance in a 1940s costume and hairstyle, she could finally see the appeal. She'd already practiced her lines over and over again. She'd filmed herself saying her dialogue, then listened to the audio portion on the plane ride to Montana. By the time they'd landed, she had her part completely memorized.

The initial texted instructions from her mother had been general, but soon after she'd heard from Felix Worthington's assistant, Milo, who gave her specific detailed directions. It seemed that Felix Worthington and company had thought of every detail regarding her visit. They'd flown her to Montana in a private jet. A limo driver met her at the airport and drove her to the Worthington ranch.

Hailey had arrived the day before the funeral and spent the night in Felix's ranch home. The only other person she saw was the housekeeper, Vicki, who'd greeted her and served Hailey both dinner that night and breakfast the following morning, accompanied by small talk about the weather. On several occasions, Hailey had tried to text her mother, but she got no response. This wasn't unexpected, though, and soon enough both of them would be flying home together. There would be plenty of time to talk then.

Walking through the door of what looked like a warehouse on the outside and finding Haven on the inside had been a total mind-blowing trip. Even though she'd already been styled and costumed and knew what to expect, it still took her by surprise. It was a step back in time. The assistant who escorted her, a woman about Hailey's age named Flora, kept the 1940s conversation going. Hailey suspected her name was not actually Flora, but since none of this was real, it was easy to play along. For whatever reason, the team had allowed Hailey to use her own name, even though it wasn't a good fit for the era.

"Such a tragedy about Bud Barlow," Flora said as they walked down the sidewalk. Like Hailey, she wore a dark-colored 1940s dress in preparation for the funeral. "I went to school with Dorothy, and Bud was about my cousin Daisy's age. You're a distant relative, I understand?"

"Yes, I moved away, but I came back for the service today."

"I'm sure it was a shock to hear about his death. I'm so sorry."

"Thank you. You're very kind." Hailey was grateful for all the times she'd watched the Haven episodes online, because it gave her an idea of how the characters spoke. Hearing about Bud's death had been a shock. She'd known the child actor had left the show during the first season, but she'd never heard the details. Milo had explained that this storyline would bring closure for the fans who'd wondered what had happened to him. Hailey patted her handbag, glad to have her speech printed on a sheet of folded-up paper inside. She imagined she'd be able to look it over one last time before it was her turn to speak.

Hailey had never even been in a school play. The closest she'd come to acting was running lines with her mother, and even that hadn't been recently. She wasn't quite sure she was up to the task, but when she'd hesitated during their initial Zoom call, Milo had jumped in to reassure her. "Fans are going to love knowing that the woman who made a guest appearance is Meri Wetzel's daughter in real life. Believe me, they'll eat it up." He was such a big guy that he filled up the screen. Hailey would have assumed he was a bodyguard, not an assistant.

"I'm not a trained actor," she said. "I mean, I'll do the best I can, but I can't promise a great performance."

"You're going to be amazing!" he said, with an enthusiasm that made her wary. "And if you make a flub, no worries. We can always do another take later and fix it. The magic of editing."

That did make her feel better. "Good to know."

The next thing he said clinched the deal. "Felix Worthington is willing to pay you sixty thousand dollars for one day's work on the show. Plus, we'll take care of all the travel details."

In disbelief, she made him repeat the number. Coincidentally, her student loans had capped out at just under $42,000. Even after paying taxes, there was a good chance she'd be able to completely pay off her loan, and wouldn't that be a relief? Now she wouldn't have to rely on her mom to help. Before he could change his mind, she said, "You can count on me! I'll do it."

"Wonderful!" Milo clapped his hands together. "Felix will be delighted to hear you'll be joining us."

"And my mom will be excited too. Will you let her know? I haven't been able to get ahold of her recently."

"Ah." Milo shook his head. "She's pretty firmly embedded at this point, so we might not be able to give her an update, but you'll see her at the funeral. Don't break character, though. I know it will be tempting, but until they announce filming is over, you're just Bud's distant cousin who's come for the funeral and she's Marion Barlow."

"I understand," Hailey said. She had sixty thousand reasons to remember.

Walking with Flora made it easy to remember she wasn't herself when she was in Haven. They passed a woman pushing a pram, and Flora stopped to fuss over the baby, who wore a ruffled bonnet and had a metal rattle clutched in her hand. "Her name is Amy," the young mother said in answer to Flora's question. "Amy Margaret Coats. She's five months old."

"Amy!" Flora said. "What a beautiful and unusual name."

Hailey added, "She's beautiful." She leaned over and waved. In response, the baby shook the rattle so vigorously that if it had been any closer to her face the little one could have given herself a black eye.

After they'd continued on, Flora turned at the corner. "Not much farther." They passed a barbershop with a revolving pole next to the door. Inside, a man was getting his face lathered up for a shave. A customer in the chair next to him, a newspaper in his lap, chatted with the barber, who'd paused while holding a pair of scissors in the air. Hailey and Flora went past several more businesses until they came to the Haven Funeral Home.

Flora bypassed the columned front entrance and guided Hailey through the parking lot to the back of the building. She knocked on the door, and when it was answered, they were greeted by Milo Lappin, who broke into a broad grin. "Hailey Wetzel!" he said, extending a hand. "I'm so glad you're joining us! Felix isn't here at the moment, but he's looking forward to meeting you later. He told me to convey his appreciation that you were able to fit us into your schedule."

Her schedule? She'd had to take two days off work, but that was a minor detail considering she'd end up $60,000 richer. For that amount of money, her schedule could become very flexible. But if they wanted to play it like she was doing them a favor, that was fine with her. "I'm glad I could make it," she said.

After saying goodbye to Flora, she followed Milo inside. He walked her through the funeral home, where a staff of five people, two men and three women, were setting up wooden folding chairs and carrying in enormous floral arrangements. "As you can see, we're still getting things ready." He pointed to a table by the back wall. "The casket will be right here, and the podium will be in front of it. When I give you the cue, you'll come out from behind the curtain, step up to the podium, and deliver your lines. After you're finished, stand next to the reverend. He'll be announcing the service is over. At that point, leave the room with the rest of the people in attendance."

"Besides my mom, does anyone else know I'm coming?" Hailey asked.

"No one." He shook his head. "Felix thought it would be best if it was a surprise. He's a fan of the authentic reaction."

"I see." Hailey took in the velvet floor-to-ceiling drapes currently covering the windows and the large floral arrangements being placed on stands lining the walls. She thought over what he'd just said. *A surprise. The authentic reaction.* "I'm not going to get any surprises, am I? I have to be straight with you and tell you I'm really jumpy."

Milo appeared perplexed. "I'm not sure what you mean."

"The kid's not going to sit up in the casket while I'm talking or anything like that?"

He laughed. "No, nothing like that. This will be the same as attending a regular funeral. I assure you that Bud Barlow will not move at all. No practical jokes, just a lot of people talking about their memories of a small boy." He nodded. "It should be a very touching scene."

Hailey breathed a sigh of relief. "Good." Now all she had to do was wait, and soon she'd be reunited with her mom. Milo had told her on the phone that he'd arranged for them to take the same flight home. Hailey couldn't wait.

Milo said, "The funeral doesn't start for another hour or so. In the meantime, I'll show you where you can stay. There are drinks and snacks if you're hungry and magazines to read to help pass the time." He beckoned for her to follow and led her behind the curtain to the back room. "Make yourself comfortable, Hailey. I'll be back soon to check in with you."

Chapter Forty-Eight

When the family came down the stairs the morning of the funeral, they found a note from Grandma on the kitchen table.

I had some visits to make today. I'll be at the funeral home in time for the service. Please feed Beau.

Love, Grandma

Tom couldn't imagine what kind of visits she had to make—she was an animatronic figure, for God's sake, constructed of metal, plastic, rubber, and moving parts. Powered by electricity. She had more in common with a blender than any of the people in Haven. But of course, that wasn't the point. The note was clearly just an excuse for the team to move Grandma while they were sleeping and get her to the funeral home.

After reading the note, Ann immediately sprang into action. "I'll take care of Beau," she said. The rest of them nodded as she scooped up dog food and headed outside. When she came back inside, she said, "Beau seems different

293

today." Her comment prompted a family field trip out the front door to the porch.

Beau was different. Instead of sitting up, ready for a head pat, he now was down on all fours, his nose resting on the floor of the porch. Was this a different dog, or had they missed the fact that he was posable? "You okay, buddy?" Marion asked, reaching down to give him a rub behind the ears. The dog whined in response.

"I think he misses Bud," Ann said softly.

Tears welled up in Dorothy's eyes, and she turned abruptly and went back inside. *Good Lord,* Tom thought. *Oh, the drama.* He knew that they were all supposed to play the grieving family, but even so, her reaction was over-the-top. Tom's creative choice was that of a brother in shock. So much easier to play, and truer to real life as well.

Their porch gathering was interrupted by Francine Rathman and Teddy, who walked over from their house to deliver their funeral clothes. "Not a wrinkle to be found," Francine said solemnly when she arrived at the house. "And Teddy shined the shoes so you can practically see your reflection." Marion thanked her profusely, while Tom and Ann stepped forward to take the clothing from Francine's arms, then carried all of it inside to distribute them to the appropriate bedrooms. When they returned to the first floor, the Rathmans had already left.

By the time all five of them headed to the funeral home, the rest of the family's mood had rubbed off on Tom and he was feeling properly depressed. The dark-colored clothing helped set the tone, along with his tight dress shoes, which, to Teddy Rathman's credit, were indeed the shiniest he'd ever seen.

The funeral parlor was uncomfortable as well, overly warm in temperature, with fussy décor including velvet drapes, plum-colored carpet, and floral-patterned wallpaper. Two stiffly upholstered sofas had been placed on either side, while the center of the room was lined with row after row of wooden folding chairs.

Walking into the room, they noticed that one of the dozens of chairs was already occupied. Grandma. She sat in the front row, head bowed, eyes closed, and hands folded in prayer. Tom smirked at the sight. As promised, she'd finished with her visits and was there in plenty of time.

One long table in the back displayed black-and-white family photos alongside a guest book, a fancy fountain pen, and a stack of prayer cards. Tom recognized one of the family photos as the one used for promotional purposes when the show had first aired. Farther into the room, an ornate chandelier hung overhead. The overpowering smell of the freshly cut flowers gave Tom a claustrophobic vibe. He itched to remove his suit coat but sensed it would be inappropriate.

In the front of the room, a half-open casket revealed Bud, his head covered with a newsboy cap. He wore a white dress shirt and a tweed vest. His expression was peaceful, and his hands were interlaced across his torso, holding one white lily. A thought crossed Tom's mind: *They did a good job of covering up his head injury.* An instant later he shook off the ridiculous notion. This wasn't a real person. Tom might as well be looking at a doll.

Shortly thereafter, visitors drifted in, their steps careful and voices quietly respectful. They signed the guest book and stopped to stare at the photos, then came to find a family member to pay their respects. Tom listened politely as neighbors and friends gave their condolences. He shook hands and said "Thank you for coming" so many times he lost count. Across the room, he spotted Marion in full-on mother mode, hugging each person in turn as they stepped forward to speak with her. Meanwhile, Gerald stood mutely next to her, his face the picture of sorrow. He spotted Ruby talking to Dorothy, while Ann had clearly taken the easy route, sitting sedately next to Grandma, her face aimed downward, her fingers tented in prayer. She sat on the aisle, so no one could sit next to her during the service.

He wished he had thought of that first. Pretend praying looked a lot like taking a nap. He reached up to loosen his tie and inwardly cringed upon seeing his mother's friend Gloria heading his way. He was played out in terms of receiving insincere sympathy.

Just then, as if to rescue him, three of his fair coworkers walked into the room. Tex, Herman, and Otis. He would have known them anywhere. Even dressed up for the occasion they still looked a little rough around the edges. Tom had never been so happy to see anyone in his life. He pivoted away from Gloria as if he hadn't seen her and went to greet them, arms extended. "Fellas," he exclaimed. "I can't believe you're here." Tom was genuinely glad to see them. He'd enjoyed their company and now fondly associated them with his own bad habits. That morning, without the benefit of their bummed cigarettes, he'd had to resort to a nicotine patch to take the edge off his craving. He didn't suppose there was a good time to sneak a smoke at his own brother's funeral, but he still connected the men with good times. There was something about being in their presence that made him feel right at home.

"Of course," Tex said. "We had to come."

Tom thought he caught a wink on the word *had*, which made him smile. It was code, meaning they literally had to come since it was written into some script somewhere. The four of them talked about Bud's passing, with Tom telling them all that had transpired at the hospital. The story must have loosened up something inside of them, because each one felt compelled to share a similar tragedy. Otis had lost an older sister in a car accident; Herman's cousin had just been diagnosed with a brain tumor; and Tex mentioned the untimely death of his favorite dog, Chester. "Not the same as a person, I know," he added hastily, "but I've never loved a human being as much as I loved that dog. And he'd a done anything for me. I just know it." He wiped his eyes with his knuckles. "Sorry about that. He used to travel with me to work, so I had him around all day." He gestured to his workmates. "They all knew him."

Herman nodded. "Chester was a good dog. We miss him."

"He got took from me way too soon," Tex said with a sniff. "Always thought he had a few more good years left to go."

"I'm so sorry," Tom said. Maybe when he got back to his real life, he'd look into getting a dog. He'd always felt like they were too much work, but now he wondered if he was missing out.

When a portly man with bushy black hair, wire-rim glasses, and a brown suit walked into the room, a hush fell over the crowd like he was a celebrity. Herman leaned in and whispered, "Must be the reverend. I heard he was out of town and rushed back for the service."

Otis nodded. "I heard that too."

Reverend Malone strode to the podium in front of the casket and addressed the crowd in a firm tone. "Everyone, if you'll take your seats, we can begin the memorial service."

Chapter
Forty-Nine

The Barlow family went to claim their spots in the front row. Marion had hoped to sit next to Grandma, but Tom had taken that spot, so she resigned herself to sitting between Gerald and Dorothy. The minister gazed down on them, his expression quietly benevolent. He gave a nod that seemed meant just for her.

When the noise of the crowd taking their places had subsided, the service began. "For those who don't know me," he said, "I'm Reverend Malone, the head of the church here in Haven. I've known the Barlow family for many years. In fact, I knew Gerald and Marion before their four children were born." He gazed out over the audience. "I know so many of you here today. Friends. Neighbors. Relatives. And most importantly, children of God, just like our dear Bud."

Marion thought back to the television show. There had been a Reverend Malone in the cast. The actor's first name was Bill. *What was his last name?* She remembered getting Christmas cards from Bill and his wife for a few years after the show ended. Straining to remember how they were signed, she had a flash of memory: *MaryAnn and Bill Schaefer*. Bill Schaefer had been a large guy with a head of thick dark hair, just like the man who stood before them, but this was not the same person. Presumably, the original Bill, a friendly guy who was always professional, couldn't make it. She hoped he was alive and well.

Reverend Malone continued. "Little Bud Barlow should have lived a good long life, but a tragic accident took him from us far too soon. All of us loved Bud, and while it's human nature to wish he was still here with us, we need to accept his untimely death." He paused to wipe away a tear. "It's hard to understand why these things happen. They say God works in mysterious ways. It would be easy to assign blame. Did someone put this accident in motion? Could we have done something different? Perhaps we'll never know. Those who don't have a clear conscience will have to find a way to live with the guilt."

Dorothy put a hand over her mouth to cover a gasp, and Marion knew the words had hit home.

"All I can say with certainty is that Bud was loved and will be missed. Now please stand for a prayer."

Everyone in the room rose to their feet and dutifully bowed their heads as Reverend Malone prayed for Bud's soul, as well as praying for the family in their time of grief. He mentioned each family member by name and paused to lock eyes with each person in turn. He finished by saying, "Please join me in reciting the Our Father."

The voices of those present rose and fell as they said the timeless words. Marion snuck a glance down the row and noticed that even Tom joined in on the prayer. *Good.* She was glad to see he was making an effort. It was the least he could do.

When the prayer was done, Reverend Malone invited those who wanted to speak a few words about Bud to come forward. Ann went first. "Bud was the best little brother anyone could ever have. He was such a good boy." Getting choked up, she paused for a moment to gain her composure. Finally, she said, "All he wanted was to be liked. He was too good for this world." She sat down, and then each family member got up one by one and said their bit, all of them variations of how much they'd loved him and would miss him. Even Tom managed to say a few appropriate words, sounding sincere. One of his better acting jobs.

Robot Grandma apparently wasn't up to the task, preferring to stay in praying mode.

Dorothy was the last family member to speak. She stood, looking stricken, and took a deep breath but didn't say anything for what seemed like a long time. Just when Marion was about to get up to join her, Dorothy managed to force out her part. "I'm Bud's older sister, Dorothy," she said, looking back at the casket. There was a long pause, and then she continued. "It's such a shock to see him like this. So quiet. He was always so full of life. Couldn't sit still. He used to tag along with me and my friends. I wasn't always so nice to him, and I regret it now. Rest in peace, Bud."

Gerald reached over and took Marion's hand, grasping her fingers. When he'd touched her during the first part of their stay in Haven, it had felt intrusive, unnatural, but now there was something comforting about it. They had a shared history, even if it had ended badly. And now, having gone through these ten days, she felt a sense of closure. Her bitterness had melted away. Too, she was impressed with his lengthy sobriety. It took a strong person to stay the course when the pull of addiction was so powerful. Her prism of resentment had been refocused, forcing her to see him in a new light. She didn't want him in her life going forward, but if they met up again, it would be a connection of old friends.

Once Dorothy sat down, Reverend Malone invited the rest of the attendees to share memories of Bud. One by one, community members went to the podium. Grade school teachers. Neighbors. Parents of Bud's schoolmates. Judging by what was said, Bud wasn't the extra Barlow child at all, but a valued member of the town of Haven. As his first grade teacher said, "Not a mean bone in his body. He just wanted to be everyone's friend. Bud was the best of us."

When the last person sat down, an hour and a half had passed, and Marion surmised that they were nearly done. Thank goodness they weren't doing anything at the cemetery. She didn't think her heart could stand it.

Reverend Malone said, "Thank you, everyone. Before we conclude this service, there's one final mourner who'd like to say a few words today. A distant cousin of the Barlows, Hailey Wetzel, has traveled a long distance to pay her respects. Please give her your full attention."

Hailey Wetzel. Even as a flash of confusion came over her, Marion felt the hairs on the back of her neck stand up. Had she heard him correctly? Hailey? She couldn't think of any reason why her daughter would be here. She watched as Hailey, *her own Hailey*, dressed in period garb, her hair styled similar to Dorothy's, stepped out from behind the curtain and walked past the casket. She knew Hailey would never have volunteered to do such a thing, so she could only guess that she'd been contacted by the Worthington team.

Seeing her daughter, her heart caught in her chest. They'd been apart too long, and she'd missed her with a painful intensity. It was all she could do to stay seated.

The reverend stepped aside to let Hailey take her place at the podium. Scanning the crowd, she spotted her mother, and her mouth quirked in recognition.

Clutching both sides of the podium, she began. "Thank you, Reverend Malone. I'm glad I could be here for my relatives, but I'm so very sorry it had to be for such an occasion. Losing my little cousin at such a young age is a tragedy. I think back to a visit I made when he was an adorable baby with wispy brown hair and dimpled hands. What I remember most is that he was so loved. I admit I was a little envious. Myself, I was raised in a small family, just my mother and me, but Bud had parents *and* a brother and two sisters. I was most jealous of my cousins' father. Uncle Gerald was such a devoted dad to his brood." She scanned the faces of the crowd, locking on Gerald's. "When you saw the whole family together, you could feel the love. I never knew my own father. The only thing I have of him would be my gray eyes."

Marion didn't dare look at Gerald, but she felt the clasp of his hand tighten. So now he knew the truth——she hadn't lied. There was no turning back.

Hailey continued, her eyes scanning the crowd. "But the Barlow children had the love and presence of both parents.

And now, in losing one of their own, Bud, who was the sweetest little boy in all the world, they will at least have each other to help get them through this difficult time." She paused and then added, "Rest in peace, Bud." She stepped aside, and the reverend returned to his place.

"This concludes our memorial service," he said. "Please take a prayer card on your way out. It's a lovely way to remember Bud." As the mourners stood, he directed his attention to the front row. "The family needs to stay, however. We're not finished yet."

Chapter Fifty

Hailey's words hit Gerald like a wallop between his shoulder blades, making it difficult for him to get air into his lungs. He clutched Marion's hand as he viewed Hailey's departure from the room with troubled eyes. Marion had to be behind Hailey's appearance, but why she'd chosen to reveal the news in Haven was beyond him. "Why didn't you tell me?" he whispered to Marion.

"Tell you what?"

He thought about how to answer and still stay in character. "About the gray eyes."

Marion shrugged. "She has her father's eye color."

"I put that much together. I just . . . why am I just hearing about this now?"

"Seems like I tried to tell you more than once and you accused me of lying." She pulled her hand away from him and sat up straight in her chair.

More than twenty-five years had passed, but he distinctly remembered when she gave him the news. At the time he was separated from his wife, but there was a chance of them reconciling. By then, *A Little Slice of Haven* had been canceled, and his drinking, never good, had been at an all-time

305

high. Or all-time low, depending on how you looked at it. Every day he sank deeper into despair.

It felt like life was trying to drown him, and just when he thought it couldn't get any worse, Meri came along and told him she was pregnant. Their affair had been secret and short-lived, and at that point, they hadn't been together for weeks.

After they broke it off, there'd been talk she was dating one of the crew. He'd never told her about his almost nonexistent sperm count, so he thought her pregnancy announcement was an attempt on her part to manipulate him, something that had infuriated him.

They'd parted ways, and although he'd heard she had a baby, he never gave it much thought. If it had been his, why didn't she hit him with a paternity suit to get child support? That's what most women would have done. And in all these years she'd never informed him he had a child? It didn't make sense to suddenly see a grown woman and find out she was his daughter. He was willing to do a DNA test if required, but there wasn't a doubt in his mind. Hailey looked identical to photos he'd seen of his own mother when she was in her twenties. Beautiful, with dark hair, high cheekbones, arched brows, and intense gray eyes.

The eyes, that was the clincher. Identical to his own.

I have a daughter. He marveled at the news, dumbstruck that life could still surprise him, even at this point. The truth was that he'd never imagined having a child. He'd always thought he'd live and die and never leave a trace of himself anywhere in this world other than his work in film and television. Crappy acting roles that didn't come close to showcasing his talents. And now to find out he had a daughter? The realization was overwhelming.

Conflicting emotions churned inside him, making it difficult to know how to react. Momentarily, he set aside his anger with Meri and reveled in the knowledge that he was a father. *A father*. He took in a deep breath, willing his pounding heart to slow. When he got out of Haven, he wanted to connect with Hailey, maybe build a relationship. With the $2 million, he'd have the money to give Meri a lifetime of child support. That would go a long way toward redeeming himself.

But first to get through the rest of the day.

Reverend Malone addressed the remaining members of the room, all six of the Barlows, if you wanted to include Grandma. "Well," he said, giving them a broad smile. "Day ten is finally here. For some of you, it was a long time coming. For others, it probably went by in a flash." He pulled back his sleeve to look at his watch. "In just two hours, all of you will be out of Haven and heading back to your everyday lives. I'm sure that will be a relief."

They all nodded and murmured in agreement. Tom had a big grin on his face.

Two hours? Gerald had thought they'd have to stay until the end of the day. Knowing it was wrapping up early was a weight lifted. At one point he'd have said Gerald Barlow had the better end of the deal, but he now saw the benefits of being Jeff Greer once again. Jeff was the one who would reap the financial rewards of his time spent in Haven. He planned to use the money to start life once again, a do-over that came complete with a new daughter.

Reverend Malone continued. "But before you leave Haven, there are still some issues that need to be addressed. Milo?"

Milo Lappin popped out from behind the curtain. Seeing him again was like running into an old friend at the end of a long, hectic day. A welcome sight. "Hello, everyone!" he said, raising his hand in greeting. "You got through the ten days! Congratulations!"

Smiles broke out among the group. Tom fist-pumped the air, while Dorothy murmured, "Thank God." Two young guys wearing jeans and T-shirts came out from behind the curtain and effortlessly lifted the casket. In a matter of moments, they'd disappeared, along with the dearly departed Bud.

"But we still have a few things to go over before you walk out that door," the reverend said. "Milo, would you lower the screen?"

Nodding, Milo took a remote control out of his pocket and aimed it at the curtain. Within seconds, a large monitor slowly descended from the ceiling. The reverend moved the podium to one side so they'd have an unobstructed view.

Milo said, "What you're about to see are the highlights from your ten days in Haven. After that, we'll go over your performances and determine if any missteps were taken. Those who broke character will be shown visual proof and will not be awarded the two million dollars."

Tom leaned back in his seat and raised his hand. "I have two questions."

"Yes?"

"Are we ever going to meet Felix Worthington?"

"Yes." Milo took a step closer. "Next question?"

"Can we skip the highlights reel and go straight to the part where we find out about the money?" He leaned over and scanned the row. "I think I speak for all of us when I say that's our primary interest."

"Sorry. Not an option."

Chapter Fifty-One

Before she'd even stepped foot in Haven, Ann had known what would be happening to the other members of the cast during the ten days. Still, she was eager to see the film. This was her chance to see what everyone had been up to when she wasn't close by.

The lighting in the room dimmed at the same time as the screen flicked on with the scene that had played out at the bank between Gerald and the bank examiner. It began with Mr. Brown pointing a finger at Gerald and saying, "You, sir, are a liar and a thief!"

Gerald responded with wounded outrage. "I'm telling you the truth!"

Ann felt a surge of satisfaction in seeing his reaction. As planned, this turn of events had clearly taken him by surprise and made him uncomfortable and left him feeling diminished.

They watched the whole scene play out without comment. When it was done, Milo said, "Now on to Tom's most outstanding scene." Across the screen flashed an image of Tom and a beautiful blonde woman dancing at the fair. Within seconds, a larger guy came between them and accused Tom of dancing with his girlfriend. The woman smiled and stepped away as the brute grabbed hold of Tom's shoulders and said, "I have half a mind to beat you senseless." Even witnessing the scene secondhand, Ann felt the threat. In person, it had to have been terrifying.

Tom's response was downright pitiful. He practically begged for mercy saying, "You don't need to do that. It was an honest mistake. I swear I won't have anything to do with Elizabeth from now on. I wish the two of you the best."

Ann glanced over at Tom, who looked completely mortified. Good. The desired result had been achieved.

The scene switched to the Ferris wheel. Milo said, "And now Dorothy's Academy Award–winning moment." He gave a wave toward the footage of Dr. Reed darting out of his seat at the last minute, leaving Dorothy to ride alone. Fear played across her face, but her expression didn't turn to terror until the ride ground to a halt, leaving her stranded at the top. She screamed and carried on and sobbed, her fear so visible that you'd have to be completely insensitive not to feel for her. Ann hadn't expected to empathize with any of the cast, so the rush of sympathy she had for Dorothy was startling. Right after she yelled, "Help me! Someone help me! Get me down!" the image froze, and Milo said, "Now we switch to Marion's moment of glory."

From the base of the Ferris wheel, Marion called up. "Amanda, hang on. I'm going to help you." They all watched as she carefully and nimbly climbed up to the top, eventually ending up next to Amanda in the seat, putting her arm around her shoulder, stroking her hair, and providing the necessary calm.

"And now Ann's greatest moment," Milo said, playing the clip where she rallied the other fairgoers and had them pull on the ride to manually bring each car down to the ground, ultimately freeing the passengers. "Quite a good idea," he said, approval in his voice. She smiled, feeling a surge of pride. Unlocking the ride and moving it by hand had not been planned ahead of time. She'd come up with it on her own at the very last minute. A perfect ending to the scene.

The screen went blank, and the lights in the room brightened. "Well done, all," Milo said. "You've provided Mr. Worthington with many satisfying entertainment hours."

Dominick stood up. "Yeah, about that." He pointed an angry finger at Milo. "Whose idea was it to cast my ex as the love interest? And what kind of psychopath has a guy threaten to beat me to a pulp? He knocked me down on my ass, and it still hurts. Seems like someone was out to get me."

Jeff joined in. "And in what universe would Gerald Barlow steal money from the bank safe?"

"What about me?" Amanda cried out. "Everyone knows I'm not crazy about heights. Why would they set it up so I'm trapped at the top of a Ferris wheel? That was unnecessarily mean."

Milo turned to the reverend. "You want to take this one?"

"Certainly. You all have valid questions, which I'd be happy to answer if you'll give me a minute to change clothes." Reverend Malone shook off his suit coat, then stood while Milo lowered a zipper on his back. The reverend then stepped out of his shoes and peeled off the rest of his clothes, revealing a much thinner man wearing a T-shirt and jeans. The reverend costume had made him look about a hundred pounds heavier. He kicked the bulky clothing to one side, then took off his glasses and handed them to Ann before pulling off his dark wig. Underneath, he had a head of light-brown hair. He ran a hand through his hair, smoothing it to one side.

"No way," Tom said, his mouth dropping open in amazement. "Felix Worthington?"

"In the flesh," he said with a grin. Ann stood up and handed him a handkerchief. He mopped his perspiring brow, then turned to address the group. "Thanks for giving me a moment. That suit was hotter than I anticipated. I'm glad to be done with it."

"Have you been in Haven this whole time?" Amanda asked.

"No. Just today. Otherwise, I've been in the control room watching." He cleared his throat. "Now about your questions. You're wondering why you were given challenges beyond the usual scenarios in the show."

"I want to know why you decided to torment us," Amanda said, exchanging glances with Jeff and Dominick. "I thought you were a fan of *A Little Slice of Haven*, so it doesn't make sense. Why would you be so cruel?"

"It did seem cruel, didn't it?" Felix said thoughtfully.

"Damn right it did!" Dominick said.

"Amanda, would you say you were terrified?"

"Of course! I've already said as much."

"And, Jeff, how did it feel to be called a liar? To know that you're telling the truth but that no one believes you?"

"It was terrible, of course. I mean, I knew it was happening to Gerald Barlow, but it still felt like a gut punch. I'd be lying if I said it didn't bother me."

"Dominick, you mentioned that your ex was cast as your love interest. That's exactly right. It went well at first, but then you realized she'd betrayed you and set you up to get pummeled by her boyfriend. That feeling of having your trust violated is awful, wouldn't you agree?"

"Without a doubt." Dominick frowned. "But what's the point of all this? I mean, why was Jaime even there?"

"I suspected it would feel more personal when it was someone you knew," Felix said, shrugging. "And Jaime was more than agreeable. She was paid well for her part in this, just so you know."

"I don't care about that." Dominick's words came out in an explosion of fury. "I'm asking why you found it necessary. The show was about a loving family. All of their problems were minor and solved in a loving, kind way. Why in the world would you want us to suffer? I don't think we deserve that kind of treatment."

A shrill voice answered from the front row, startling all of them. "You don't think you deserve that kind of treatment?" Startled, all of them turned to see Grandma jump to her feet. "You little pissant. Who the hell do you think you are?"

Chapter Fifty-Two

"Excuse me?" Dominick said, stunned.

Grandma strode over and smacked him across the back of his head. The sound of her hand making contact made Meri think it really hurt.

"Ouch!" He put his hand up and glared in her direction. "What the hell?" He turned to Milo. "You made it so she can walk now?"

"You always were an idiot," Grandma said, fixing him with a critical expression and a shake of her head. She walked over and stood next to Felix. "I'm Catherine Sedgwick. A real person."

"Catherine Sedgwick?" Jeff and Amanda said in unison.

Their reaction reminded Meri of the big reveal in a *Scooby-Doo* episode.

Catherine said, "That's right. In the flesh. I've been here the whole time, trading off with the fake me. She's in storage right now, in case you were wondering."

Meri herself was speechless. Over the years, she hadn't heard anything about Catherine. Google came up with nothing as well, so given her age, Meri had always assumed the woman had died. Now it was as if Catherine had been resurrected from the grave by Felix for the sole purpose of hiding in their midst. The billionaire and the cranky old actress. She couldn't think of two less likely allies.

Dominick must have drawn the same conclusion, because he asked, "How did the two of you connect?"

"Funny you should ask that, Dominick Ingrelli." Catherine spat out his name with an air of contempt. "I think that brings us to part two of the presentation, doesn't it?" The question was aimed at Milo, who just nodded.

Meri's breath caught in her chest. She had barely processed seeing Hailey, the shock of having Jeff learn he was the father of her child, and the existence of Catherine Sedgwick, and now there was more? Her career had been in playing other characters, in total make-believe. Meri was used to working with actors who wanted to improvise which sometimes threw her off course, but this was completely out of her territory.

She wasn't sure her heart was up to this.

The lights dimmed again, and they all watched the images flickering across the screen, a silent montage of family moments from *A Little Slice of Haven*. "Once upon a time," Felix said, "there was a little boy named Sean Knight who was cast as Bud Barlow on a television show on a major network. He wasn't particularly good at acting, but he tried his best." A close-up of Bud's face came next. Meri was reminded again of how sweet and little he'd been. His big eyes gave him an endearing look, and his rosy cheeks were the kind you'd want to pinch. She'd been so consumed with her own worries at the time that she'd barely paid attention to him. He was just another kid on the lot. "Sean tried to be friendly with the other actors, but the only one who was nice to him was another child actor named Lauren Saunders. Lauren played his sister, Ann."

Under his breath, Dominick muttered, "I'd love to know where this is going."

"Quiet!" Felix ordered.

A close-up of the tree next to the house flashed on the screen. Felix said, "Once when almost everyone had left the set for the day, two of the other actors, Dominick and Amanda, thought it would be fun to trick little Sean. Even though they'd been repeatedly mean to him, he wanted to believe that this time they were sincere, so when they encouraged him to climb the tree and told him that there would be a surprise for him at the top, he believed them." Felix let his gaze travel over the faces of the cast. "There was no surprise," he said after a long, uncomfortable pause. "The two of them found this very funny. Once he'd climbed all the way up, they left, laughing."

"I wouldn't say laughing," Dominick grumbled.

Felix ignored him and carried on. "Sean felt terrified. He also felt betrayed by those he'd trusted. He tried to climb down, but the tree wasn't made for climbing and the surface was slippery. He fell, breaking his arm, several ribs, and smashing two bones in his left leg. He was on the ground, in agony, for a long time. Fortunately, his only friend, Lauren, noticed he wasn't outside waiting for his mother, so she came back to find him. She ran to get help and found Catherine Sedgwick, the only adult nearby. Catherine called for an ambulance, and she and Lauren stayed with little Sean, comforting him while they waited."

A photo of Sean in the hospital came next.

Amanda said, "That's not exactly how it happened. You can't just take their word for it."

"I'm not done yet," Felix said harshly. "Sean wound up in the hospital for several weeks. Eventually he healed, although his one leg was never quite right, and it still causes him pain to this day." There was a click as the image switched to one of young Sean standing with crutches. "His mother sued for lost wages, pain and suffering. She claimed the management was at fault since they did not protect little Sean from being abused by his coworkers, which eventually resulted in the injury. These claims created quite an uproar. Dominick and Amanda disputed his account of the event, saying he was lying and that he'd climbed the tree of his own accord." He raised his eyebrows and shook his head. "Jeff Greer and Meri Wetzel claimed not to know that the two had been bullying little Sean all along. But Catherine Sedgwick? She was the only adult who stood by him and told the truth. And for that, her role in the show was relegated to an old lady in a rocking chair rather than a valued part of an ensemble cast. She was demoted as a punishment for being honest."

"This was twenty-five years ago," Dominick said, irate. "Who can even remember?"

Felix ignored him. "The emotional pain turned out to be worse than the physical pain. Sean wondered—How could people he trusted treat him this way?"

Meri felt a pang of guilt. Everything Felix said was true, but there'd been no malice on her part. At the time, she'd shrugged off the interactions between the younger actors in the cast as kids being kids. Sean was a tagalong; the teenagers didn't want him around. It didn't seem personal. If there'd been any bullying in her presence, she would have put a stop to it.

Felix, his glare still fixed on Dominick, kept going. "Sean's mom was required to hold the million-dollar settlement in trust for him, something that infuriated her. She took it out on him, physically abusing him and berating him at every turn. He received the money when he reached adulthood, then changed his name and broke ties with his horrible mother and other family members. The only relative he continued to keep in contact with was his little sister, Ruby. He had years to think about what he wanted to do with such a financial windfall, and what he really wanted to do was build an empire. When the time came for Sean to get the money, he took some major risks, but it paid off in a big way and he became incredibly wealthy. You'd think that would seem like a suitable revenge for what he'd gone through, but it wasn't enough for him. He wanted the people who'd hurt him to know exactly what they'd done. He wanted them to know what it felt like to be called a liar, to feel betrayed, to feel helpless, to be completely terrified."

For a long moment, the group was silent as realization washed over all of them. Jeff spoke the words just as Meri was thinking them. "You're Sean Knight."

Dominick stared at him. "You've gotta be kidding me."

"Sean?" Amanda squeaked.

Lauren leaned back in her chair, folded her arms, and smiled.

Chapter Fifty-Three

Felix shook his head. "The person you knew as Sean Knight no longer exists, which is for the best. By all accounts, he was one sad, dejected little boy. Nowadays, I only answer to Felix. But yes, all of you used to know me in a past life."

"How is it that no one knows this?" Amanda asked. "I'm in the news business, and no one's ever mentioned that Felix Worthington had a name change."

Felix grinned. "I've managed to cover my tracks pretty well. It helps that I have more resources than the average person."

Dominick stood up and waved a finger. "So all of this, building Haven and getting us here, paying us two million bucks each, everything was for the sole purpose of getting back at us for something that happened when you were seven years old?"

"Almost eight, to be precise," Felix said. "And it wasn't just *something that happened*. It was a formative event, the ripples of which I live with to this day. As I mentioned before,

I still have pain in my left leg, and I find it very difficult to trust people. I've had therapy, but that only goes so far. In my experience, traumatic childhood events follow you around for the rest of your life."

Jeff watched, not saying a word. He'd known that the older two kids had been picking on Sean on the set. They'd once closed him up in a closet and secured it by shoving a chair under the knob. Another time, Dominick gave him candy that had been licked by the dog and then told him so after it was already in the younger boy's mouth.

It wasn't that Jeff had been insensitive to Sean's problems, but Sean had a mother on set, and he'd figured it was her job to protect him. Besides, just showing up on time and saying his lines required a gargantuan effort on Jeff's part. His life at the time had been a confusing mishmash of work, drinking, and arguing nonstop with his wife. His dalliance with Meri had given him some joy, but even that had been short-lived and tarnished by guilt.

Now, being reminded of how he'd handled the situation made him flush with shame. Even though he had known what was going on, he'd denied it when the studio was trying to settle the lawsuit. At the time it had seemed an easy out, but in retrospect it was cowardly. He'd failed a little boy.

"You're blaming us for all your problems?" Amanda scoffed. "If anything, you should be thanking us because it looks like your life turned out pretty damn well."

"I'm blaming you for the aftermath of what you put into play," Felix said, calmly answering Amanda. "So what if I was an annoying child? You could have ignored me, but you deliberately chose to attack me, to make me the brunt of your jokes."

"I'm sorry you got hurt, but you climbed up the tree without any help," Dominick said. "It was a fair assumption you could climb back down again. When we left, you were fine."

"I wasn't fine. Even thinking back on my time working on *A Little Slice of Haven* was so painful that when I had the means, I arranged for one of my companies to buy the rights to the show so it would never air again," Felix said. "I only leaked the episodes online after I dreamed up the idea of re-creating Haven and bringing all of you here."

"You did that?" Dominick asked, outraged. "You're the reason none of us ever made a penny from residuals?"

"That's correct."

Jeff stood up and sheepishly met Felix's eyes. "I'm sorry," he said. "You're right. I did know, and I didn't stick up for you. I don't have any excuse for my conduct. None whatsoever. I can't go back and fix it, but for what it's worth, I am sorry."

Felix nodded. "I appreciate it, Mr. Greer."

Hearing him say "Mr. Greer" took Jeff back to the days on the show. Sean had been such a quiet, respectful kid, always calling adults by their surnames. Miss Wetzel. Mr. Greer. Mrs. Sedgwick. Really, the child had just wanted to be liked and accepted. He wasn't asking for much. He felt a flush of remorse and regret.

"I'm sorry you fell," Amanda said, although her tacked-on apology didn't sound nearly as heartfelt.

Felix nodded. "I think it's time to wrap this up. To keep it simple, I'll just read off the names of those who fulfilled the conditions of the agreement. Those cast members will have the payment wired into their bank accounts immediately. After that, I've arranged flights home for all of you. As a reminder, these are the rules, which all of you read and signed off on." Milo handed him a document, and Felix proceeded to read aloud.

Gerald sensed a shift in the room as Felix recited the rules. Everyone was impatient to get their money and go home.

"All of you remained for the full ten days, but unfortunately several of you broke character." His tone was measured, like he had all the time in the world. "It's sad when things don't work out, isn't it?"

"For God's sake, just tell us," Dominick said.

Felix beamed. "All right, have it your way. The cast members who stayed in character during their time in Haven are Lauren Pisanelli and Catherine Sedgwick. Both of them will be getting the promised amount of two million dollars. The rest of you will get a lovely gift bag as a thank-you for participating, and a ride home."

"That's bullcrap," Dominick said, standing up. "Show me one time I broke character. Every inch of me was Tom Barlow the entire time."

"Same for me," Amanda said. "I was really careful. Believe me, I was Dorothy through and through."

Puzzled, Jeff said, "I would like to know what I did."

Felix laughed. "I had a feeling you'd want proof. Milo, would you mind rolling the tape?" The video played showing Tom Barlow taking a puff of a cigarette. "I think we can all agree that the Barlow children are known for being well-behaved good citizens. I contend that Tom would not have smoked or drunk beer at the fairgrounds."

"And I contend that he would have." Dominick threw it right back at him. "Even teenagers who are model citizens smoke and drink. Tom was coming into his own as a man. It would be completely in character."

Felix shrugged in a way that was instantly recognizable to Jeff. He could remember Sean lifting his thin shoulders in just the same way. "You might be right, but even if that were the case, you'd be disqualified for bringing in contraband."

Dominick made an exasperated noise. "Contraband? What the hell are you talking about?"

"Rule number three: All personal effects and clothing must be relinquished prior to the beginning of the project and will not be allowed in Haven." He gave Dominick a long look. "Did you or did you not bring nicotine patches into Haven?"

"You've gotta be joking. How would you even know that?"

"Not only that," Felix continued, "but you referred to Elizabeth Ness by the actor's name, Jaime. Turns out you were guilty on multiple counts."

"You're going to ding me for saying *Jaime*?" Dominick's face reddened. "That was one word, spoken in a moment of surprise."

Felix smiled. "Don't feel too bad, Dominick. Everyone makes mistakes." He turned to Milo. "Next!" Two short clips of Amanda as Dorothy played, one on the Ferris wheel and one in the hospital room. In the first she mentioned "Chips Ahoy cookies," something that Felix pointed out didn't exist in the 1940s; in the other, she called her television mother by the actor's name, "Meri."

"Those were such small things I don't think anyone even noticed," Amanda said, looking stricken. "I was one hundred percent Dorothy for nearly the entire time. All ten days. I made sure of it." Her eyes filled with tears. "I quit my job thinking I was getting paid two million dollars. I can't just walk out of here with nothing. Isn't there some way you could overlook my mistakes?" She put her hands together, pleading.

"Sorry!" Felix said brightly. "Rules are rules." He glanced around the room. "Who's left? Oh yes, Mr. Greer. You wanted to see what you did?" Before Jeff could answer, footage flashed on the screen showing Gerald talking to Mr. Brown on the porch after Bud's death. When the conversation ended and they parted ways, Gerald muttered, "Good riddance, asshole." Jeff had nearly forgotten he'd said that and was honestly surprised the hidden microphone was able to pick it up. Felix said, "I think we can all agree that Gerald Barlow would never have used such language."

Jeff couldn't argue the point. With a sinking heart, he realized he'd have to borrow money from his brother to pay off his gambling debt. It was official: Jeff had been given every advantage and still managed to be the family screwup. When would he learn?

"This is crap," Dominick said, standing up. "You set all of us up to fail, and you're being unreasonably picky and vindictive. No one could have stuck to your stupid rules. I don't care if you are a billionaire. You were a pathetic, annoying little kid then, and you're a complete prick now." He turned and stalked out of the room, deliberately knocking over a chair as he went.

"Don't forget your gift bag!" Felix called after him, but Dominick was already out of earshot.

Milo said, "I guess he doesn't want it."

Felix turned his attention to the others in the room. "Who does that leave?"

"Just me." Meri held up one finger. "But you don't have to play back my footage. I know what I did, and I accept your decision."

Chapter Fifty-Four

When the others were looking through their gift bags, Meri took the opportunity to talk to Felix privately. "Can I ask you something, Mr. Worthington?" she said.

"Of course, but call me Felix."

"You set up the others to go through horrible situations so they'd understand what you went through, but you didn't do that to me. Why?"

His intense eyes met hers. "But I did. It just didn't work out the way I intended."

"I'm sorry, I don't understand."

"I know how compassionate you are, and I knew it would kill you to see Amanda in distress at the top of the Ferris wheel. I wanted you to experience the same feeling of helplessness that I went through."

"But then I climbed up . . ."

"Yes, you did." He grinned. "You had to know that doing so would ruin your chances of getting the money."

"I was pretty sure," Meri admitted. "I can't imagine Marion Barlow doing such a thing. And I think I called her Amanda at one point too."

"You did." He tilted his head to one side, giving her a long look.

For a brief moment their eyes met, and she caught a glimpse of the thoughtful, sensitive child inside the adult man. It was curious how every person was a compilation of all their younger selves combined.

He said, "If it makes you feel any better, you lost out on the money but won my admiration."

"That does make me feel better." She grinned. "For the record, I never saw Dominick and Amanda bullying you. I knew about the name-calling and that they kept ditching you, but I ascribed it to typical kids' stuff. If I'd been paying attention, I might have been able to save you from being tormented and getting injured. I'm sorry."

"I appreciate that. I accept your apology."

"Can I ask another question?"

"Have at it." He grinned, giving the impression he was enjoying the unraveling of everything he'd set in place in Haven.

"Whose idea was it to have my daughter come today?"

"Mine," Felix said, looking pleased with himself. "She knew what the role entailed and what her compensation would be, and she gladly agreed. For the record, Hailey is pretty excited about flying back home with you. She missed you while you were gone."

"I missed her too." Meri dreaded having to tell Hailey she couldn't pay off her student loans after all, but they'd be fine. They always were.

"She was nervous about reciting the speech at the funeral, but I think she pulled it off perfectly. Every word, just as written."

"Did Hailey write that speech?"

"No." He shook his head. "That was done by me."

"But how did you know that Jeff was her biological father?" Meri asked, puzzled.

"Lauren told me. As a kid, she overheard you telling Jeff you were pregnant. She didn't put it together until she was older. And then, of course, both Hailey and Jeff have the same distinctive gray eyes. That made it obvious to me."

Meri shook her head. "I didn't think anyone knew except for me and Hailey. I kept it to myself all these years because I didn't want him to have any rights to her."

"She's an adult now and can make her own decisions. Besides, she told Milo she'd like to get to know him. She never brought it up to you because she sensed you'd disapprove, and she loves you. Which reminds me." He reached into his pants pocket. "I believe I have something that belongs to you." He handed over her cell phone.

"I wondered where that went," she said dryly.

"I hope you don't mind, but I used it."

"Really?" She raised an eyebrow.

"Just once. For something important."

She had to smile. "Well, as long as it was for something important."

Chapter Fifty-Five

After the cast and the rest of Haven's population had departed the warehouse, Milo and Felix walked the streets of the town, once again taking it all in, their footsteps echoing in the emptiness. When they got to the Barlow home, Felix pushed open the gate and bounded up the walkway. Beau the dog appeared to be waiting for them on the porch.

Felix seated himself in one of the rocking chairs and gestured for Milo to take the other. They rocked in silence for a few minutes, until Milo said, "Well, I have to say I was surprised to find out you were once Bud Barlow."

Felix heard the hurt in his voice and knew Milo felt he should have been informed. "I trusted you to keep the secret, but after I told my sister, Ruby, what I had in mind, she disagreed with my plans and felt compelled to warn the cast. I couldn't take a chance that anyone else might sabotage my big reveal. Sorry for that."

"Finding out at the same time as the cast was an interesting experience," Milo admitted. "It was a complete mystery to me, but I'm surprised *they* didn't put it together sooner."

"I've always found that people believe what you tell them when you present it as fact, especially if a large sum of money is involved. It's a curious thing."

Milo rested his elbows on his thighs and tented his fingers together. "So would you call this experiment a victory?"

Felix took a deep breath and shook his head. "I know what victory feels like, and this isn't it, exactly." He idly pushed off with the toe of his shoe. "I'm not sorry I did it, though."

"So it was worth doing?"

"I'd say so." He spoke thoughtfully. "You know, they say there's no point in dredging up the past, but I disagree. Sometimes the past needs to be revisited, if only to hold it up to the light. People need to be held accountable for what they've done. Confronting all of them was far more satisfying than seeing them suffer. That surprised me. It turns out that inflicting pain seems like justice in theory, but in practice it's gut-wrenching. I was glad when Meri climbed up the Ferris wheel to comfort Amanda. Seeing her so terrified and knowing I'd caused it . . ." He exhaled. "That's not who I want to be."

"But you didn't mind withholding the money from them."

"No." A slow smile crossed his face. "Although I wish Amanda hadn't quit her job."

"Not her smartest move."

A breeze kicked up, making the leaves in the trees rustle. Overhead, lazy clouds drifted across the sky. Felix said, "I wanted them to know what I went through, but I don't think that was a realistic goal. All of us are on a different journey, with our own joys and sorrows and pain. We can empathize with others, of course, but to really understand what I went through they'd have to have lived my life, and my life is unique to me and me alone."

Milo absentmindedly reached down to pet the dog. "You did get a few apologies out of it, though. That has to count for something."

"It did count for something." He leaned back in the chair and took in the street before him. "And this experience has softened my memories of Haven. I understand now why people find the town and the television series so charming." Laying the past to rest felt restorative. He'd let his awful childhood take up too much space in his mind. Time to let it go.

"Are you going to try to make a limited series out of the footage?"

Felix looked pensive. "I'm open to the idea, but I'd have to get everybody on board, and as expected, Lauren's not keen on the idea. Ruby is going to try to convince her. We'll see."

"If anyone can persuade her, it would be your sister."

It was true. Ruby had an enthusiasm for all things Haven, and her attitude was downright contagious. Despite the eight-year difference between them, Felix had adored his little sister from day one. His mother had mellowed somewhat by then, so Ruby's childhood had been a bit gentler than his own. Still, it was not the nurturing, supportive environment children deserved. Maybe that's why Ruby loved all things Haven, especially the episodes her brother had appeared in. Felix waved a finger up and down the street at all the charming houses. "Such a shame to have built all of this only to dismantle it."

"Maybe you don't have to tear it down," Milo said. "I've been giving it a lot of thought. Meri Wetzel said something when I gave them the initial tour, and it gave me an idea for the use of this property. If you'll hear me out, I think it's something you'll want to consider."

"I'm all ears." Felix listened thoughtfully while Milo earnestly laid out his proposal. Without factoring in an analysis of cost versus potential revenue, there was no way of knowing the profitability of such an idea, but in theory, it had potential.

And maybe it would be fun to do. There was value in that as well.

"So what do you think?" Milo asked when he'd finished.

Felix gave an approving nod. "It just might work."

Chapter Fifty-Six

Haven Con – 2019   Chicago

Meri had to give Ruby Sapp credit—as impressed as she'd been during her last visit to McCormick Place in Chicago, this year's Haven Con surpassed it in every way. Meri was prepared this time, mentally ready for greeting the fans and signing photos. So much had happened since leaving Haven in Montana, it was dizzying. Her ten days living as Marion Barlow had been a trial, but the aftereffects had only been positive.

The first good thing that happened? Being reunited with Hailey, of course, and finding out her daughter was able to pay off her student loans with the payment from the funeral speech. She hadn't been thrilled to find out that Felix had texted Hailey pretending to be her in order to get her to agree to come to Montana, but Hailey had actually laughed it off when she found out, and ultimately it had worked out, so it was hard to stay mad. A case could be made that it was her own fault for sneaking a cell phone into Haven in the first place.

The second good thing was discovering that Meri's parting gift bag held assorted gift cards for restaurants, stores, and massages at a local spa near her house. Since then, she and her daughter had indulged in some shopping sprees and upscale dinners.

After that came other assorted Haven opportunities. About three months later, the series had magically been picked up by one of the streaming services, and they'd all begun getting royalty checks. Every time she checked her rising bank balance, Meri said a silent thank-you to Sean, the little boy who'd grown up to be Felix Worthington. She hoped that letting go of past grudges had been cathartic for him. She had firsthand knowledge of how holding on to hard feelings eroded a person's sense of well-being.

Now she stood backstage with Jeff Greer, Catherine Sedgwick, and Amanda Waddell, waiting to be introduced for the panel discussion. Both Lauren and Dominick had taken a pass on attending the con, which didn't surprise the rest of them. Lauren had also nixed the idea of turning the ten-day Haven footage into a limited series. In retrospect, it was for the best. What kind of storyline could they have cobbled together from the events of their time there? No matter what they came up with, most likely it wouldn't have been on-brand for the Barlows. And adults playing teenagers? Awkward.

Now her only problem was Jeff Greer, who was determined to win her over. Hailey had met with him several times and thought he was great. "I love how when you talk to him, he really listens," she'd said. "He's also not afraid to talk about his mistakes and his mental health issues, which isn't something you get from most guys. There's something really sweet about him. And, Mom, he says you're the one who got away." From Hailey's expression, it was clear she found this romantic.

Meri felt like getting away had been in her best interests, although she had to agree that Jeff had always been an exceptional listener. Today, he was thrilled that Hailey would be in the audience. He'd talked about the three of them going out for a family dinner on Sunday night.

A family dinner.

Before Meri could respond, Ruby, who'd overheard, had said she'd made reservations at a local restaurant in the hope the cast could join her for an evening meal. "My treat!" she'd said. "And Hailey is included too, of course."

"We'd love to come," Meri said, and then Jeff had no choice but to say he'd go as well. Later she heard that both Catherine and Amanda had agreed to join them, so that put an end to the talk of a family dinner.

From her point of view, a person couldn't randomly decide they had a family and expect one to materialize just like that.

From behind the curtain, they heard the crowd file into the auditorium, their voices rising excitedly. Once everyone was seated, Ruby didn't waste any time. She greeted the audience and said, "I know you're all looking forward to the Q and A with our cast members, and believe me, they're just as excited to meet all of you, but before we do that, I have a short film presentation for you. Something very exciting!" Dramatically, she stepped to one side of the stage, pointed to the screen behind her, and said, "Roll the tape!"

Backstage the cast watched on their own monitor as a commercial for Havenwood in Montana ran. The voiceover was done by Felix Worthington as drone footage showed the streets of Haven, occasionally darting into buildings to show the interiors.

Jeff and Amanda were in the clip, alongside animatronic versions of Meri, Lauren, Catherine, and Beau. The narration said, "Not a theme park or a tourist attraction, but a trip back in time." The voiceover went on to say that the number of people allowed on site each day would be limited, and each visitor would be given a role to play. "Interact with the Barlows and the other residents of Haven. Walk the streets. Stop to talk to Doc Tartar. Have lunch at Charlie's Family Restaurant. Join us for the Haven experience!" Judging by the way the audience screamed in approval, Havenwood was going to be a huge success.

"And now," Ruby called out after the film was done, "the Barlows! Meri Wetzel, Jeff Greer, Amanda Waddell, and Catherine Sedgwick!" They all trotted out one at a time. At eighty-six, Catherine wasn't quite as quick as the rest of them, but she was surprisingly spry for her age. Meri had been shocked to find out she'd only been sixty-one at the time the show had aired. She'd always seemed much older. Probably because she'd been so grouchy.

Meri wound up on the end, right next to Jeff. It made sense since they were a couple on the show, but she wasn't overjoyed with the way he moved his chair closer. Still, there wasn't much she could do without looking too obvious. Best just to put on a happy face and get through the Q and A.

This time around, she had done her homework and was prepared to answer questions about the family and their time working together. A young woman stood up and said, "This one is for Meri Wetzel. I'm wondering how it feels when you watch the episodes now, especially because the show has become such a big deal on Netflix?"

Meri knew what the fan wanted to hear and answered appropriately. "I have so many great memories of that time, so seeing the show again is like watching happy home movies. I feel lucky that we get to unite for events like these. And of course, none of it would be possible without the fans." She blew a kiss to the crowd.

A man went next. "This question is for anyone. Why aren't Tom and Ann here today?"

"I can answer that," Amanda said, her hand popping up in the air. "I just talked to Dominick Ingrelli, who played Tom, and he recently started an exciting new job and couldn't get the time off at this point. I don't want to give anything away, but if you check out his Instagram account, you can find out more about it. As for Lauren Pisanelli, our Ann Barlow, she's at home with her family. She loved acting in the show, but as an adult her focus has changed and she prefers to live a quieter life."

The next question was for Catherine. "We haven't seen much of you since the show aired. Did you give up acting?"

Catherine smiled. "I switched to a different kind of acting. I've been doing voice work for children's cartoons. You won't find my name in the credits, but I'll let you in on a little secret. I'm actually the voice behind Great-Aunt Mudgie on *Call Me Crazy, You Big Silly*." A gasp rose out of the crowd.

Meri had never heard of *Call Me Crazy, You Big Silly*, but apparently it was well known to the audience.

Most of the questions after that were addressed to Jeff or Amanda. Amanda in particular charmed the crowd. At one point, a lady raised her hand and said, "I'm Tammy Gulling, and I'm your biggest fan! My question is about Havenwood. I saw Gerald and Dorothy in the clip, but I'm wondering if the rest of you have been there?"

Amanda answered on behalf of all of them. "All of us were able to visit several months ago, and we were absolutely enthralled by the attention to detail and how they'd managed to re-create the feeling of the town. In fact, Jeff and I are going to be working there for the first few months of the grand opening, playing our parts and interacting with visitors. We can't wait. Right, Jeff?" She looked to Jeff, who nodded in agreement.

Meri added, "All of us agreed that Havenwood was magical."

Ruby stepped forward. "I think we have a photo taken from the cast's visit." She indicated the screen, and up popped an image of all of them together on the porch. "They thought it would be fun to visit in character." The crowd cheered and clapped. If they were that excited to see a picture of them in costume, there was a good chance that a limited series might have gone over well after all. Oh well. That decision had already been made.

The questions after that concerned what it had felt like to be in Havenwood and in costume again. Amanda leaned forward and in a conspiratorial whisper spoke into the microphone, saying, "Just between us, I kept that dress! I love the styles of the forties and am excited that I'll be able to dress that way at Havenwood."

Jeff broke in. "For me, being in Havenwood felt like going home."

A ripple of applause rose up from the audience. Meri could have laughed at the contradiction between how Amanda and Jeff portrayed their recent Haven experience and the reality of their time there. If only the assembled fans could see how Jeff had sweated when he was accused of stealing money at the bank and how happy Amanda had been to leave on day ten. Good actors created magic.

Ruby held up her hand. "I think we have time for one more question."

A man in his thirties stood up with his cell phone aimed at the stage. "I have a question for Meri Wetzel. Is it true that your daughter's father is Jeff Greer?"

Meri felt the blood drain from her face. Her throat closed. Maybe she should have anticipated this, but she hadn't, and she wasn't prepared. Words wouldn't come out. Luckily, Jeff spoke up.

"I can answer that. Yes, it's true that Hailey Wetzel is my daughter. I wasn't involved in her life when she was younger because of my alcoholism, but we're getting to know each other now. She's an incredible young woman. I wish I could take credit, but her mother did an amazing job raising her all on her own. I feel fortunate to be in her life at this point."

Ruby jumped in. "That's all the time we have. I want to thank all of you for—"

Jeff rose to his feet. "Sorry to interrupt, Ruby, but I have a question for Meri."

Oh God. What could this be? She tried to keep the expression on her face pleasant, even as all the possibilities played out in her mind. When he came around to the end of the table and dropped to one knee, the audience screamed and clapped their approval.

She looked down at his sweet, earnest face and thought, *If he proposes right now, I'm going to kill him.*

Ruby ran over and put her microphone up to his mouth. "Meri?" he asked, taking her hand. "Will you go out on a date with me?"

Relieved, she said, "Of course I will."

He rose to his feet, and she joined him, both of them taking a bow to wild applause. Later they would have words, but for now, this was the perfect way to wrap up the appearance.

Chapter
Fifty-Seven

Wild Rose, Wisconsin

His break from work over, Dominick took one last puff, then dropped his cigarette into the dirt and ground it out with the tip of his toe.

"Weather's perfect today," Tex said, "but it's going to be a hot one tomorrow."

"It can't get hot enough for me," Herman said. "Sticky and hot is my preferred temperature, for both the weather and women."

One of the other guys started riffing on the innuendo as they made their way to the truck. Dominick loved all of it: the guy banter, the physical labor, the travel, and working outdoors. It was like the job was custom-made for him. He'd been an official employee of Mike's Premier Midways ever since his contract at the radio station had lapsed. One of the guys from the fair had messaged him on social media, and Dominick had been astounded to learn that setting up rides and concessions was an actual job, and that his friends at the Haven fair weren't actors but actual employees of Mike's, a company that traveled the country setting up fairs, festivals, and other events.

It was more fun than acting or arguing with people on the radio. And he was able to bring his dog, Nellie, too. He'd taken on Nellie when a friend's wife had twins. With two babies in the house, something had to give, and it turned out to be the dog, a mixed breed brown-and-white female who lived to fetch balls. Dominick had agreed to take her without a moment's hesitation, and they'd become best buddies ever since.

Even better, his relationship with his ex, Jaime, had improved. She'd said she felt awful about betraying him in Haven. "It was in the script, though," she said. "So it really wasn't up to me." Remembering how much she'd seemed to enjoy it, he had his doubts. Still, something good had come of it. Playing the role gave her the urge to start working again, and a friend had matched her up with an older actress who needed someone to run lines with her. The woman didn't mind if she brought little Nick along, which was a definite bonus. When Dominick wasn't on the road, he took over, picking up his son for some quality father-son time. Luckily, Nick really loved the dog, which made everything easier.

Now that he had this new job, he felt like he had nothing to complain about.

As they were unloading the truck, Otis said, "Dominick, is it true they made a robot version of you for that new Havenwood deal?"

"Yup." He lifted his end of the strut, making sure to use his back. "I'm licensing my likeness to the company." His younger self would be depicted, which was fine with him. There was something nice about knowing that somewhere in the world there was a version of him that would never age.

"And you get paid for that?"

"Sure do."

"And you're getting money now that the TV show is on Netflix, right?"

"You are correct, my friend."

"Why are you working here, if you're getting money for free?" Otis sounded perplexed.

"'Cause there's nothing I'd rather be doing." Absolutely true. This job was an adventure. Of course, it helped to know he didn't *have* to do it and could quit anytime. When the day came that it seemed like a chore, he'd bow out and not give it another thought. Until then, he liked being one of the guys.

Chapter Fifty-Eight

Kansas City, Kansas

When Aaron came inside after cleaning and covering the grill, he found Lauren seated at the kitchen island, staring at her open laptop.

"What are you watching?" he asked.

She glanced up and met his eyes. "You won't believe this." Returning her gaze to the screen, she said, "Felix Worthington announced today that he's starting his own aerospace company, and guess what? He's calling it Space Haven. He said his goal is to eventually make space flight accessible to ordinary citizens."

"Ordinary citizens who have a lot of money," Aaron said wryly. "Well, at least he's not dwelling on the past anymore."

"Yes, I definitely get the feeling he's moved on."

Aaron got two wine glasses out of the cabinet and opened a bottle of pinot noir. The cork came out with a satisfying pop. He held up the bottle. "You up for this?"

"Just half a glass for me," she said. "I still have to pick up Emily and her friends from the movie."

"I can do it."

She shook her head. "I don't mind. I like listening to them talk in the car. It's like they forget I'm there. I hear all the best stuff that way."

He laughed. "Probably better if I don't know."

Lauren gestured to the laptop. "While you were outside, I was watching clips from today's Q and A panel at Haven Con. At the end of it, Jeff got down on one knee and asked Meri out on a date. The look on her face!" She laughed. "You can tell she was afraid he was going to propose."

"Did she say yes to the date?" Aaron handed her the glass, which she accepted with a nod of thanks.

"Well, yeah, but she really had to, seeing as how the audience was all-in." Lauren paused the clip. "I don't know. Those two might get together yet." She turned to face him. "I saw something there—not a spark, exactly." She sighed. "An understanding, maybe? They do have a daughter in common, and that's kind of a big deal."

Aaron raised his glass and took a sip. "Do you wish you had gone?"

"Me?" Lauren laughed. "No." She thought about what it had been like sitting at a table on stage in front of an adoring crowd. If she was honest about it, the attention had made her uncomfortable. Going to Haven for ten days had given her all the closure she needed, and she only did that after getting the phone call from Felix Worthington and learning that he was Sean Knight. She had gone to Haven as a favor to her old friend. She'd sensed he needed something to end his lingering feelings of resentment, and it seemed as if he'd gotten it.

More recently, she'd agreed that they could use her likeness at age fourteen for an animatronic version to be used in Havenwood, with one provision—she would only be seen waving from the upstairs bedroom window. She didn't want people touching or interacting with her doppelgänger in any way. Just too creepy.

"Are you sure?" Aaron grinned. "You could be there right now, signing photos and having people screaming your name."

"They'd be screaming for Ann Barlow, not me."

"But it was your acting ability that gave them Ann Barlow."

"That was a lifetime ago," she said. "Trust me, I'm in a good place. I love living in Kansas City, teaching third graders about fractions, and spending time with the love of my life and our two daughters." Lauren smiled at her husband and lifted her wine. As they clinked glasses, she added, "All I ever wanted is right here."

Acknowledgments

I owe an enormous debt of gratitude to my early readers, all of whom are simply the best of the best.

MaryAnn Schaefer, you have an eagle eye and an incredible way of reassuring an insecure author. Plus, you're a speedy reader, which counts for more than I can say. Thank you for being the first!

Michelle Watson, a high five for always bringing the levity and finding some great catches, including palazzo pants. You've been a great supporter since day one, something that warms my heart.

Charlie McQuestion, no one has a brain like yours, and for that I'm glad. Your notes on this manuscript were a gift. I'm grateful for your help, and I'm also proud to be your mom. (Sorry for not using Tominick! Maybe in another book?)

Freida McFadden, when you offered to beta read, I was floored. Who wouldn't want a bestselling thriller author to critique their manuscript? I loved all your suggestions and appreciate your insights.

Barbara Taylor Sissel, your time and valuable story-editing skills were so helpful. Anyone would be lucky to have you as an editor, and this time around I'm glad that the fortunate one was me.

Jessica Fogleman, where should I begin? As the last line before publication, I'm always in awe of your editorial skills and attention to detail. The way you respect an author's vision makes you a pleasure to work with. Thank you from the bottom of my heart.

To my review team: a million thanks for reading and reviewing the book prior to publication. I don't take your time or efforts for granted. Hopefully, I remembered to include all of you: Elaine Sapp, Amy Barbaro Coats, Angela Sanford, Ann Marie McKeon Gruszkowski, Bambi Rathman, Bethany Danielle Luther, Bri Ruffin, Carol Sigle Doscher, Carol Zuba, Catherine Bonner, Christie Watson, Crystal Vargas, Danielle Williams, Darlene Rose, Elizabeth Ness, Gabrielle Land Reed, Jackie Shephard, Jaime Trotter, Jamie Onderisin, Jeanne McAvoy, Jenn Bentley, Joyce Stewart, Julianna Odom Shields, Kathy Aden, Katie Waddell, Keenalynn Pratt, Kelly Dineen, Kelly Olshefski Brown, Kris Lewis Lescinsky, Kris Rubi, Linda Foust, Linda Nadwodny Moore, Linda Smith, Lynda Spliethof, Marie Lappin, Martha Burlingame Morin, Marti Wilson, Mary Clifton, Melodie Lyon Nielson, Michelle Jaretsky Stuck, Nikki Wilhelm, Pam Fleming, Pat Tarter, Phyllis Saunders, Rhonda Canfield Sedgwick, Robin LoBollita Ruiz, Ruby Sloan Greene, Shannon Dolgos, Sheri Powers, Tammy Gulling White, Tammy Mondry Leon, Tammy Morse, Teresa M. Carter, Tiffany Whalen, Tracy Smelco, Vicki Hardman, and Brandi Reyna.

Thank you to my foreign rights agent, Taryn Fagerness, for her tireless work, honesty, and always answering my emails on a timely basis. Taryn, I appreciate you more than I can say.

Elizabeth Mackey, once again, thank you for the cover design. You have a great eye and always go the extra mile to make sure the image perfectly fits the story and genre (even when I can't define the exact genre).

Stacey Glemboski, thank you for your excellent narration of this novel for the audio version. Your voice talents are second to none.

To Tess Thompson, my friend and podcast cohost, I raise a glass for all the times you listened to me go on about this book. I feel lucky to have you in my corner.

As always, I'm extremely grateful for my readers. Without you, this book wouldn't exist. Thanks for your messages, emails, comments, and reviews. I love hearing your thoughts on my stories, and on those days when I'm in the weeds, your words spur me on to keep writing.

Greg, Maria, and Jack, thank you for helping brainstorm plot points. A special shout-out to Jack, who came up with the name of the television show: *A Little Slice of Haven*. Besides this bit of brilliance, I appreciate how you never hesitated to tell me when one of my ideas was terrible. Your honesty is appreciated, more so in retrospect than it was at the time.

And last, but never least, none of it would count for anything without my family. To Greg, Charlie, Rachel, Maria, and Jack, I send my love and give thanks for your support and encouragement.

About the Author

Karen McQuestion is the author of more than twenty novels and has sold over two million books worldwide. Her publishing story has been covered by the *Wall Street Journal*, *Entertainment Weekly*, and NPR and she has appeared on *ABC's World News Now* and *America This Morning*. She lives in Hartland, Wisconsin.

Printed in Great Britain
by Amazon